Practically Married

Karin Beery

GUIDING LIGHT
WOMEN'S FICTION
COMPELLING STORIES, BEAUTIFULLY WRITTEN

PRACTICALLY MARRIED BY KARIN BEERY
Published by Guiding Light Women's Fiction
an imprint of Lighthouse Publishing of the Carolinas
2333 Barton Oaks Dr., Raleigh, NC 27614

ISBN: 978-1-64526-236-7

Available in print from your local bookstore, online, or from the publisher at ShopLPC.com

For more information on this book and the author, visit: www.karinbeery.com

This is a work of fiction. Names, characters, and incidents are all products of the author's imagination or are used for fictional purposes. Any mentioned brand names, places, and trademarks remain the property of their respective owners, bear no association with the author or the publisher, and are used for fictional purposes only.

All Scripture quotations, unless otherwise indicated, are taken from the Holy Bible, New International Version®, NIV®. Copyright ©1973, 1978, 1984, 2011 by Biblica, Inc.TM. Used by permission of Zondervan. All rights reserved worldwide. ww.zondervan.com. "NIV" and "New International Version" are trademarks registered in the United States Patent and Trademark Office by Biblica, Inc.TM.

Brought to you by the creative team at Lighthouse Publishing of the Carolinas (LPCBooks. com):
Eddie Jones, Shonda Savage, Karin Beery, Irene Chambers, Brenda Kay Coulter, Kelly Scott

Library of Congress Cataloging-in-Publication Data
Beery, Karin.
Practically Married / Karin Beery 1st ed.

Printed in the United States of America

It isn't hard to keep turning pages when you have swoon-worthy characters who find themselves in potentially crushing circumstances. Unexpected chemistry and fast friendship make this story a delightful read, and author Karin Beery's deft words, wisdom, and wit make it a memorable one.

~Kaley Rhea
Co-Author of *Turtles in the Road and Messy to Meaningful*

A sweet contemporary romance with endearing characters who don't follow the typical path to their happily-ever-after. Beery's writing shines with humor, witty dialogue, and charming moments that'll have you rooting for Ashley and Russ till the very satisfying end.

~Susan L. Tuttle
Author of *At First Glance*

Don't you just love coming across characters you'd like to know better? Like, let's-have-coffee-and-talk-this-out kind of know them better? Karin Beery has introduced me to some new friends in Practically Married and placed them in a not-so-traditional romance with a clever twist. So fun!

~Rhonda Rhea
Award-winning humor columnist
TV personality
Author of sixteen books

ACKNOWLEDGMENTS

Most of the magic of writing and publishing a novel happens alone while sitting behind a computer, but that doesn't mean the experience is a solitary endeavor. I could probably thank a hundred people for their help, influence, and encouragement with this book, but I'll try to be brief. (Refills coffee cup.)

To Lighthouse Publishing of the Carolinas. You've given me so many opportunities to learn and grow as an author and editor. I honestly don't know where I'd be without your willingness to take a chance on me. Thank you.

To Pegg Thomas. I'm not even sure where to start. Thanks for being an amazing friend and mentor.

To Steve and Ruth Hutson at WordWise Media. Thank you! It still amazes me that you've stuck with me for so long.

To Irene Chambers. Thank you for not being afraid to use your red pen. My story is better because of you, and that's such a wonderful gift to give an author.

To my husband. You're an amazing provider and encourager. I truly couldn't do this without you. You're my favorite.

For my Lord and Savior, Jesus Christ. Thank you for being with me through the rejections, the rewrites, the tears, the frustrations, and the celebrations. As much fun as it is to publish another book, it doesn't compare to the grace and mercy you show me every day of my life. I'm blessed not because I'm able to write books for a living but because you loved me enough to save me. May I never forget that.

Dedication

For Aunt Linda

CHAPTER 1

This is Tom, please leave a message.

Ashley disconnected, unwilling to leave another voicemail. Tom had promised to check his messages during his hiking trip, but that was ten days ago. He must've had a signal at some point since then. How could an entire section of Michigan function without phones? Unless something had happened to him. She stared into the living room, tapping her fingers on the Formica table, her nails clicking in time with the scenarios flying through her head. Her aunt and uncle's afghan-covered furniture and beige, contractor-grade carpet offered little counsel.

The bedroom door squeaked behind her. "Good heavens, you're up early, sweetheart. Is everything okay?" Rose managed to sound chipper despite the hour.

"I couldn't sleep. I still can't reach Tom." Ashley spun the useless phone on the table.

Rose patted her shoulder on the way to the kitchen. "Maybe you should postpone the move, at least until you hear from Tom. You're welcome to stay with John and me until then."

"Thanks, but I'm ready to go. In all fairness, Tom warned me I might not be able to reach him, but I didn't expect total radio silence." In the kitchen, cupboards thudded, dishes clinked, and silverware rattled. When Rose finally returned, her pink shirt glowed behind a short stack of butter-yellow plates and glistening silverware. "Do you usually set the table for breakfast?" Ashley asked.

"Of course not, but you don't usually join us either. Are you sure you don't want to go back to sleep for a while? It's barely eight."

Ashley laughed. "I'll survive, though I don't think I've set my alarm this early since high school."

Her aunt set down the plates, then grabbed Ashley's hand and gave it a squeeze. "That was a lifetime ago, wasn't it?"

Ashley nodded. The pain had dulled, but the reality of her parents' deaths never disappeared. "Living my entire adult life without Mom and Dad isn't how I would have planned things, but it's worked out. I can't imagine life without you and Uncle John at every turn."

"We've gotten spoiled." Rose kissed the top of Ashley's head. "I'm not excited about sharing you with anyone, especially someone who's not as crazy about you as we are."

"No one will ever be as crazy about me as you are, but Tom and I are great friends. Mom always said she was glad she married her best friend. I think she'd be happy that I found someone like him."

"Maybe. Are you sure you want to spend your life with a man who would marry a woman he's never met?"

"It's not like we're complete strangers. We text and talk all the time, plus we video chat, which at least lets us see each other."

Rose shook her head, her long, silver hair swaying around her shoulders. "I'm glad I met John before all your worldwide Google dating. There's nothing more romantic than a handwritten love letter. Now, what would you like for breakfast?"

"Why don't I make breakfast for you today?" Ashley hopped up. "What would you like?"

"Do you know how to make breakfast? I thought you only woke up for lunch." Rose winked before heading into the white-tiled kitchen.

Ashley followed, missing her already. "I hope I'm still full of sass when I'm seventy-five. Sometimes I wonder how much trouble you and Mom would have gotten into if she was still here."

"I wouldn't get into any trouble. I had a way of tricking your mom into making all the bad decisions."

Ashley's laughter mingled with her aunt's—the same tone, but decades older. They worked side by side, whipping up eggs and chopping vegetables.

"Could you reach my serving bowl on the top shelf there?" Rose pointed to the far cabinet.

Ashley pulled a blue ceramic dish from above the microwave. "Did you buy a stepladder for when I'm gone?"

"Nonsense. John can reach it for me."

"And what if he's gone?"

"Where would he go without me? He's eighty years old."

A deep chuckle rumbled through the kitchen. "Eighty's the new sixty." Ashley turned and smiled at her uncle as he toweled his hair in the bedroom doorway, his blue eyes twinkling in the morning light. "What in the world are you doing up?" he asked. "I wasn't expecting to see you until noon."

"My flight's at noon, Uncle John. We need to leave for the airport by ten."

"Good grief, that's a long time to hang out at the airport. Why don't you stay with us for a while longer?"

"Your retirement community doesn't allow thirty-five-year-olds to live here."

"Ah, they're old. Mumble when you talk to them. They won't understand, but they'll be too embarrassed to ask you to repeat yourself."

Ashley laughed, but she appreciated the sentiment. "I think it's time for me to move on, don't you?"

"What do I know? I'm an old man." John walked over and wrapped an arm around her. "I want you to be happy, even if that means moving to the tundra." He shivered as he said the word. "I can't imagine why you want to move there in November, but I don't understand much about how you do things these days."

Ashley leaned into him, happy to reassure him again. "Lots of people meet online. Tom's a good man. We have the same values, and we make each other laugh. We'll be good for each other."

"Bleh." Rose wrinkled her nose. "This isn't an arranged marriage. You can take time to date and fall in love."

Ashley cringed. "Love doesn't always last. Tom's sister and one of his cousins married for love, but they fell out of love, divorced, and remarried. Tom and I have a lot in common, including our frustration with dating. We're tired of being alone, and we're committed to making it work.

"My mom and dad were friends who fell in love and got married. Tom and I will be friends who get married, then fall in love." Hopefully. Returning phone calls might speed up the falling-in-love process. "Besides, I have to move now. The photographer I told you about is expecting me to start my internship after New Year's. I want to be there early so I can get settled."

Rose scooped eggs into the serving bowl. "You take beautiful pictures already. Why do you need an internship?"

"Because I'm not good enough yet to make a living at it. I've only been able to sell a few landscapes and still-life photos, but if I can learn how to take portraits, too, I could make a decent career for myself as a photographer."

John shook his head. "Why do you need to make a career for yourself? You're getting married."

Ashley rolled her eyes. "Yes, and I can have a career too. This isn't the Teddy Roosevelt era anymore."

He tugged on Ashley's hair. "You have my blessing to go now."

"That's all I've ever wanted." She let herself lean against him a while longer, soaking in his support and love, as she had for the last decade and a half. His spring-fresh scent mixed with the savory aroma of her aunt's sizzling sausage, the same brand Ashley's mom used to cook. "I think Mom would've liked Tom."

Rose turned to her. "Are you still reading through her journal? Haven't you memorized it by now?"

Ashley glanced at the worn blue notebook on the dining room table. "I only found it two years ago. I never realized how much Mom supported me. Even when she wanted me to take more English classes in high school, she encouraged me in math and started researching possible engineering careers for me."

What would her mom think now, knowing Ashley lived in the same house she grew up in, working out of the living room as a medical transcriptionist? Not the life Mom had written about for her only daughter, but Ashley was changing that. She would make her mom proud. "The one thing Mom wrote consistently about was being a grandma someday. Did you know she had given up on having kids a year before she found out she was pregnant with me?"

Rose chuckled as she rushed around the kitchen dishing up food. "I remember the day she found out. I went to the doctor with her. We thought it would be a quick stop, then we were going shoe shopping. That doctor said 'pregnant,' and we bought half the baby clothes in JCPenney. When your daddy came home, he stared at your mom like he didn't know where babies came from."

Rose told the rest of the story—the baby shower, the delivery, the crying—as Ashley set the table. By the time Rose finished, she'd piled food onto each plate. As they sat down, Ashley's stomach rumbled.

John patted her hand. "Why don't you go ahead and call that boyfriend of yours? I'll feel better dropping you off at the airport if I know he's going to meet you on the other side."

Ashley picked up her phone from the table and stuffed it in her pocket. "He's still out of range, but I've left him a few voicemails. I'm sure Tom will be there."

****

The phone rang again, the obnoxious chirp echoing through the house. Russ took his time walking down the stairs, fastening the last button of his oxford before tucking it into his jeans. Thick cotton socks muffled his slow steps. No reason to rush. He had no idea what he'd say if he answered the phone anyway.

At the base of the stairs, he caught sight of his reflection in the glass covering an old family picture. Dark eyes stared back at him. Mom would ask him to cut his hair when she saw him—the curls were popping out again. She wouldn't mention the beard. Though she hated it, she'd been losing that battle for twenty years. Tom had always kept a clean face. Her baby-faced nephew.

A familiar pain pressed against Russ' chest. He didn't have time for that. His family would start arriving soon. He glanced at the clock behind him, the second hand ticking in front of pictures of Tom's favorite northern birds. Any minute now the front door would open, but the phone kept chirping.

By the time Russ reached the dining room, the ringing stopped. He pulled the phone out of the hutch drawer. *Ashley* flashed across the screen an instant before the phone beeped. Another voicemail. If he had the passcode, he could find out who she was and why she kept calling, but he didn't have the strength to talk to her anyway. She'd been calling for two days, though. He really should call her back. Later. After he figured out what to say.

The front door groaned. A hundred footsteps thundered against the hardwood in the foyer. Two soft steps padded toward him. Russ smiled. He tossed the phone back in the drawer and looked up as three-year-old Phin plowed into him.

The typically unrestrained boy wrapped his arms around Russ' legs, his blue eyes wide and wet. "Mama cwying."

Russ scooped up the little guy. "I know, bud. Uncle Russ cried a little bit too."

That innocent face brightened. "You did?"

"I did."

"You cwy now?"

"I'll try not to. We'll leave that to your mom and aunts."

"Aunt Wiz cwy?" Phin's bottom lip trembled.

Oh no.

Rachel and Chad ushered their other boys into the adjoining, open-concept kitchen. Russ couldn't be responsible for making her baby cry. Holding Phin out in front of him, he tossed the boy in the air.

"Again!" Phin squealed as his older brothers ran at Russ.

"Me too!"

"My turn!"

Their dad pulled them away, throwing one over his shoulder and tucking one under his arm as if wrangling six-and eight-year-olds were easy. "We'll let Mommy talk to Uncle Russ. Let's find you a movie." More squeals and cheering filled the room as Phin squirmed out of Russ' arms to run away with his brothers. That left Rachel and Russ alone, staring at each other, the loneliness of the house closing in around them.

Tears rolled down Rachel's cheeks. "I'm so sorry."

"It's not your fault, Rach." She nodded but didn't stop crying. He pulled her into a hug, summoning all of his remaining strength for her to absorb. "Thanks for coming over."

She nodded, wiping her tears and nose on him. Maybe he should have worn a work shirt instead of his church shirt. The door opened again, followed by more footsteps, voices, and the throaty cry of his only niece.

Rachel stepped back, squeezing Russ' hand. "Carrie was right behind me, and I think I saw Liz pulling in too. You go greet everyone. I'll get the food out."

"I don't have any food."

She laughed as she walked into the kitchen.

Russ moved through the randomly furnished living room. A fire popped in the cobblestone fireplace, throwing soft, warm light onto the mismatched couch, loveseat, and oversized chair. Before he made it to the foyer, his oldest nephew jumped onto the chair, his feet dangling over the arm while he fiddled with his phone. Russ walked toward the front door, but a pile of coats and boots blocked his path.

Liz looked at him, her young eyes red and tired. "The diaper bag spilled in the car, and I can't find Kristy's snacks. Do you have anything she can eat?" She passed off the crying infant to Russ. "I'll nurse her in a bit, but I need to clean up the mess and see if I can find that tube of rice puffs for her."

"How about yogurt?" The one thing he stocked especially for Kristy. That little girl owned his heart like his three sisters never had. He was pretty confident the feeling was mutual. Kristy dropped her bald head onto his shoulder, grabbed the dry half of his collar, and stuffed it into her mouth. He turned back toward the kitchen, but someone grabbed his elbow and steered him around.

Liz hugged him. "How are you doing?"

He wrapped his free arm around her. "The house is quiet."

"We can take care of that for a few hours." His youngest sister held him tighter than Rachel had but without the tears. "Thanks for letting us come over."

"Like I had a choice."

She smacked his chest before walking back outside.

Russ stepped over the great coat divide, passed the staircase in the foyer, and trekked into the family room. Little boys covered the sectional. Five nephews aged three to twelve climbed over and around each other as a cartoon played on the flat screen. Their dads talked in the corner, one facing the kids while one watched the kitchen. Russ walked by them, nodding as he passed. They offered the same salute.

As soon as he stepped onto the gray kitchen tiles, Rachel and Carrie stopped talking. Somehow, they'd covered the island countertop with food. They removed lids and foil from pots and pans. Buttery, garlicky aromas floated through the air. Rachel rushed over to steal Kristy, but the baby burrowed into Russ' neck.

He smiled at Rachel's fake hurt expression. "Could you get her something to eat?" he asked.

She nodded, her eyes still pink and puffy. Their oldest sister, Carrie, walked over and squeezed him and Kristy in a quick, tearless hug. He could always count on her for emotional stability. Carrie was the closest person he had to a brother, besides Tom.

"How are you doing?" she asked. "Can I get you anything?"

"Shouldn't I be asking you that? This is my house."

"Yes, but you're a man. We brought our own comfort food."

His stomach growled. "What kind of comfort?"

Carrie grinned. "Mom's bringing the pie."

Russ salivated. Mom's comfort always came baked between two perfectly flaky crusts. "I hope it's apple."

"She's probably bringing pumpkin, cherry, blueberry, *and* apple."

"She trained us. You know there'll be too much food." Rachel returned with a bowl of banana pieces.

"I don't mind at all." Russ took the bowl and sat at the large oak table with Kristy on his lap. He gave her one piece at a time, the way his sisters had taught him.

Chatter and laughter filled the old farmhouse, warming it in a way the fireplace never could. Carrie's husband stepped into the kitchen and snagged some food, taking a moment to wrap his arms around her and kiss her hair. Two boys stormed through the house laughing and yelling. They charged toward the dining room and right into Rachel. Blessed chaos.

Something warm and wet pressed on Russ' hand. He looked down at Kristy, eyes closed, head resting on his hand, and drool rolling down onto the table. Her tiny pink shirt stretched and contracted with her rapid baby breaths.

Russ hadn't wanted his family over. He'd thought he needed time to process, to let reality sink in, but having them there was what he really needed. He would never understand how his sisters realized that about him, but he liked it. Maybe not the drool, but everything else he liked.

Another whoosh of air caught his attention. Russ leaned back, trying to see through the living room and its walls to the front door. A puffy purple sleeve swung into the foyer. Mom.

She and Liz marched toward him balancing pie plates on their hands. If they ever showed up wearing the same outfit, it would be like watching past and present versions of the same woman. Carrie met them midway, taking all three pies to the kitchen.

Russ' mom stepped behind his chair and wrapped her arms around him. "You are a wonderful man, Edgar James Russell. I'm so proud to have you as a son."

Her words strangled his heart. He forced down tears and nodded. "Thanks, Mom. How're Aunt Rita and Uncle Bill?"

She walked around the table and sat across from him. "They're doing okay. The girls came home this week, so at least the family's together. They asked about you. You were closer to Tommy than either of his sisters, and they wanted to make sure you're okay. I can't imagine losing a son, especially this close to the holidays."

Liz set a plate of food in front of Russ before scooping up Kristy. "Thanks. Do you want anything, Mom?"

"No, I'm fine."

Liz took an empty plate from the island and set it in front of their mom. "Just in case."

Russ watched his family roam around. They didn't ask anything of him, didn't make him talk. It wouldn't last long. Rachel would eventually come up with her thousand questions, but for now she respected his space. He ignored his plate and simply enjoyed watching them. His little sisters, all grown up. Wives and mothers. Three great men who loved them, wrangling kids in the other room. All of them giving him the support he needed. Until they left. Then he'd be alone again. He'd never envied his sisters' marriages until then.

He didn't have time to worry about that, though. The farm needed constant attention, and Russ would have to work for two people next year. Starting his own family would have to wait awhile. None of the women in the kitchen would like that, but he couldn't control everything.

Besides, he had two more years before he hit forty. Plenty of time. Two years to find a woman more interested in a marriage than a wedding, someone committed to as-long-as-they-both-shall-live, not simply as-long-as-the-romance-stays-alive. Maybe two years wouldn't be long enough, but right now he only wanted to—needed to—appreciate his family. Nothing else mattered.

Chad sauntered into the kitchen, his large frame dwarfing the women as he passed. He pulled out the chair beside Russ and dropped onto the seat. "We need to talk about the farm."

CHAPTER 2

The sharp edge of reality sliced through Russ' heart. "I haven't thought much about it yet. Can this wait?"

"Probably, but I thought you should know the township called."

Great. Pressure from small-town government weighed on Russ like a sack of fertilizer. "Now what? Do we owe them money? Did I forget to fill out some paperwork?"

"Not that I'm aware of. First, they offered their condolences. Then, they mentioned a new program at the college that preserves historical agriculture or something like that."

"I don't even know what that means."

"I don't either, but Wayne Dunville—"

Russ groaned.

"—said they're trying to preserve farmland in the township, and somehow our farm can help."

"Our land *is* preserved. We're farming it."

"All I know is the college approached the township, and they're putting together a program where the history and science departments work with local farmers. I think students actually work the farm."

"He wants kids running my farm? That man is crazy."

Chad shrugged. "I don't have all the details, but Wayne has them. Think about it. Free labor."

Laborers he didn't need. Russ needed someone in the office with management skills. "I don't know."

"At least call them back. We've got plenty of help in the orchard, but that still leaves you and me with a lot of paperwork."

Work that Tom had done with ease, but the mere thought of desk work made Russ' head ache. He and Tom could have worked the orchards with their eyes closed and hands tied. They grew up walking the fields with their dads, the dew wetting their pant legs while the rising sun blinded them through the branches. They'd enjoyed more than a few mornings among the cherry trees, Dad and Uncle Bill sipping coffee while Tom and Russ ate fresh-picked fruit. The farm had practically raised them.

Chad didn't share those memories, though. His farming career revolved around Rachel. Russ lived for weather roulette, planning one day at a time and praying for a good harvest. He loved the anticipation of spring, when he could dig his fingers into the ground and examine the roots and plants.

Russ loved farming. Chad loved Rachel. Not quite as motivating. Russ couldn't imagine working a job he didn't love for the sake of a woman. He wasn't sure if that made him or Chad crazy.

Rachel sat down next to Chad. "What're you two talking about?"

"Nothing," Russ said.

Chad looked at her. "The farm."

Her mouth dropped open, and she stared at Chad like he'd suggested slugs for dinner.

Russ laughed. "Seriously? You don't know my sister well enough yet to keep your mouth shut?"

Rachel shook her head. "Do you really need to talk about the farm now? Mom's here. The kids are in the other room. There has to be a better time to discuss this."

Chad deflated as she chattered on.

Russ shoveled food into his mouth to hide his smile. At least some things hadn't changed. A little more consistency and life would be back to normal in no time.

* * * * * * *

Alone in the Traverse City airport. No help. No luggage. No fiancé.

Ashley stood next to the luggage carousel, watching a pea-green duffle bag slide past for the fourth time. Apparently, no one wanted the ugly beast. Maybe that person had run off with her suitcase since no one could seem to find it. Half of the fifty seats on that plane had been empty. How could the airline lose her luggage?

She glanced around the airport. A few people walked about, most wearing name tags and logoed polo shirts. None of them appeared to work for her airline, though, and there was no sign of the young employee she'd spoken to earlier. The one person she knew in town wasn't answering his phone.

Great. She didn't have a car, but then, she didn't have directions either. As much as she wanted to hear a familiar voice, she couldn't call Rose or John. They didn't need another reason to worry.

She sighed. Time to call Tom again, not that she was hopeful.

Ashley pulled out her phone, then pressed speed dial four. He had to be back from his vacation. He'd told her he'd be at the airport.

"Huwo. Biwings."

Finally! "Hi, this is Ashley. Is Tom there?"

"I Phin. Unca Tom gone."

Maybe he was on his way to pick her up. "Is there an adult there I can talk to?"

"I at his house. We watching a movie."

Music blared in the background, mixed with people talking. Was that a baby crying? He must be with his family. Tom had told her all about his cousins and their kids. She couldn't wait to meet them. Hearing them hanging out and having fun quickened her pulse. They must be expecting her.

"Phin, did your Uncle Tom go to the airport?"

"Pwanes! And hewicoptehs. I wike hewicoptehs."

"Me too, but I'm sort of stuck here. Is there an adult nearby? Can I talk to your mommy?"

"Mommy cwying."

"How about your daddy then? Is your daddy there?"

"Phin, gimme that."

"No!"

"Hey!" Thump. Shuffle. "No!" BEEP!

Silence.

"Phin. Phin! Can you get an adult for me? Phin?"

Silence.

She stared at her phone, willing it to ring. They had to wonder who Phin was talking to, especially on Tom's phone ... but if Tom was on his way to pick her up, why would a little boy have his phone?

"Excuse me, ma'am?" The long-lost airline employee approached her. "We found your suitcase. It missed the plane in Detroit and will be on the next flight here."

"Perfect. When will that be?"

"Tomorrow morning at nine."

"The world hates me." Ashley dropped onto the edge of the carousel, her strength and hope missing with her suitcase, and Tom. The attendant shuffled from foot to foot. No need for him to be uncomfortable too. "I guess I'll have to come back tomorrow," she said.

"Yes, we'll have it then."

"Thanks."

The young man nodded, then dashed away. Ashley sat next to the ugly green bag, empathetic to its plight. This was not working out. What would her mother think? She unzipped her large red shoulder bag and dug out her mom's journal.

"Inspire me, Mom." Ashley flipped open the spiral-bound book. She wouldn't find anything new, but maybe one of the entries would help her figure out what to do. She went to the middle of the journal.

January 15 –

It snowed today! Not a dusting, either. Five inches of snow last night. Needless to say, school is closed. I snuck in and shut off your alarm this morning. I thought you'd enjoy sleeping in. Instead, you woke up in a panic at 9 a.m., certain you'd lose credit for missing your science lab …

Ashley had memorized the rest of the entry. She'd layered on clothes and walked into town to catch a matinee at the movie theater, the only customer there. The manager gave her free popcorn for braving the storm. A fun story, but not very helpful. She flipped back to the first half of the book.

August 26 –

I can't believe you're starting middle school tomorrow. I'm trying to decide if I should be sad or excited, so I'm switching between the two. You grew four inches this summer and don't fit into any of your old school clothes. We went shopping yesterday, and your saving skills amaze me. I gave you $100 *and told you to spend it however you wanted. You went from store to store, checking prices and substituting clothes. Your Aunt Rose …*

… would be proud. Yeah, Ashley knew how that one ended too. As much as she loved connecting with her mom's words, nothing in the journal was going to tell her what to do when abandoned by a fiancé and stranded at the airport in a strange city. Without clean underwear.

Ashley closed the journal, looking around the cavernous terminal. A lighted billboard caught her attention—FREE SHUTTLE! Those big, brilliant words beckoned her. She'd get a room for the night, in case Tom didn't show up. Tomorrow she'd pick up her suitcase, rent a car, go find her fiancé, and figure out what was going on.

She pulled out her phone and dialed one more time.

"This is Tom, please leave a message."

"Hi, Tom, it's Ashley again. I'm not sure what happened, but it's almost eight o'clock, and I'm still at the airport. I'm going to get a room at the Bay Resort for the night. If I haven't heard from you by morning, I'll rent a car and come find you. I'll be honest, this probably isn't the best way for us to meet. I hope everything's okay. I guess I'll find out tomorrow. Please call me when you get this message."

She ended the call and sighed. Part of her hoped everything was okay, but another, smaller part hoped he'd broken a leg and was stuck in a hospital that didn't allow cell phones. Ashley didn't want to believe that she'd promised to marry a man who could forget about her for a week. Either way, they needed to have a serious talk.

CHAPTER 3

Ashley wrapped her hands around the white coffee mug. The hot ceramic warmed her chilled fingers. If only it would warm her heart. She could forgive Tom for the missed phone calls, possibly even for forgetting to pick her up, but she'd been in Boyne Heights for two hours and still couldn't find him. Her patience had walked out with the last diner patron.

The waitress returned and refilled mug. "Are you sure I can't get you anything? At least let me get you a piece of pie."

Ashley smiled at the kind woman. Her name tag said Pearl. Judging by the salt-and-pepper hair and creases around her mouth, Ashley guessed she was her mother's age, probably had kids of her own. Maybe grandkids. Taking care of people most likely came second nature to Pearl. "Thank you, but I'm fine," Ashley said. "I won't be here much longer, I promise."

"Take as long as you need. You look a little worried is all. Are you waiting for someone?"

"How could you tell?"

Pearl's laughter rolled through the dining room. "Most strangers pass through. I make a decent cup of coffee, but no one's ever stayed two hours to enjoy it."

"I'm waiting for my friend. He'll be along soon. I hope." Maybe. Ashley offered another smile, but the waitress didn't smile back.

"I've lived here my whole life and know pretty much everyone. Tell me who you're waiting for, and I can probably find him for you."

"I'd appreciate the help. I was supposed to meet Tom—"

"Tom Russell?" The waitress frowned.

"You know him?" Sweet relief! "Thank goodness. I don't have his home address, only his cell number, but he's not answering. Could you tell me where I can find him?"

"You stay right there." Pearl set the coffeepot on the table and pulled the apron over her head. "Get whatever you want. It's on the house. Lou! Get this girl some food!" Pearl leaned over, eye to eye with Ashley. "I'll be right back. Don't go anywhere."

Ashley didn't have a clue where she'd go, and she didn't have time to ask. Pearl ran down the hall before she could say anything. As soon as the waitress disappeared, a skinny teenage boy set a giant sandwich in front of Ashley. "Are you Lou?"

"No, that's my dad. He said to fill you up. Sorry about Tom."

"Uh, thanks. I really don't need all of this food, though." The kid shrugged, took the coffeepot, and walked back to the kitchen. Tom had joked about the solitude of his hometown and the characters who lived there, but he'd never mentioned how hospitable they were.

Ashley's stomach growled. She checked her watch. It had been four hours and eighteen minutes since she found her luggage, rented a car, and finally made her way to Boyne. Maybe she should eat something.

She made quick work of the sandwich, popping the last bite into her mouth as Pearl emerged from the back of the restaurant. Behind her walked a tall, brooding man. Dark hair stuck out from under his ball cap, and dark whiskers shadowed his face. Like Pearl, he looked at her without smiling. Warning tingles raced over Ashley's spine. She kept her eyes on the frowning man who slid into the booth across from her.

Ashley forced a smile. "Can I help you?"

The man nodded, his brown eyes locked on hers. "Pearl said you're waiting for Tom."

Ashley's pulse kicked up. "Yes. And you are?"

"Russ. I'm his business partner."

That's right. Tom's cousin. "He's mentioned you. Can you tell me where to find him?"

Russ looked up at Pearl, then back at Ashley. Suddenly the booth seemed too small, too crowded. The stranger across from her didn't flinch. "I'm sorry, ma'am, but there was an accident. Tom's dead."

* * * * * * *

The woman's hazel eyes blinked twice. She opened her mouth but quickly closed it.

Russ had never seen her before. Other than the gal who wouldn't stop calling Tom's phone, he didn't know his cousin associated with women outside the family. His death had left plenty of surprises. At least this one was pretty.

She looked at Pearl. "Could I have a glass of water, please?"

Finally. Anything but uncomfortable silence. Pearl rushed away while he studied the woman.

"You're Tom's cousin, right?"

"Yeah. And you are?"

"A friend of his. He told me about you. You run, er ran, the farm together, right?"

"Apparently you two talked a lot." More than he and Tom, obviously. Too bad Tom never mentioned this woman.

When Pearl returned, the brunette downed the water. She shook her head as she set the glass down, her gaze avoiding Russ'.

"I'm sorry I had to tell you like this," he said. "I would have called, but I didn't know Tom was expecting you. Are you staying long?"

"I, um …" She scratched her arm, and Russ saw a thin, gold band on her left hand. Oh, Tom. A married woman?

Russ adjusted his cap as he waited for an answer. When she didn't explain, he assumed the worst. "It's not my business. Sorry I asked. The memorial's in a few days if you want to go." He slid toward the edge of the booth, ready to be done with the awkward situation his cousin had left behind.

"Wait, please." She reached out but stopped an inch before touching him. She finally looked at him. "How did he die?"

Russ paused, watching her as she studied him. "Hiking accident. He slipped, hit his head."

"Did he suffer?"

"No." Russ swallowed, pushing down the pain. "The doctor said he probably died instantly."

Her eyes glistened as she pulled her arms in to her chest. "Thank you."

"I wish we could have met under better circumstances."

"Me too." She offered her hand. "I'm Ashley Johnson, by the way."

He accepted her handshake and tried to remember his cousin talking about her. "Ed Russell. Everyone calls me Russ."

"I know. Tom mentioned it."

"He never mentioned you."

Her eyebrows pinched together. "Never?"

"Not that I recall." Russ motioned toward her left hand, hoping. "Are you married to someone he knows?"

"What?" She looked at her hand, the color draining from her cheeks. "A friend gave it to me." As she twisted the metal band, it caught Russ' eye. The band spun around again. The engraving. His grandmother had a band with a cross carved into it exactly like that one.

As the ring went around again, Russ snatched Ashley's hand, pulling the ring close. "Where did you get this?"

"I told you." She pulled her hand back. "A friend gave it to me."

"That's my grandmother's wedding ring."

She hugged her hand against her chest, dropping her gaze to the table.

What was going on? "How exactly do you know my cousin?"

Barely green eyes flashed at him before turning back to her lap. "We were engaged."

Ashley. The phone calls! "You're the Ashley who keeps calling Tom's phone." Oxygen abandoned his lungs. "You and Tom?"

"Yes, me and Tom."

Someone dropped a tray of dishes, splintering the air.

"I'm sorry, what?" he asked.

She stared at him, equal parts innocence and terror flashing in her eyes. "We are—were—engaged."

"Wow." Russ scrubbed his hands over his face, trying to push the information into his brain. "I had no idea."

"I noticed." Ashley sat up straighter. "I suppose finding out like this is a little like showing up in a strange town and finding out your fiancé is dead. I'm sorry I bothered you. If you could point me in the direction of Tom's house, I'll leave you alone."

"Tom's house?" Russ lowered his hands enough to see Ashley. "Why do you need to go there?"

She slid out of the booth. "I'd like some time to process this, and I don't think Pearl's Diner is the place to do that."

"I agree, but wouldn't you be more comfortable at your hotel?" But even as Russ asked, the realization crashed into him. "You're staying at Tom's house, aren't you?"

"Yes." She offered her hand again. "It was nice to meet you. Thank you for telling me what happened, but I think I'd like to be alone for a little while."

Russ looked at her hand, level with his nose. He didn't want it that close to his face when he told her the rest of the story, so he slid out of the booth and stood in front of Ashley, surprised to find her nearly eye-to-eye with him.

"Don't thank me yet." He tugged his hat down low. "Tom and I live together."

CHAPTER 4

Ashley stood in the expansive front yard. The large white farmhouse—complete with a wraparound porch, wooden rocking chairs, and a faded, red barn in the background— overwhelmed her. Devastated her. Excited her. It was exactly as Tom had described it, except he wouldn't be inside.

"Are you coming in?" Russ asked from the porch. He hadn't acknowledged her since telling her to follow him. He'd simply jumped into his truck and waited for her to climb into her rental car. She had no idea how far they'd driven before she finally spotted the driveway, but that was only the beginning. They'd driven at least a mile before reaching the house.

"Ashley?"

How could Tom have forgotten to mention his roommate? She cozied up to the side of her car. "This doesn't feel right."

"I know today has been a shock, but I'm inviting you in. I thought you'd like to look around before you go."

Go? Go where? To her aunt and uncle's? Move back to Ohio? A smart woman would sit down with Russ and hash it out immediately, but that was more drama than she cared to face at the moment.

Ashley stepped away from the safety of her car. She should have been approaching the house with Tom, asking questions about the farm, the house … their wedding. Instead, Russ stood in front of her, his eyes as dark and melancholy as his attitude. When she reached the steps, close enough to notice the scar above his left eye, he turned and led her into the house.

The front door groaned as Russ entered, his boots thudding on the hardwood floor. Ashley's feet were glued to the distressed gray boards of the porch as she peeked in at the wide, carpeted staircase. One step and she'd be in the house she had planned to share with Tom.

Russ cleared his throat.

"Coming." Sorrow clutched at her chest as she lifted her foot. "I didn't think it would be this hard. It's just that ..."

"Tom should be here." His eyes softened.

She recognized that look—pity. Straightening her spine, she hustled past him. "I'm fine."

Her shoes clicked as she walked through the foyer and into the bright living room. A faded, paisley rug covered the center of the floor. An antique couch, a mismatched loveseat, and a fat, brown chair sat around it facing the stone fireplace. Family photos covered the sky-blue walls. Dark floor-to-ceiling shelves—overflowing with books—filled a third, partial wall. The smoky aroma from the fireplace filled the room as she walked toward the bookcase.

Agricultural textbooks. Computer coding for kids. Tom Clancy and Carl Hiaasen novels. Tom had mentioned his library and promised to show her his favorite books. Did Russ know which ones were his favorites?

She continued to explore, moving past Russ, back through the foyer and into the family room. The biggest, bluest sectional she'd ever seen sat against the far wall, fitted with recliners at each end. A massive flat-screen TV hung above another stone fireplace, but movies and games filled this room's shelves. Between the fireplace and the sectional sat a dingy brown steamer trunk with cracked leather straps. In the far corner, an unfinished puzzle filled the top of a two-person chrome dinette set. Like the living room, nothing matched. No wonder Tom suggested she bring her favorite furniture. Nothing would clash with his current motif.

Russ hustled by her, picking up paper plates and plastic cups as he moved through the family room. "I wasn't expecting company." A napkin drifted to the floor as he disappeared through a doorway at the end of the room.

Ashley followed, stepping into the open dining room and kitchen. The granite-topped island separated the stainless-steel, gourmet kitchen from the family-sized dining room with a ten-person, light-wood table and matching hutch.

No wonder Russ had rushed away. In addition to the disposable dishes on the island, empty foil baking pans covered the table. Grabbing the nearest pans, she stacked them together and filled them with dirty plates. She was on her way to the sink, hoping to find the trash, when Russ returned from a back hallway with an industrial-sized garbage can.

His eyebrows shot up. "What are you doing?"

Ashley dumped her haul into the can. "Cleaning up."

"You don't have to do that."

"I don't mind."

"I do." He dropped the container, then sighed. "My family was here a couple of days ago. I would have cleaned if I'd known you were coming."

If he'd known she existed.

"My mom taught me better than to ask company to clean up."

"And my mom taught me better than to watch while someone else does all the work. Besides, technically I'm not company. I promise you, I don't mind."

He sighed again, but this time he held out the garbage can. Ashley took her cue and dashed around the room, trying to clean up as much as possible before he changed his mind. After the last fork landed in the trash, Russ retreated again to the hallway.

When he came back empty-handed, she motioned toward the family room. "Can I see the rest of the house now?"

"Sure." Russ pointed as he walked. "Kitchen. Dining room. Family room." His voice faded as he rounded the corner. Ashley ran after him, catching up as he climbed the staircase. Unlike the wood floors on the main level, the carpeted stairs cushioned each step. The wooden handrails could use a polish, but the intricate swirls and leaf etchings more than made up for it. As they neared the top, she counted three doors to the left, one in front of her, and one to the right. More family pictures hung on the walls, though they were older, with several black-and-white photos in the bunch.

"There are four bedrooms up here. A couple of bathrooms. Nothing special."

To the point. An edge in his voice. She'd used a similar tone after her parents died. When she wanted the conversation to end so she could stop the memories. No one had appreciated it when she took that tone. Now she understood why. When they reached the top landing, she touched his hand. He flinched but didn't pull away.

"You're doing a good job," she said.

"With what?"

"Keeping it together. A dirty dining room is nothing to be embarrassed about. It's not easy losing a loved one."

Russ snorted. "You're handling it fine."

His words hit her like a blast of cold air. "Excuse me? I'm not 'just fine,' and I haven't had the chance to process this yet." She sucked in a breath, taking advantage of every bit of her height. "Please don't judge me." She didn't need anyone scrutinizing her or her grief again.

Russ scanned her face. She stared right back. His cheek twitched, and his jaw tightened.

What was she doing? He'd just lost his cousin. So what if he judged her? That didn't mean she had to be rude. Ashley forced her shoulders to relax. "I understand that you're hurt. I don't mean to make it more difficult."

His cheek twitched again, but his expression didn't crack. Those deep eyes searched hers. He must have found what he was looking for because Russ nodded. "It's okay." He pointed to the door on the right. "Grandma and Grandpa's room. Guest room. Bathroom. My room. And this"—Russ knocked on the nearest door—"this is Tom's room."

Ashley's nerves hitched. "Can I ... can I go in?"

Without a word, he opened the door. Dark-green walls. Dull, wood floors. Musky, earthy air. Was that Tom's cologne? Would the smell of his skin have reminded her of walks through the woods?

Against the far wall sat a dresser. On top of it, leaning against the wall, was a photo of her at a Reds baseball game. She'd emailed it to Tom a few months ago. They'd planned to see a Tigers game together next year. He said he'd buy the tickets, but he also said he couldn't wait to tell his family about her. A wave of emotion crashed into her, weakening her knees.

Russ' strong hand squeezed her elbow. He led her to a rickety chair next to Tom's bedroom door. "You look a little sick. Are you okay?"

Ashley pushed back the grief as Russ hovered. She needed space. "Could I have something to drink?" He dashed out of the room.

The solitude consumed her. She'd never officially met Tom, never touched him, yet the intensity of the loss surprised her. She hadn't expected the hollowness.

While she waited for Russ, Ashley familiarized herself with the rest of Tom's room. A blue, green, and tan star-patterned quilt covered the queen-sized bed. A simple, slatted headboard rested against the wall. Through the open closet door, she spotted several long-sleeved flannel shirts in a rainbow of colors. The midmorning sun shone through a sheer white curtain covering the bottom half of the double hung window. Two books sat beside a clock on the nightstand, but she couldn't see what they were.

"Here." Russ forced a glass of water into her hand, splashing half of the contents onto her legs. "Sorry."

"It's okay." She sipped the water, thankful for the excuse to sit in silence. Russ shifted beside her, then shifted again. When he moved the third time, she pasted a smile on her face, but it faded when she saw that awful, sad look in his eyes. "Really, I'm fine." Pushing herself off the chair, she took one more glance around the room. "Can I see the guest room?"

Stone Face didn't argue. He led her down the landing and swung open another door. The room was stuffy but cheery. Pink-and-tan plaid wallpaper met brown carpeting. A patchwork, pastel quilt covered the queen bed supported by a white metal footboard and headboard. A faded photo hung on the far wall. Over a distressed wooden dresser hung a rectangular mirror in a gold, leafy frame. Cozy country. Ashley could picture herself in that room.

Time to rip off the Band-Aid.

She turned to Russ and flashed what she hoped was her nicest smile. "I'll take it."

"Take what?"

Slipping off her shoes, she walked across the lush carpet and pushed open the window. Crisp, chilly air bit at her cheeks. "I think I'd like to stay here instead of in Tom's room."

"What?" His voice cracked.

She steeled herself before facing him. Russ stared at her as if she'd grown a third arm. Time to come clean. "I came here to start a new life. I'm staying."

CHAPTER 5

"What do you mean you're staying? You can't live here." The crazy woman moved around, opening drawers and looking under the bed. Cold air swirled through the room. Would she really move in?

Ashley pulled on the closet door. "I have to. I sold my house and donated most of my furniture, not to mention I start my new job after the holidays." She twisted and yanked, but the door stuck.

Russ had been meaning to fix that handle for years, but they never had enough visitors to justify the time. He crossed the room in three steps and moved Ashley out of his way. With a twist, lift, nudge, and pull, he opened the door. She slipped in front of him and peeked inside.

Taller than most women he knew, she blocked his view of the closet. As she moved, her hair shifted, sending silky brown strands sliding across her shoulder. Leaning back, she bumped into him. Cinnamon and orange. A scent as unexpected as her presence, both of which were more pleasant than he cared to admit, but that didn't mean they had to be permanent. "You're homeless, but you have a job?"

"Yes, with John Miller, a photographer in Boyne." Ashley looked back at him, whipping her citrusy hair across his face. "And I'm not homeless. Tom told me I could live here. Of course, I was supposed to be his wife."

Those wild eyes flashed at him—not really green, not quite brown, but fierce and focused. And dry. Not a tear in sight as she talked about his dead cousin. He should be grateful, but suspicion invaded his mind. His sisters had cried more than this woman,

Tom's supposed fiancée. Something was off. He needed more information so he could figure out what. "January's two months away. John would understand if you gave notice."

"I don't want to give notice. I want to learn how to become a portrait photographer."

"Fine, you need to stay in the area, but you don't need to stay here. If you sold your house, then you should have money available. Buy another one."

"It's not that easy. I—"

The front door slammed. "Yoo-hoo!"

Russ closed his eyes. It had to be his imagination. She wasn't supposed to arrive for hours.

"Russ? Whose car is that?"

Nope, not his imagination. "I'm upstairs, Mom!"

Ashley's eyes widened. "Does your mom live here too?"

"She's staying with me until the memorial. She didn't want me to be alone."

"That's nice."

"Honey, who's here? That car is adorable."

Russ motioned toward the door. "I suppose I need to introduce you."

"Probably. If Tom didn't tell you about me, then I doubt your mom knows."

Her body remained rigid, but her eyes narrowed. It didn't take a genius to recognize that look, but it didn't hurt that he'd grown up with three sisters. Ashley put up a good front, but it had to be hard to pretend like she wasn't upset with Tom's … oversight.

Russ offered his arm. "I'll introduce you." Those beautiful eyes looked into his, then down at his arm. She slid a steady hand around his bicep. A surge of energy shot across his skin as her fingers tickled him through his sleeve.

"Thanks."

He nodded but couldn't seem to move. Soft fingers. Pink cheeks. Strong spirit. She wasn't like any of his sisters.

Ashley's eyebrows pinched together. "Russ?"

"Oh! Um, let's go." He took off, pulling her alongside him.

"Honey?"

"Comin', Mom."

"I brought Robbie Kraft with me. He wants to talk about Tom's will."

They met his mom at the bottom of the stairs. Curly, graying ponytail, sparkly seasonal sweatshirt, and electric-blue sneakers, same as always. A welcome sight after a day full of surprises.

"Hey, Mom." Russ hugged her. For no good reason, it disappointed him that she didn't smell like oranges. "This is Ashley Johnson. She's a friend of Tom's. Ashley, this is my mother, Kathleen Russell."

"You're Ashley?" Mom's eyes widened. "Robbie was just asking about you."

Rob walked in from the kitchen, an apple in hand. His wife's influence seemed to be working. "I stole one of your candy bars." So much for that theory. He extended a hand.

Russ shook it. "Good to see you again. What brings you out to the house?"

Mom took Ashley's free hand and led her toward the kitchen. "Tom's will. Ashley, why don't we get you a cold drink? I know my son. He didn't offer you anything, did he?"

"No, but I didn't ask."

A spark of panic ignited in Russ' chest. He wasn't sure he wanted those women talking about him.

Rob smacked Russ on the back. "Where did she come from?"

"Ohio."

"I can't believe you guys didn't mention her before."

"I've never met her until today. How do you know about her?"

"I need to talk to her about that. Come on, let's get this over with."

Russ followed his old high-school classmate through the house. In the kitchen, Ashley sat at the island with cold cuts, cheese, and lemonade, none of which had been in the house when Russ left that morning. Mom's hospitality skills amazed him.

"Robbie, can I get you anything?" she asked.

"I'm fine," he said, waving his apple. "As long as we're all here, let's get started."

"This is private. I should let you talk alone." Ashley slid off the stool.

"No, you need to be here." Rob dropped his briefcase on the table. "I need both of you here."

Russ leaned against the island beside Ashley. "Both of who?"

"You and Ashley."

"What?" Ashley's voice harmonized with his. They faced each other. She looked as confused as he felt.

Russ shook his head. "Just when you think the day can't get any weirder."

Mom handed him and Ashley each a glass of lemonade as her phone rang. She checked the screen and frowned. "It's Liz. I'd better take this," she said as she stepped into the living room.

"Before Tom left for his trip, he called me and scheduled an appointment," Rob said. "He wanted to talk about adding Ashley to his will." He glanced at her. "I assume he meant you."

Perfect. Russ looked at her now. "I didn't know Tom had a will. Did you?"

"No. That's ridiculous. He wouldn't include me ... would he?"

"No." Rob's shoulders relaxed. "He died before the appointment, so we never talked, but I wanted to see if he'd spoken to either of you or given you a copy. If neither of you has anything in writing from him, then we're all set. His will stands."

Russ held up his hands. "Don't look at me. Tom knew better than to give me hard copies of anything."

"Our only written communication was through email and texts," Ashley said. "Actually, he did send me one letter, but it doesn't mention his will."

"A letter?" Rob walked toward them. "May I see it?"

Her face brightened to the cutest shade of pink. "I, I guess. You're not going to read it out loud, are you?"

"Not if you don't want me to, but I'd like to see what's in it."

"Okay, sure." She left the kitchen, the clack of her footsteps fading as she disappeared around the corner.

Russ refocused his attention on Rob. "Why do you need to see her letter?"

"I want to check something."

Rob said something about his kids, but Russ' ears focused on Ashley's steps as they padded around above them. A door slammed overhead. Her footsteps hurried to the kitchen, slowing as she approached the island. She held a piece of paper against her chest, her gaze honed in on Rob. "For your eyes only, right?"

"I promise."

With two slow steps, she walked to Rob and handed over the page. "It's just a letter."

As he read, she twisted her fingers and shifted her weight. Russ wanted to ease her discomfort. Would she want a hug? A drink? A kind word? Was it even his responsibility?

Rob blew out a loud, long breath.

A weight settled on Russ' shoulders. "That doesn't sound good."

"Congratulations, Ashley. You own this house."

"What?"

Russ couldn't tell who yelled the loudest, but Ashley definitely won the wide-eyed, drop-jawed contest. Tom left her the house? Anger coursed through Russ' limbs, tensing every muscle and joint, threatening to crush his bones and sanity. "Did you say Ashley owns this house? The house that my grandpa built? The Russell family home?"

Rob nodded. "If Tom legally owned the house, then he can legally will it away."

"I don't know who technically owns the house." Russ clenched his fists. "Grandma and Grandpa lived here until they died. By then Tom and I were working the farm full time, so it made sense to move in. Tom knew all of this. He kept the paperwork. Uncle Bill probably has a copy of something, but his son just died. I'm not going to burden him with a nonsense legal matter based on a letter."

"But how?" Ashley wrapped her arms around herself. "It's a letter."

Rob held up the paper. "May I read a section out loud?"

"If you need to."

"This is what I was looking for: 'I'm sorry about the fight. Our relationship is more important than any trip. I know how important a family and home are to you, and I will do everything in my power to give you everything you need. My house is yours.'" Rob tossed the letter on the table. "In court, that could hold up as a holographic will. Tom gave Ashley the house."

My house is yours. The words lingered in the kitchen. Ashley got her wish—she wasn't homeless anymore. Russ was. "What about the farm? Does she get everything?"

"I'd like to read the rest of the letter and do a little more research on holographic wills. This is the first one I've handled, so I want to be certain before I offer advice."

"It doesn't make sense." Frustration ripped through Russ' body as he turned to confront Ashley. "If you only emailed each other, why did he conveniently write that letter?"

"Conveniently?" The soft lines of her face hardened as Ashley pulled her shoulders back. "That letter was an apology. Tom and I got into a fight a few weeks ago because he wanted me to move here, but he was going on that camping trip and asked me to fly up as soon as he got back. I was mad because we wouldn't be able to talk until the day I flew in. I don't like traveling alone, and I wasn't comfortable relocating my whole life without having a contact here, but he wouldn't cancel his trip.

"The letter says he wrote it in Marquette. It's dated the first day of his trip. It wasn't 'convenient.' It was heartfelt and thoughtful. And it was the last thing he said to me before he died. He may not have talked about me, but at least he was thinking about me."

Mom shuffled back into the kitchen. "What did I miss?"

Russ crossed his arms. Ashley could deal with it. Instead of responding, she pressed her lips into a thin, white line.

Rob picked up the letter. "Tom left Ashley the house."

"What?" The color drained from Mom's face. "Can he do that? Why would he do that?"

Russ suppressed a groan. He and Ashley had enough to figure out. He wouldn't unleash the Mother Inquisition on her now. "It doesn't matter. Besides, we don't need to understand why he did it. We need to figure out what to do about it."

"We can fix it, though, right?" Ashley's song-like voice raked his nerves. "I can sell the house to Russ."

"I don't have the money to buy it, and I've got a giant mortgage on the new farm equipment." The sterile white walls of the kitchen closed in on him, threatening to consume him. He needed a solution. He paced across the tile, trying to relieve the pressure.

With limited space and options, he stopped at the island, gripping the cold granite countertop.

A warm hand landed on his shoulder. "It's okay. We'll figure it out."

Ashley's touch soothed his tense muscles. Why did she have to be so charming? "I'm sorry about this mess," he said. "It's bad enough that you just found out about Tom—"

"What?" Mom spun Ashley around and pulled her into the death grip of comfort, the same stifling hug she'd given Russ every day for a year after his dad died. He'd never been able to avoid it. Small chance he'd be able to rescue Ashley.

When Ashley wheezed, Mom stepped back. "Robbie, thank you for coming out here, but this is too much for today." Her hands framed Ashley's face. "Honey, we don't need to worry about the house right now. You can stay here as long as it takes to figure this out."

CHAPTER 6

The following afternoon, Ashley stuffed another sweater in the drawer, finally filling the oak dresser. With her clothes unpacked, she inspected the sparse bedroom. The sunny, friendly room didn't feel right under the circumstances. Invading Tom's room, however, seemed morbid.

Someone stomped through the hallway, the footsteps fading down the stairs. Russ. Tom talked about his cousin more than anyone else. Why didn't he mention their living arrangement? She should have figured it out, though. They did everything together, from working on the farm to playing in a winter basketball league. Tom called it necessary, both of them having grown up surrounded by sisters.

Now, instead of meeting those sisters, Ashley was trying to figure out ways not to annoy Russ any more than she already had. She'd imagined them being friends, not strange roommates, though his hospitality was more than she would have extended. But how long could they live like that?

Her cell phone jingled. Rose. Ashley had talked to her aunt when she landed but hadn't called since then, and she'd ignored both of Rose's calls. She and John were worried enough. How would they take the news of Tom's death, especially considering Ashley's decision to stay in Michigan without him? Of course, the truth couldn't be worse than any tragic scenario Rose would concoct if Ashley didn't talk to her soon. Rose deserved better than that.

With a deep breath, Ashley answered her phone. "Hi, Aunt Rose. Sorry I missed your call last night."

"That's all right. I thought you might be busy but wanted to call anyway. Did you make it to Boyne okay?"

Ashley glanced at the family picture on the dresser. Sorrow clogged her throat. "Yes, everything's fine."

"And Tom made it to the airport for you?" Rose's voice lowered.

Ashley could picture her aunt's creased face with her eyebrows pulled together and her lips pinched as they did when delivery drivers left her packages in the rain. She wouldn't lie to Rose, but she couldn't add to her aunt's worries either. "He wasn't able to meet me, but I'm at his house now. His aunt and cousin are here too. I'm looking forward to getting to know them better." Which was true, but Ashley couldn't control the hitch in her voice.

"Is everything okay?"

"Yeah, I'm fine, just"—her voice caught—"a little tired."

"You should rest. I know I haven't been completely supportive of your decision, but I'm proud of you. This is a big change, and it's not an easy thing to do. I don't know how you found the courage to do it, but I admire you for doing it."

Her praise pierced Ashley's heart, pushing her tear ducts past full. "Thanks, Aunt Rose."

"Now go get some rest."

Ashley ended the call, but the tears continued to fall. She should be celebrating, not mourning. Rose believed Ashley was starting a new life, but it was more of the same. Another death and another funeral. Another hole in Ashley's heart, filling in with loss and pain instead of growth and joy. Life in Michigan wasn't supposed to happen that way. Tom was young and healthy. A friend. Her new family.

And now he was gone.

God, not again. Ashley sank to the floor and sobbed.

* * * * * * *

Russ headed back upstairs to look for his watch. It had to be on the nightstand. As he reached the top step, he couldn't miss the closed door in front of him. For eight years he'd looked at the door without giving it a thought. He'd already noticed it three times that day.

What was Ashley doing in there? She'd closed herself in after dinner the night before and hadn't come out since. He walked past the door and paused. Crying? But her short gasps weren't the cause of the chills down his spine.

"I can't." She sucked in a deep breath. "Not again."

Again? He clenched his fingers together. Another fiancé, or something else? Every shaky breath Ashley drew weakened his resolve. Her arrival and the will had surprised him, but until that moment he'd never thought about how hard it must be for her. At least he had his mom and sisters nearby. Who did Ashley have?

Staring at the glossy black doorknob, Russ raised his hand. Before he could talk himself out of it, he knocked.

Ashley coughed, then cleared her throat. "Yes?"

"It's Russ. I, uh, I wanted to see if you need anything."

"I'm fine, thank you."

"It sounds like you're crying." She blew her nose but didn't respond. Now what? His sisters always wanted to talk, but he never knew what to say. Maybe Ashley was more like him. "Want to go for a drive?"

More sniffling. "A drive?"

"Grab your coat."

She shuffled around behind the door, then the knob turned. Ashley peeked through the narrow crack, her eyes red and swollen. "Where are we going?"

"It's better if I show you."

She stepped back, allowing the door to open more, and rubbed her fingers under her eyes. "I'm not really presentable."

Not presentable? He'd never known jeans and a sweater could look so good, but he couldn't say that. Instead, he shrugged. "No one else will see you."

"Do I need to bring anything?"

"Just your coat."

Ashley pressed her lips together, her eyebrows pinched above her nose. For a moment, he thought she might close the door in his face, but her chin bobbed slightly. She pulled her coat out of the closet before meeting him at the door. "Okay, let's go."

Russ led the way downstairs. Ashley sniffled behind him, but her footsteps fell into sync with his. Neither of them spoke as they trekked out the front door and to Russ' truck. The engine turned over easily, and they rumbled along the dirt driveway before turning onto the equally bumpy road. Out of the corner of his eye, he watched Ashley brace herself against the door. At least she'd stopped crying.

They rode in silence for nearly twenty minutes as Russ navigated the familiar unmarked roads through acres of woodlands. As he guided the truck up the last hill, peace washed over him. Hopefully, Ashley would find the same comfort there.

As they approached the top, the trees thinned out until the truck pulled into a clearing. Fluffy clouds dotted the blue sky above them, and miles of orchards stretched out below. Smatterings of green grass circled the dormant trees as the last, desperate leaves clung to barren branches.

Ashley gasped, leaning closer to the windshield. "Is this your farm?"

"The western fields are, but the rest belong to our neighbors." Russ backed the truck up until the bed and cab leveled out, then he killed the engine. "Let's go."

"Won't you need a jacket?" Ashley asked as she zipped her coat.

He reached behind the seat and grabbed his Carhartt and an old blanket. "I rarely leave home without them."

"Even in July?"

He couldn't stop his smile. "Fifty-degree nights can happen." Her eyes widened, but she didn't flinch. Instead, she opened her door and stepped out.

Following her lead, he climbed out. The air wasn't yet cold, but he knew how the chill could eat at one's skin. He slid into his coat, preferring to maintain warmth rather than trying to create it. As Ashley stared into the distance, Russ reached into the truck bed's toolbox for his seat cushions. When he unlatched the tailgate, she turned around. Her eyebrows popped up.

"What?" he asked.

"You seem very … prepared."

"I am. For unplanned fishing trips or visits from the nephews." Russ tossed the cushions on the cold metal tailgate, resenting the need to defend himself. He dropped the blanket next to the cushions. "It's northern Michigan. Even in the summer, the weather's unpredictable."

Pink colored her cheeks, and he instantly regretted his tone. He'd brought her out there for comfort, not chastisement. Adjusting a cushion, Russ sat to one side on the tailgate and turned his attention to the view. Ashley took her time shuffling over, stopping at the other side. Without looking at her, he nudged the other cushion toward her.

She hopped onto the tailgate, barely rocking the truck. "How did you find this place?"

"I don't remember exactly. It was sometime in high school. I was probably out exploring."

"It's beautiful."

"I know."

She shifted and shimmied beside him, bouncing the entire truck. When she finally stopped moving, she sighed. "Thank you for bringing me here."

"You sounded like you needed to get out."

"Thanks for noticing." A few minutes later she started kicking her feet, once again rocking the truck. When she started blowing on her fingers, Russ smiled, reaching into his pockets for his gloves. He handed them to her.

She hesitated but took them. "Is there anything you don't carry with you?"

"Not when it comes to staying warm."

"Do you usually come out here when it's this cold?"

Pain clenched at his heart. "I haven't been up here for a few years … since my dad died."

"I'm sorry."

"I've had time to get over it."

"You never get over it."

He looked directly at her. "You lost your dad?"

She met his gaze. "And mom. Seventeen years ago." A half smile tugged at her lips. "The pain never really goes away, but you adapt."

Seventeen years without parents? They must have died when she was in high school. Russ couldn't imagine all of that time without his folks. What would it have been like?

Ashley groaned, pulling her legs up in front of her. "You're looking at me like that again."

"Like what?"

"The poor-little-Ashley look. It doesn't matter how many years pass, people always look at me like that when I tell them my parents died when I was eighteen. That's one of the things I liked about Tom. He never looked at me that way."

"You two met?"

"No, but we video chatted. He never pitied me. He always treated me like I was everyone else."

"How did you two meet anyway?"

"The internet," Ashley said as casually as she might tell someone they met at a coffee shop or birthday party. If it didn't bother her, who was he to judge, but why hadn't Tom ever mentioned it? "I still can't believe he never told you."

Russ sighed. "He might have. I didn't always pay attention."

"That's not what he told me."

Interesting. Giving her his complete attention, Russ swung his legs up and crossed them in front of him. "What did he say?"

She turned toward him, copying his posture. "You were best friends and the only boys in the family. He knew everything about you. I assumed you knew as much about him."

"I thought I did too."

Ashley sank back against the side of the truck. "This whole situation is surreal." She shook her head, looking down. "I don't even … I mean, this was arranged, but … why wouldn't he—"

"What do you mean arranged?" It wasn't possible, was it?

She glanced up, her eyes red. "What?"

"You said it was arranged. What was arranged?"

"The, um"—her face flushed—"the engagement."

No way! Russ leaned forward. "Did he actually talk you into it?"

"Talk me into what?"

He scrubbed a hand over his face, trying to disguise the surprise. "An arranged marriage. Two years ago, his sister got a divorce. We couldn't believe it. She and her husband seemed so perfect, but she said they didn't love each other anymore."

"And Tom said that didn't matter." Ashley's eyes brightened. "He said it was a commitment, a covenant, that if people could fall in love once, they could fall in love again as long as they honored their promises to each other."

Had Tom found a woman who agreed with his beliefs about marriage? "Do you really believe that? Would you marry a stranger because of a commitment?"

She lifted a shoulder. "I would never marry a complete stranger, but the concept has merit. My mom kept a journal that talked about how happy she was to have married her best friend. The more Tom and I talked, the more I enjoyed it. I wasn't in love with him, but he was one of my closest friends.

"One day it hit us. Instead of being best friends who fall in love and get married, like my parents did, we could be best friends who got married, then let love happen." Ashley didn't crack a smile or break eye contact. Everything about her demeanor screamed sincerity.

A bizarre amount of admiration welled up for her. A woman who wasn't chasing a wedding or prince charming. This woman wanted an honest-to-goodness lifetime commitment. How had Tom gotten so lucky?

"Do you think I'm crazy?" she asked, crossing her arms. "Because my aunt and uncle weren't exactly supportive of this."

"That's probably a reasonable reaction."

"You too?" She threw her hands in the air as she rolled her eyes. "It's not like we're eighteen-year-old kids who just met. We're adults, and we're making a practical, intelligent decision. I'm thirty-five years old, and I'm tired of being alone. I want a marriage like my parents had, and Tom and I have a chance at that. Well, we had …" Her face crumpled.

"I'm not judging you. You didn't let me finish. I can understand your aunt and uncle's reaction. It's a shocking concept for most people. Tom and I talked about it before, but you still surprised me. I just don't understand—"

"Why Tom didn't mention me." She sagged against the truck.

No tears, but Russ recognized the grief and pain that tugged at Ashley's face. She might not love Tom, but she and Russ had both lost their best friend. That he could understand. And maybe he could help. "I don't know why Tom didn't tell me about you, but I know Tom. He never meant to hurt anyone, but he never thought much about how his actions affected others. I'm not making excuses for him. That's the kind of man he was. At least he told you about me. Tom didn't trust me enough to tell me he was getting married, and he usually told me everything."

Ashley nodded, but her posture didn't change. That wasn't why he'd brought her to the most beautiful view in Boyne Heights.

Russ hopped off the truck. He grabbed the edge of her cushion and spun her toward him. "I'm not very good at consoling people. That's why I brought you here. I don't have all of the answers, and I'm not sure I want them, but here I can forget about it for a while. I can be quiet and enjoy the orchards, and sometimes that's the best therapy. Do me a favor and sit here for a minute."

Eyes wide, she nodded. Stepping aside, Russ sat beside her and let the view hypnotize him. The midday sun illuminated every visible acre—his family's history and, he had assumed, his and Tom's future. Now what?

"Will you tell me about your farm?" Ashley asked. He glanced at her. Moisture clung to her eyelashes, captivating his attention. She tucked a strand of hair behind her ear as she gazed out over the orchards. "I didn't mean to interrupt you, but I've spent a lot of time alone, so I have a hard time passing up a conversation."

"That's okay. I don't mind talking about the farm."

"Really? Because I don't want to bother you."

His arm brushed hers, and he noticed how close their legs were. Bothering him? Yes. Putting some space between them,

Russ looked back at the apple trees. "My great-grandpa bought this farm, and I plan to keep it in the family as long as I can."

CHAPTER 7

Bacon.

Ashley inhaled the savory scent as she rolled over, pressing her nose into the soft, wet pillow. She rubbed her face, wiping drool off her chin. Sleep clung to her eyelids, but she pried them open.

Darkness. Who cooked bacon in the dark?

She searched for her clock. More darkness. What was going on? She pushed herself up and looked in the direction of her nightstand. Reaching for the tabletop, her hand flapped through the air.

No nightstand.

Bacon.

Darkness.

Tom.

The past few days rushed back at her. She was at Tom's house. No, her house. And someone was cooking breakfast in the dark. Ashley's mouth watered as her brain struggled with the details.

Swinging her feet over the edge of the bed, she ran her hands across the soft patchwork quilt and down the side of the bed until she located her pile of clothes on the floor. She slipped out of her pajamas, then stuffed her arms and legs into different pieces of clothing, hoping she wouldn't look like a four-year-old who'd dressed herself. Shuffling around the bed, she made her way to the door, drawn by the sliver of light peeking under the bottom.

Ashley opened the door to more heavenly aromas. Bacon. Coffee. Butter. They beckoned her toward the light at the bottom of the stairs. The bare floors chilled her feet, but hunger propelled her through the house and into the blinding light of the kitchen.

As she squinted in the brightness, she spotted Russ by the stove, his eyebrows raised and a flowered apron around his waist. She had to be dreaming. She blinked a few times, but he didn't move. The apron kept its flowers. Why would he wear that? She should ask, but she needed to wake up first. "Coffee?"

Russ pointed his spatula at the far counter.

"Cups?"

The spatula rose, indicating a distant cupboard.

Ashley nodded, her bare feet smacking against the floor. She filled a mug, then turned to the island, where Russ had set a bottle of creamer. Considerate. She took the creamer and poured until the coffee turned a familiar tan, then pressed the warm mug against her lips and sipped. Smooth, nutty perfection. She'd never dreamed about coffee this good before. "This is really happening, isn't it?"

"What?"

"The bacon. Coffee. Apron." Ashley leaned to the left to peek around Russ at the stove clock. "At five a.m. Good Lord, you're crazy."

"No, I'm a farmer. What are you doing up?"

"Bacon." Ashley cradled the mug in her hands before making her way to the table. She kicked out a chair and plopped onto it, tucking her feet beneath her to warm them.

"You got up for bacon?"

"No, I smelled bacon. That made me hungry. I got up because I'm hungry." Ashley tried to look at Russ when she spoke, but the stove light assaulted her retinas. She stifled a groan as she crossed her arms on the table and rested her head on them. Her mouth watered, but exhaustion weighed her down. Metal scraped metal as food sizzled and popped around her. A hinge creaked. Muted thuds. Her breath flowed in and out.

Mom humming. Dad bellowing about the city council as he turned the pages of the newspaper. Ashley sitting at the kitchen table as Mom flipped eggs and buttered toast. Dad hugging them both, growling as he squeezed her until she giggled. Every Sunday, breakfast … with bacon.

A once-familiar peace settled over her. Ashley hadn't thought about those breakfasts in years. She might have forgotten them completely until Russ and his apron. She should thank him and drink her coffee and get some bacon. As soon as she could open her eyes. And pick up her head. The kitchen table wasn't a bad place for a nap.

Warmth wrapped around her. No, not warmth—arms. Someone picked her up. Ashley forced her eyes open long enough to get a blurry look at Russ. "Is breakfast ready?"

"You fell asleep."

Her head dropped onto his shoulder. "Just resting."

"Sure."

"Coffee?"

"You can get it when you wake up." Russ' voice rumbled in his chest, soothing her. As quickly as he'd picked her up, he set her down on a velvety bed. She should really get up, talk with Russ about what they were going to do, but a heavy blanket covered her, sealing in the warmth. Every last ounce of resistance melted away as Ashley surrendered to the welcoming pillow.

"Sleep well."

"Mmmmm."

* * * * * *

Russ tucked the last edge of the quilt under Ashley's shoulder as she mumbled. Bunching the quilt in her arms, she rolled away from him, her long hair falling across one of his mother's stitched pillows.

"Good morning. What are you up to?"

"Shhh." Russ pointed at the couch. "Ashley."

His mom stepped beside him and leaned close. "Why is she on the couch?"

"She said she wanted bacon, then fell asleep at the table."

Mom chuckled. "Poor kid. Come on. I'll eat her bacon."

Russ smiled. He hadn't wanted Mom to stay with him, but the last week had been so quiet that it was nice to have the company. He draped an arm around her shoulders and led her into the kitchen, where two plates full of food sat on the island. "You're just in time."

"Lucky for me she fell asleep. Oh, it looks good." Mom carried the plates to the table while Russ refilled his coffee mug. As he sat, she took a sip from Ashley's mug. "Mmm, perfect. I'll take care of this for her too."

"How nice of you." Russ grabbed his fork and attacked the food, his stomach growling its thanks.

"Tell me about Ashley."

Eggs clogged his throat. He coughed around the food, desperate for air.

"Oh, honey. Are you okay?"

He pounded his chest. "Fine. Fine. Do you need me to warm up your coffee?"

"I've barely touched it. What's going on?"

"Nothing." Russ picked up his fork again, but iron fingers clamped around his wrist. He locked eyes with her. Sweet, gentle caregiver when she wanted to be. Steel-jawed alligator the rest of the time.

"I'm going to ask you about Ashley," she said. "I'd hate for you to choke again."

He sighed. "You know as much as I do. She's Tom's friend. Moved here from Ohio. Works as a medical transcriptionist, but she's an amateur photographer. She starts an internship next year. Most of what I know she told us both at dinner."

"But Tom left the house to her? It's been in the family for generations. I don't understand how he could do this, or why."

Russ took another gigantic bite. How could he explain it when he didn't understand it himself?

"I wonder if there's anything we can do about it."

"You heard Rob. We'd have to find the original paperwork, and I have no idea where to look." She pursed her lips the way she did when he and his sisters didn't take her advice, so Russ patted her hand. "Don't worry. I'll take care of it, even if I have to hire someone to help us out."

"You take such good care of me." She squeezed his hand. "Your father would be so proud."

"Thanks."

"Now about Ashley—"

"Mom."

"Is she single?"

Russ shoveled eggs into his mouth. The sooner he got away from his matchmaking mother, the better.

CHAPTER 8

Ashley stretched her arms over her head, flexing her feet against the soft fabric. Light shone against her eyelids and warmed her face, but she wasn't ready to get out of bed yet. Pulling the blanket back around her shoulders, she rolled onto … nothing.

THUMP!

Ouch.

"Everything okay in there?"

Ashley squinted against the sun. Why was she in the living room? She'd been dreaming of Russ and flowers, or had that really happened? Her stomach growled. Why did her mind keep going back to bacon?

"Good morning." Kathleen strolled into the room. "Are you okay?"

Ashley rubbed her palms over her thick eyelids. "It's so early."

"It's almost nine o'clock."

"Ugh. I don't like mornings."

"I've noticed." Cool fingers pulled Ashley's hands away from her face. When Kathleen smiled, delicate lines framed her dark-brown eyes. "Let me make you breakfast."

"Didn't I eat breakfast?"

"You tried. Come on. I saved some for you." Kathleen pulled her up.

Food first, then coffee. Ashley trudged into the kitchen for the second time that morning. In an hour or two, she might be coherent enough to carry on a conversation. When Kathleen pushed a mug into her hands, she noticed the rich coffee aroma.

"I put cream in it, just like you had it before."

Ashley sipped the perfectly flavored liquid, letting it warm her to the core. "Thank you."

"You're welcome." Kathleen practically danced around the kitchen, waving pans and spinning utensils, faster and more efficiently than Rose. "You're a rare breed around here. We're so used to waking up early that we sometimes forget there are people who don't get up with the sun."

"I love the sun. I just don't like watching it come up."

Kathleen's hearty laugh lightened Ashley's spirit. She sat at the island, working on her coffee while Russ' mom worked on breakfast. "Do you have any plans for today?" Kathleen asked.

"Not yet. I was supposed to be with Tom today." Blinking back tears, she looked down at her coffee as she tried to control her grief.

"Oh, honey."

Summoning her I'm-okay face, Ashley put on a smile and gave Kathleen her attention. Russ' mom stood in the middle of the kitchen, watching her with sad eyes. Ashley straightened her spine, no longer tired. "I guess I'll have breakfast, then go exploring. I'm sure there's lots to see in town."

"There is, but you don't know which shops are the best. I'll take you."

"I don't want to interrupt your day."

"You won't." Kathleen turned back to the stove and flipped the food. "I'm an old retired woman with four kids who take care of me. I can spend my days however I want. Once I'm done with breakfast, we'll see the sights. I'd like to spend some time getting acquainted with Tom's friend."

Friend. Fiancée. Whatever.

"Did you two meet in college?"

Every muscle in Ashley's body tensed. She'd tried to prepare herself for that question, but panic still threatened. She took a deep breath and willed her body to relax. The truth was always the best answer. "We met online."

"How did you manage that?"

"I was researching northern Michigan and found a blog post Tom wrote about the farm."

"He wrote blog posts?"

"He posted once a month for a website about fruit farms. He was the only farmer from northern Michigan, and I loved his pictures and descriptions."

Kathleen carried a plate piled high with eggs and bacon to Ashley. "Well, I'll be. I had no idea."

"I don't think many people did." Ashley's stomach roared in appreciation of the food. "Thank you so much. This looks wonderful."

"It's nothing. Now tell me how this blog introduced you two."

"Tom included his email address on each post, so I sent him a note telling him how much I enjoyed his photos. He responded, and we stayed in touch."

"Why were you researching northern Michigan farms?"

"I wasn't specifically researching farms. My mom and dad used to vacation here before I was born. They brought me up a couple of times, but I was so young that I don't remember it well. My mom talked about retiring here someday. I guess I was trying to reconnect with her by finding out more about the places she loved."

"Your parents found a different place to retire?"

"No." Ashley swallowed. "My parents passed away."

"Oh, honey."

"It's okay." She raised a hand and put on a smile. "It was a long time ago. There's been enough tragedy recently. Why don't we talk about something else?"

"Okay then. It'll only take an hour or two to visit downtown, then we can see the rest of the sights. The fall colors are pretty much gone, but there are still plenty of beautiful places to see. The lake? The farm?"

Ashley bit into a piece of bacon, and crispy, salty goodness filled her mouth. She stuffed in another slice. "The grocery store. I could buy another five pounds of this stuff. It's amazing."

Kathleen chuckled. "I'm glad you like it, but we can't get it at the store. This is Russ' special recipe. He cured it himself."

Ashley hesitated to eat the last lonely strip on her plate. "Who makes their own bacon?"

"My son is a wonder."

Up at five and cooking food that he made himself? A wonder indeed. "Then maybe I'll buy him another pig. How much does that cost?"

"A few hundred, maybe a thousand. Depends on the size."

"Or maybe not."

"You don't need to replace anything. You're our guest. Let us take care of you while you're here."

"I appreciate that, but eventually I'd like to help."

"If you insist, I'm sure we can come up with something. For now, finish up, get dressed, and we'll hit the road."

* * * * * * *

Russ slammed the filing-cabinet drawer shut. It echoed through the square, cinderblock building. The farm office reminded him more of his old elementary school than an office with three Formica-topped metal desks, a gray concrete floor, and fluorescent lights buzzing overhead. He looked around the open space. Piles of paperwork still covered Tom's desk in the farthest corner. Three filing cabinets lined the wall beside it. Two armchairs and a couch sat in the adjacent corner, where Russ had fallen asleep more than once during a busy harvest season. The kitchen near the front door—including a tan electric stove, off-white refrigerator, and rarely-cleaned microwave—could have come from his college apartment. None of it, though, offered any clue as to where Russ might find a will. "Chad, do you have any idea where Tom kept his legal documents?"

Wheels squeaked as Chad pushed his chair around the cluttered office. "You're looking at them. He kept everything in those cabinets."

"Are you sure? Did he ever ask you to take anything home?"

"Not with *my* kids. Whenever he had time, he was scanning things into the computer to get rid of the hard copies, so he might've tossed some when he was done. What are you looking for?"

"Nothing." Even if Russ could find a different copy of Tom's will, chances were slim it would supersede that letter. "Thanks a lot, Tom."

"What?"

"Nothing. I'm going out." Russ swiped his keys off the desk and stomped past Chad on his tiny, wobbly chair. "You look stupid."

"I feel stupid. We need help in here. I can't handle this mess without Tom, and I don't want to try."

"Do whatever it takes to keep me out of here. I'll see you later." Russ had enough problems without worrying about organizing the office. If he got stuck doing paperwork, too, he'd leave the state and start over.

Yeah, right. The farm was in his blood. He couldn't function without it any better than he could function without lungs. If he had to work inside to save it, he would, but right now he needed to get onto the land and clear his head. In three strides, he was through the small building and out in the fresh, cool air.

He welcomed the blinding sun, closing his eyes and turning to face it. If only it could burn away all of his problems. The only thing he liked about the office was its location. Built on the opposite side of the farm from the house, fruit trees and dirt surrounded the square, one-story building. More tractors than cars drove along the road out front. When he needed space to think, he could walk in any direction and not see another building for miles.

HONK! HONK!

Now what? Russ opened his eyes in time to see Mom's rusty red truck crawl into the parking lot. She waved from the driver's seat, her giant smile warming him more than the sun. As she swung the truck around, Russ spotted a brown ponytail. Ashley said something, then she and his mom laughed. He couldn't explain why, but he wanted to see that happen more often.

The truck rolled to a stop beside him. He opened Mom's door and gave her a hug. "What are you doing here?"

"I'm giving Ashley a tour."

"How's it going?"

Mom nodded toward Ashley. Tom's fiancée wandered around the parking lot, pointing her camera at the building, the sign, him. Something turned in his chest. He liked knowing that she would have a picture of him.

"Are you enjoying your tour?" he asked.

Ashley lowered her camera and flashed a smile. "Everything's so beautiful. Tom sent pictures, but they aren't the same."

"We visited Boyne Heights, and now Ashley wants to see the orchards. I told her there's not much to see this time of the year, but she insisted. I thought you could take her around."

"I'm heading out to check on some of the trees now. I can take you guys with me."

"Not me." Mom climbed back in the truck. "I forgot about my coffee date with Rita. I'm meeting her in Traverse City, so I need to get on the road." The engine fired before Russ realized what was happening. "You can take Ashley home, can't you?"

"What?" Ashley rushed up beside him as Mom winked, then waved her way out of the driveway. "Where's she going?" Ashley looked up at him. "She's coming back, right?"

"She has lunch plans."

"But she didn't say anything about it to me. I would've driven myself if I'd known."

Russ snorted. "She didn't want you driving yourself. That's why she didn't say anything. Now I have to drive you home."

"Would she really try to set us up? Tom just died."

"But she doesn't know you were engaged. All she sees is an attractive, single female in close proximity to her only, single son. It does funny things to her grandma DNA."

"I'm sorry. If you drive me back to the house, I'll get my car and get out of your way."

"No need." Russ crunched his way across the parking lot and yanked open the passenger door of his truck. "I'm heading into the orchard. As long as you're here, I'll show you around."

She pressed her lips together, cocking her head to the side, same as the first time he invited her on a drive, except this time she didn't quickly join him.

"Is there a problem?"

She crossed her arms. "You don't think I had anything to do with this, do you?"

"Not at all."

"Because I didn't."

"I believe you."

"I'm not pretending Tom and I were in love, because we weren't, but still, I would never—"

"Ashley."

"—consider anything like this—"

"Ashley?"

"I promise."

Russ tuned out her ramblings as he moved toward her. When he finally stopped in front of her, she clammed up. "This isn't the first time my mom has tried to set me up. I wouldn't expect anything less from her."

"Oh." Those large eyes blinked. "As long as we're clear."

"We're fine. Now, let me show you the orchards. I'm sure you'll find plenty of things you can take pictures of."

The corner of her mouth twitched. "I'd love to see them."

"Then come on while it's still daylight."

＊＊＊＊＊＊＊

The gargantuan pickup flew over the dirt path, spraying rocks behind them. Ashley zipped up her coat before lowering her window, eager to feel the breeze against her skin. Ahead of them, white, billowy clouds dotted the brilliant blue sky, dancing together above the brown, wintering trees. "I didn't realize an orchard would be so hilly."

"It helps with the frost. We plant our more valuable fruit up high where there's less frost, to protect them in the spring." The truck descended along another row.

"Are these cherry trees?"

"No. We started switching to apple trees a few years ago. We're getting a better return on our investment with these."

"That sounds so businesslike."

"It is. We have to make enough money to support the families that work here."

"That makes sense. I guess I expected it to be more about the sun and soil and ... outdoorsy things."

"If it makes you feel better, there's more sun on top of the hills."

Ashley chuckled. "I feel much better now, thank you. Is all of this land yours?"

"Most of what you can see now is, but about a hundred yards that way and you'll step onto our neighbor's property."

"And you and Tom farm all of this?"

"Chad works with us, and we have a great seasonal staff."

Empty branches scraped along the cab and bed as the truck wobbled through the orchard. Everything looked dead, but with the bright sun shining from the blue-and-white canopy overhead, hope emerged. The slumbering fruit trees inspired Ashley. Did they have the same effect on Russ? "You and Chad will be able to keep things going, right?"

He sighed. "Yeah, we'll make it. As soon as we figure out how to do Tom's job."

Ashley took a good look at him. Stress lined his face, darkening his handsome features. It stirred her heart. She suddenly understood why, after her parents' funeral, people she barely knew offered to bring her dinner and mow the lawn. All she wanted was to take care of Russ, to do what she could to make his life easier. "Can I cook you dinner tonight?"

Something flashed across Russ' face. "Where?"

"At your house, or my house. At *the* house. It's not much, but I'd like to do this for you." As Russ drove in silence, a rush of doubt slammed into her. "Please?"

The truck slowed, but he kept his eyes forward. Ashley held her breath, wanting him to say yes. When he finally looked at her, the corner of his mouth turned up.

"Sure. Let's have dinner together."

CHAPTER 9

"I thought your mom would be home by now."
Russ followed Ashley into the kitchen. As expected, it was empty, not that it surprised him. Mom had been checking in with him eighteen times a day since Tom's death, but he hadn't heard from her since she'd dropped off Ashley. A piece of paper lay on the kitchen counter.

Hi Honey –

I'll be late tonight. There's meat in the sink. Go ahead and eat without me.

Mom

For crying out loud. She was supposed to be staying with him to help him grieve Tom's death, not setting him up with strange women. Not that he minded having dinner with Ashley. Not that he should be thinking that way.

"Is that from her?" Ashley's arm brushed across his as she looked over his shoulder. "Oh, so it's just the two of us?" She looked up at him, a shaky smile creasing her cheeks. "Is that okay with you?"

"You bet."

Her head cocked to the side, tossing her hair against his shoulder.

What was he doing? Russ crumpled the paper and tossed it in the trash. "We might as well make extra in case she's hungry when she gets back."

"Not we. I said I'd make dinner, remember?"

"I remember, but I'm not going to let you work while I lounge around." He leaned over the sink. "It looks like she thawed some chicken quarters. I should have plenty of food to go with them."

Ashley crossed her arms. Leaning against the counter, he mimicked her. As they stared at each other, she narrowed her eyes. He was about to argue the wisdom of them working together, considering it was his kitchen and he knew where to find everything, when she shrugged, then moved to the fridge.

Opening the door, she bent over, leaning in. "There's a ton of food in here. I can throw something together in no time."

A blast of heat shot through Russ' veins. "I'll get the chicken started. Why don't I throw them on the grill?" Outside. In the bitter winter air. Alone.

"If you want to start the grill, I can cook it."

"What kind of man would I be to leave my guest alone to cook dinner for me?" Russ reached for a platter and collided with Ashley at the island. Two plastic containers hit the floor an instant before her hands latched onto his upper arms, her fingers digging into his biceps. He anchored himself against the counter to break their fall, and her soft warmth pressed against his chest. Her breath tickled his neck. When she tried to step back, his arm stopped her, having somehow found itself around her waist. Her eyes widened.

"I, uh …" Ashley's cheeks turned red, but she didn't move. "I think I'm okay now."

He nodded, but his arm tightened. Her gaze dropped to his lips. His brain nearly misfired.

"You can probably let go now," she whispered.

"Yeah, sure." As he slid his arm from her waist, he didn't miss the fact that she took her time letting go. When she stepped back, a thin chain shifted against her neck. The thin curve of his grandmother's ring hung from it.

What was he doing? She had Tom's engagement ring around her neck. Steeling himself against her charms, Russ reached around Ashley, pulled the platter out of the cupboard, and gave his complete attention to the sink full of raw poultry.

"Why don't I put together a salad?" she asked.

"Sure."

"What do you like on yours?"

Russ tried to visualize what was in the fridge. Instead, he pictured Ashley, reaching into the refrigerator. His pulse spiked, and he dropped the pack of chicken in the sink. "Let me see what's in there." Pushing past her, he dove in and scooped up everything from the bottom drawer. "Anything from here will work. I'll start the grill." He dropped the food on the island, then stepped toward the door, but a vice wrapped around his wrist.

"I said I'd make you dinner, and you're doing all of the work. Would you please stop and let me cook?"

"I'm not going to make you wait on me. You just lost your fiancé."

"Yes, and you just lost your cousin, someone you knew much longer than I did. Death sucks, but it doesn't make us helpless."

"Exactly. I'm not helpless, so I'll grill the chicken. You make a salad."

Ashley stood her ground, her lips pressed together in what he was beginning to recognize as her frustrated, yet tempting, pout. But then her face relaxed. "You're right. I'm a bit of a hypocrite. I'll do the salad."

Before she could change her mind, Russ stepped outside and started the grill. Back inside, a serving bowl sat on the counter.

Ashley closed one cupboard, then opened another. "Do you have a cutting board?"

He grabbed a board from under the sink and set it next to the bowl.

"Thank you. It might take me a while to get used to your kitchen."

"Don't worry about it. I'm surprised you didn't bring your own stuff. When my sisters got married, they had every kitchen gadget imaginable."

Ashley chuckled. "I lived in my parents' house my entire life. Most of the furniture and appliances were thirty years old, so I sold what I could and donated the rest. I have a few keepsakes stored in my aunt's garage, but I wanted to start fresh, so I got rid of most of it."

"My mom and aunt stocked Tom and me with everything they could think of. What else do you need?"

"I don't need anything."

"I don't doubt that. How about you tell me what I can do to help?"

She opened the package of lettuce and tore into the bright-green leaves. "Dressing?"

"Sure." He took every bottle out of the refrigerator and set them on the island before stepping around to the other side, giving himself space.

"You're the dirt guy, right?"

"I'm the what?"

"The dirt guy. That's what Tom used to say."

He would. "I have a degree in crop and soil sciences from Michigan State University."

"What do you do with a degree in crop and soil sciences?"

"I analyze the soil and study the crops."

Ashley's eyes shone. "So you work with the dirt."

Russ laughed. "Yes."

"At least you get to work outside."

"That's why I like it. It keeps me out of the office."

"Which is why you didn't mind playing hooky with me today."

"Exactly." That, and because he didn't mind spending time with her.

While Ashley chopped, Russ checked the grill. He didn't have to, but he wanted to clear his head. He fiddled with the grill's dials and thermometer, trying to make it look like he needed to be out there. When he stepped back inside, Ashley smiled at him over her shoulder.

"If I'm completely honest," she said. "I would probably ask for your help with the chicken anyway. I've never been very good with a grill."

"On the rare occasion that I cook dinner, I prefer to grill, so I'm your man." The chopping stopped as Russ realized what he'd said.

Ashley cleared her throat. "So, you don't usually eat dinner?"

He stalked to the sink and ripped the plastic off the chicken. "Of course I eat dinner. I don't like to cook it, though."

"You seemed comfortable in the kitchen this morning. I figured you were an all-around chef."

"I'd like to be, but it's harder to cook after fourteen hours at work than it is after six hours of sleep."

Ashley gasped.

Russ glanced at her.

She stared at him with a contorted expression, as if he were covered in slugs. "What do you people have against sleep?"

He laughed. "Six hours isn't that bad. You need to get on the right schedule. It works."

"Ugh. I like my schedule exactly as it is. It includes a solid eight hours of sleep that don't end before ten a.m."

Russ stepped around her to grab the barbecue sauce. She slipped in front of him to rinse carrots in the sink. They shifted and turned in the kitchen, moving around each other in silence without missing a step. Easy. Comfortable. He'd never enjoyed cooking with someone so much.

He walked in and out between the kitchen and the deck to watch the chicken while helping Ashley. She handed him potatoes, he peeled. He pointed to the salt and pepper, she passed them. She didn't force him to talk about the big issues, and he avoided the small talk. She kept the evening casual, and he liked casual.

Russ moved back outside and lifted the grill lid. Sweet, tangy heat billowed into his face, making his mouth water.

"That smells amazing." Ashley's hand pressed into his shoulder. She leaned against him, bringing her warmth with her. Her face appeared beside his, mere inches away, but her gaze never left the grill. What would it take for her to look at him that intensely?

"It needs a few more minutes," he said.

"Perfect. The potatoes are almost ready." She smiled at him before stepping back inside. Russ had never missed having his personal space invaded until then.

Wrong thinking. She was Tom's fiancée. Well, ex-fiancée. Sort of. Russ watched her through the glass door. She'd found placemats and a small centerpiece he didn't know he owned. He picked up the tongs but couldn't pull his attention from her.

Life with sisters should have prepared him for cooking with a woman, but it had never been this distracting. Why was Ashley so captivating? She was about the same age as Carrie. As tall as Rachel. Her hair length and color reminded him of Liz. But he'd never paid attention to how they smelled. Or smiled. Or moved.

Ashley looked out at him, her head cocked to the side and eyebrows pulled together. A piece of hair slipped across her forehead. As she walked toward the door, Russ realized the food was still on the grill and he was staring. Turning his back to the glass door, and Ashley, he lifted the chicken off the grates.

The door slid open behind him. "Everything okay?"

"Yeah. Let me turn off the grill, then I'll be in." He handed her the platter. After closing the gas valve, he joined her inside.

"I poured you a glass of water. Do you want anything else?"

"I'm fine. Let's eat." He took the seat across from hers.

She folded her hands. "Do you mind if I say grace?"

Sitting across from her, noticing every unique detail about his cousin's fiancée, he didn't mind at all. Russ needed all the divine intervention he could get.

CHAPTER 10

BAM!
Russ shot out of bed. Something shattered in the distance. His clock read 4:59. His heart banged in his chest as he stood in the dark, waiting for the adrenaline to wane. Mom must have gotten up early. He couldn't remember the last time anyone had beaten him out of bed.

A little disoriented, he skipped the overhead light and grabbed the clothes off the chair where he'd thrown them the night before. By the time he was dressed and in the hallway, the scent of coffee greeted him. After thirty-eight years, he could cook for himself, but he had to admit, it was nice to think of food waiting for him in the morning. He thumped down the stairs, then toward the kitchen, his socks sliding over the hardwood.

"Hey, Mom." He hit the kitchen tile, and his legs froze. Ashley sat at the island, her head resting on her arms. A mess of hair spilled onto the countertop and around her shoulders, hiding most of her face. She wore fuzzy purple pants and a pastel patterned shirt he'd not seen before. A broom leaned against the wall beside her. Pieces of blue-and-white ceramic, the same shades as his dishes, filled a dustpan on the floor.

"Ashley?"

"Hmm."

"Are you awake?"

"Mmm."

He couldn't stop his smile. She shifted on the stool.

Russ shuffled through the kitchen and poured a cup of coffee as quietly as he could. He poured a cup for Ashley, too, adding the creamer. When he sat on the stool beside hers, she leaned into him. Her finger-sicles wrapped around his arm, freezing his skin through the sleeve of his shirt.

"Ashley?"

She shifted again, spilling a piece of dark hair across her milky skin. Her light-pink lips moved silently, capturing his attention.

Tom did well with this one. He hadn't dated many women before Ashley, and none of them had impressed Russ as quickly. Of course, none of them had been engaged to Tom either. Still, Ashley was different—special—and that twisted Russ' gut. She moved her hands, sending a different kind of chill across his skin.

She moaned. "Mom?"

"No, it's Russ."

"Am I late for school?"

"What?" He moved the hair from over her eyes. Still closed. "Are you awake?"

"Coffee."

"Right here."

"Bed."

"That's upstairs."

"Noooooo." Her voice pitched up, stretching into a whine that rivaled any of his nephews'.

"Would you like me to take you back upstairs?"

A puff of air burst from her lips, shooting the hair out of her face. "School?"

Okay, she was out of it. He definitely needed to put her somewhere more comfortable—and warmer—to sleep. Russ grasped her arms and stood her up, turning her toward him. She moved without protest.

Ashley's eyes flickered open, sleep heavy on her lids. "I made coffee."

"Thank you."

"I'll make breakfast in a minute. First, I need …" Her eyes closed, and she tipped to the side.

"No, no, no." Russ tightened his grip and held her up. "Let's get you to the couch."

"I don't want you to go."

"I'm not going anywhere." He tugged on Ashley's arm. "Come on, let's move." Her knees buckled, dropping her back onto the stool. Was this really happening? "Ashley?"

"Please stay."

His chest tightened. "I said I'm not leaving. Now help me out and stand up."

"Are you sure she's not asleep?"

Russ spun around at his mom's voice. "She was just talking to me."

"Liz used to have conversations with your father in her sleep. They didn't make sense, and she never remembered them in the morning, but he would keep it going as long as he could. I even taped her one night to prove it to her."

Russ looked back at Ashley. Her eyes were closed and her face pinched. "Looks like I'm carrying her again."

"Or you can leave her there. She'll wake up eventually. Why don't I start breakfast?"

While it would be nice to have Ashley in the kitchen for amusement, Russ wouldn't condemn her to cold hands, a stiff neck, and possibly falling off the stool. "I'll put her on the couch."

Mom helped herself to the mug on the counter. "I'll take care of her coffee."

This time Russ didn't bother standing Ashley up. He scooped her into his arms.

"No." Ashley shook her head, wrapping her arms around him in a death grip. "Mom." The tightness of her tone needled at him. Her head tossed from side to side, her breathing erratic.

He looked at his own mom, but she was wrist deep in sausage. He leaned close to Ashley's ear. "It's Russ. You're okay." Her arms tightened. Legs curled up. She hadn't tensed like that yesterday.

Russ slipped out of the kitchen to the ugly old loveseat on the far side of the living room. That should be enough distance to keep him out of his mother's hearing range.

"Ashley, wake up. I think you're having a nightmare."

She coiled tighter, burying her face in his chest. "No, no. Mom, please." A sob. Nails cut into his neck. "Mom."

"Ashley." Russ raised his voice. "Ashley, wake up. You're dreaming."

"Please, no." She sobbed in his arms. Warm tears ran down his neck.

"Ashley!"

She gasped, pushing herself away, eyes wide open.

Russ struggled to hold on as she flailed in his arms. "It's okay. You're okay. Calm down." He tightened his grip, pressing her against his chest until she stopped squirming.

"I'm sorry, I'm so sorry." Ashley looked at him with crazy green eyes.

He relaxed his hold. "It's okay."

Her gaze shot around the room, her breathing rapid. She squeezed her arms even tighter around his neck, collapsing against him.

Russ dropped onto the loveseat, Ashley still in his arms. "You're going to strangle me."

Her breaths stuttered as another tear rolled onto his neck. "I'm so sorry. That hasn't happened in years." Leaning back, she wiped a hand across her face. "Where did you find me?"

"In the kitchen."

She sucked in a deep, slow breath, relaxing her grip on him. Some of the tension melted out of her back and arms. "I'm sorry if I scared you. I didn't do anything dangerous, did I?"

"It looks like you dropped a dish, but at least you cleaned it up. You don't remember?"

She shook her head. "I must have been sleepwalking. I haven't done it in years. Not since my parents died."

Grief covered Russ' heart, but he worked hard to keep the emotion off his face. "Did you do it often?"

She dropped her head onto his shoulder. "I started sleepwalking after the funeral. I don't think about it much anymore, but I did some crazy things."

"Like what?"

"Laundry. Dusting. I even addressed Christmas cards one year."

"At least you were productive."

"It was August."

He chuckled. "You didn't mail them, did you?"

"No. I couldn't find the stamps."

She shivered, so Russ dragged the blanket from the arm of the loveseat and wrapped it around her shoulders. "Do you always cry when it happens?" She trembled again, so Russ rubbed his free hand up and down her back. "I didn't mean to upset you."

"You didn't. Sometimes after I would sleepwalk, I had this recurring dream."

"You kept calling for your mom."

She nodded, her hair rubbing against his chin. "My parents were killed in a car accident the week after I graduated from high school. In the dream, I'm begging them not to go, but they don't hear me, or they ignore me, or someone keeps interrupting. The distraction changes, but the dream's always the same. I ask them to stay home, but they leave anyway."

"Do you blame yourself for the accident?"

"I used to, but I realize now it wasn't my fault. There was a storm." She lifted her head enough to look at him, her eyes red and damp. "I miss them, but it was a long time ago. They've been out of my life almost as long as they were in it. I didn't think I'd ever sleepwalk again. I'm sorry if I worried you."

"I don't mind." Especially when she looked at him as if she trusted him completely. Unsure what else to say, he smiled at her.

Her cheeks tinged pink, and her back stiffened. "Thank you for waking me up. I'll be fine in a minute."

"Then stay here for another minute."

Ashley's eyebrows slid up her forehead.

"I can feel you tensing up. Relax. Everything's fine."

Her eyes scanned his face several times before she relaxed against him without argument. "I stayed with my aunt and uncle for a few months after my parents died. Sometimes I'd wake up and my aunt would be sitting by my bed, rubbing my back. She'd tell me what crazy things I did while I sleepwalked. It made me feel better knowing she was there, just in case I tried to run out of the house or anything. I didn't realize how much I appreciated that until now."

"Glad to help."

Ashley inhaled deeply as she shifted in his arms. It would probably be more appropriate to take her upstairs. Then he could help his mom in the kitchen. A dozen reasons to move floated through Russ' mind, but Ashley finally relaxed, and the selfish side of his brain figured he'd never have a good excuse to hold her like that again.

Forget reason. Russ tucked the blanket under Ashley's chin and closed his eyes. As he settled deeper into the cushions, she sank further into his arms. Her breathing slowed, warm against his skin.

"Ashley?"

"Hmm?"

"Are you falling asleep?"

"Mm-hmm."

She snuggled against him.

He could be reasonable later.

* * * * * * *

Ashley burrowed into the warm, woodsy scent. Strong bands embraced her. Light burned against her eyelids. She turned away from the brightness and into a sturdy wall. The wall moved, then yawned.

Russ.

Those weren't bands around her. She'd been sleepwalking again. He'd soothed away her panic, holding her until her heartbeat calmed.

Modesty told her to sneak away before he woke up and asked questions. Moving an inch at a time, she slipped the blanket off her back.

"Feeling better?"

So much for that plan. Looking into Russ' eyes, she offered a sheepish grin. "Yes, thank you."

He lowered his arms, taking the blanket with him. "I don't mean to be pushy, but I need to get going."

Ashley looked outside—the sun. "What time is it?"

"After eight I'd guess."

She jumped off his lap. "You must be late. I didn't ruin your day, did I?"

He chuckled. "In August, maybe. Not in November."

Thank goodness. "In that case, do you have time for breakfast? It's the least I can do. That's why I got up in the first place. I think."

"My mom was cooking when we fell asleep. There may be food in the kitchen."

"I'll check, and then I'll make coffee." She headed toward the kitchen. "I definitely need coffee."

"You already made a pot."

The muscles in her legs constricted, and her feet stopped. "I made coffee?"

"Yep."

"Wow."

"It could have been worse." Russ appeared beside her. "You could have gone for a joy ride."

"Maybe we should hide my car keys for a few days."

"If you think it will help."

"It won't, but it'll make me feel better knowing I won't have access to my car. I'd hate to drive into the side of your barn. You shouldn't have to worry about me. I'm not your problem."

"You're not a problem."

"Try to remember that when you're chasing me around the backyard."

"Have you done that before?"

"No, but there's a first time for everything."

"So there is." He picked up a mug off the counter and poured himself some coffee.

Nothing about his behavior suggested that their nap had bothered him. They could be talking about the weather for all the reaction she was getting.

"Hungry?" Russ held up a heaping plate of bacon.

"What's with you and bacon?"

"What do you have against it?"

"Nothing, but you seem to eat a lot of it." The aroma reached her nostrils, and Ashley's stomach growled.

"Looks like I'm converting you."

"Don't gloat." She took the plate, spotting a note on the counter.

Hi Kids,

You fell asleep and I didn't want to disturb you. I'm going into Traverse City so I'll be gone all day. I should be home by dinner!

Mom

Ashley pushed the paper away. "Do you want anything else with your bacon, or are you happy with a plate of pig?"

"I've got eggs and potatoes. What would you like?"

"I don't usually eat this early, so don't bother cooking for me."

Russ pulled out pans and utensils. "I'm not cooking for you, I'm cooking for me. I like a big breakfast, and you don't look like you eat enough."

"Is that a compliment or an insult?"

"An observation."

Ashley hopped onto a stool as she watched Russ slice potatoes and dice onions like a pro. He cracked and whipped the eggs, working two pans as if they were extensions of his arms. Calm and relaxed, unphased by the fact that she had delayed his start. Should she be honored or insulted that a nap together in the loveseat didn't seem to affect him?

As Russ tossed the eggs and vegetables in one pan while potatoes sizzled in the other, the warm feeling from the day before wrapped around Ashley. She should have appreciated Sunday mornings with her parents more. She'd eaten a lot of oatmeal since then.

"Why do you think you started sleepwalking again?" Russ glanced at her, his eyes ever calm. "Do you suppose it has to do with Tom's death?"

"Maybe. It's strange, though. Tom and I were good friends, but I wasn't close to him like I was with my parents. I didn't think it would affect me like that."

"How long did it last before?"

"About six months, I guess."

"I hope it doesn't last that long this time."

"Don't worry. I'm sure we'll figure out the housing situation before then."

Russ looked at her like she'd grown a third eye. "I didn't mean it like that," he said. "It sounds like the sleepwalking might be dangerous. I don't want you to worry about it for another day, much less six months."

"Oh." Her neck and cheeks warmed. "You're not the only one." Who knew where she'd end up? Years ago, she woke up in the front yard, but at least she recognized her surroundings. What would happen to her here, waking up in a strange house? Maybe it would be better if she went to John and Rose's after all. That thought wrenched her gut.

"You're looking a little green."

"Just thinking about moving to Florida for a while."

Russ dished up the food and set a plate in front of her. "You don't look like you want to go back."

"Not really."

"You don't like it there?"

"It's okay, but my aunt and uncle live in a retirement community, so it would have to be temporary." Instead of obsessing about it, she sampled Russ' food. Fluffy eggs melted in her mouth. She could get used to mornings if they all started like that. Not caring what Russ thought, she bent over and dug in.

Russ leaned against the counter with a plate in his hand. "Are you going to stay in town then?"

Ashley shrugged. "I haven't thought about it yet."

"You can stay here for a while. Things are slowing down on the farm."

"I appreciate it, but that might not be the best idea."

"Why not?"

"We don't know each other."

"I guess, but Tom knew you, and I trust him more than I trust myself. If you want to stay here, I can introduce you to the family. Show you more of the farm."

The idea calmed her, but curiosity invaded her peace. "Why?"

"Like I said, it's slow." He took a bite of food then mumbled. "It's nice having someone else in the house again."

And it was nice *being* in a house with someone. No more meals for one. Someone to watch TV with. She had that when she visited Rose and John, but it wasn't the same. Not only could she talk with Russ about things relevant to that century, but she'd get to know Tom's best friend. Tom's stories about Russ had impressed her, and so far, the person lived up to every expectation. "That's tempting."

He smiled at her.

Very tempting. "Can I ask a personal question?"

"Sure."

"Did you pick up any weird habits after your dad died?"

Russ' fork stopped moving. "My dad?"

The heat must have kicked on in the house because Ashley's clothes felt stifling. "Tom said you and your dad were close and that he died unexpectedly. I was wondering if, well …"

"If I started sleepwalking."

She nodded.

"I never had time to pick up any habits. Dad died, but there was a farm to run. We had the funeral, and I went back to work."

A new heaviness weighed on Ashley's heart. "That's terrible."

"Not really. I didn't have a chance to get depressed."

"But did you grieve?"

"In my own way, I guess."

"I hope you had a chance to grieve. It's so important."

"I take it you took time off for that?"

"I'd just graduated from high school and didn't have anything else to do. I was able to grieve as long as I needed, and no one rushed me."

Russ grimaced. "That sounds depressing."

"It *was* depressing until I moved on." The wonderous freedom of that day flooded her spirit. Ashley smiled. "I remember the day I decided I'd had enough. I broke this hideous lamp in the living room. It was this wooden, midcentury statement piece, but it reminded me of the lamp from *I Dream of Jeannie*. My first thought was that I'd never find another one like it. I even spent a couple of hours looking for a replacement online before I realized I didn't *have* to replace it. I could buy a lamp that I actually liked.

"I didn't want to forget my parents, but I didn't want to stay trapped in the past either. I love them, and I miss them, but they wouldn't want me sitting alone in their house forever." Which was exactly why she'd sold it and moved to Michigan to be with Tom.

Russ set down his plate and crossed his arms. "What did you do after your parents died?"

"I skipped college and used the insurance money to become a medical transcriptionist. I bought my own equipment, took correspondence classes, and never had to leave home."

"And you've been doing that ever since?"

"It's not a glamorous life, but it pays the bills." As she said it, the sad reality of the statement nearly gagged her. Seventeen years of the same work in the same house. Regardless of what happened with Russ and the farmhouse, she couldn't go back.

"What about your pictures?"

"What pictures?"

"All those photos you were taking. Why do you do that?"

"I needed to get out of the house. It's nice working from home, but it's lonely. For whatever reason, I felt like I needed an excuse to go out, so I picked up my camera, and I've been taking pictures ever since. It's empowering when you capture a moment in history for all eternity."

The corner of Russ' mouth twitched. "I never thought of it like that. It's a nice way to view the world."

"I think so. You did a nice job of changing the subject, by the way, but you never answered my question. What about you changed after your dad died?"

Russ picked up his plate. "Nothing."

She didn't believe him but decided not to push the subject. After all, she wasn't in a hurry to move back to Ohio. She had time to figure out Russ while she figured out her life.

CHAPTER 11

Sunlight filled the downtown building, spilling in through the windows along the front wall as Russ entered the lobby of Rob's office and passed the empty reception desk to his right. The smallish pleather couch and armchairs, both in light shades of green that complemented the dark-green carpet, reminded him more of a doctor's office than a lawyer's. And a lawyer was what he needed right then.

"I need to figure this out. Fast," Russ said as he grabbed one of Rob's coffee mugs and helped himself. The heater kicked on, forcing warm air into the suite as Russ turned around and carried his coffee across the hallway and into his friend's office. "Ashley moved in and has no intention of leaving."

"Is that a bad thing?" Rob dropped a brown, waxy bag on his ridiculous desk. Russ couldn't remember the last time he'd visited his friend at work, but it hadn't included the dining-room table pretending to be a desk.

Russ pointed at the bag. "I thought you were on a diet."

"I am, but I get a cheat day."

"How many have you had this week?"

"Instead of doing it all at once, I prefer to cheat a little each day." Rob pulled a chocolate-covered doughnut out of the bag before passing it to Russ. "Kelly knows. It's not me she's worried about. Her mom's spending more time at the house these days, and she was diagnosed with type 2 diabetes. Kelly doesn't want to tempt her, so I suffer." Rob bit into his pastry and sighed. "I can't remember the last time I had a doughnut."

"Can we stay on topic, please?"

"Right. Ashley won't move out. Legally that's not a problem. You're the squatter."

"It's *my* family's farmhouse. I don't care if Tom *did* have the legal right to will it away. I'm not letting a stranger take it. If we can't find anything to keep it in the Russell family, then I'll take her to court." Saying the words nearly strangled Russ. The farm was doing well, but he'd invested a lot into transitioning from traditional apple trees to dwarfed roots, plus the farm equipment. Next spring the house would need a new roof and furnace if they survived that long. How much would legal fees cost?

Rob reached into the bag and handed Russ a fritter. "You look tense."

"I'm trying to add up the cost, and I see my life fading from black to red."

"If you go to court, I think you have a good case. Do you have any idea why Tom would leave the house to a stranger?"

Russ looked through the doorway into the lobby, straining to see the entrance. "Anything I say to you is confidential, right?"

"If you're seeking legal counsel, yes."

"Then let's say I need counsel," he said as he faced Rob. "Ashley is—was—Tom's fiancée."

"Wha—" Rob's jaw dropped. "Are you kidding me?"

"I wish."

"Why didn't you say anything at the house?" Rob collapsed against his chair. "Wow. This clarifies a few things, but wow!"

"Tell me about it." Russ bit into his fritter as his friend processed the situation.

"Obviously, your mom doesn't know. What's with the veil of secrecy?"

"I'm not doing it on purpose. I didn't know about Ashley either."

"How could you not know?"

"Tom didn't tell anyone, not even me." The sting of that betrayal rekindled when Russ admitted it. "Ashley showed up to marry Tom. Nobody knew about her, so no one told her about the accident."

"Whoa."

"Yeah."

They ate in silence as the truth filtered through the air between them. Maybe Russ shouldn't have shared Ashley's story. A spot of guilt floated through his mind, but he squashed it. He needed help, and the one person he trusted as much as Tom was Rob. Plus, that whole lawyer-confidentiality thing had to count for something.

Bells tinkled as the front door opened. "Hello?"

Every nerve in Russ' body sprang to life. "Ashley?"

Rob's eyes lit up as he straightened his tie. "Come on in!" He made his way around the desk, slapping Russ' shoulder as he walked past. Russ' body wouldn't move. "Ashley, it's good to see you again," Rob said. "What brings you here?"

"I hope I'm not bothering you, but I wasn't sure who else to talk to. Do you have a few minutes? I might need to hire you."

"I don't have an appointment until this afternoon. Why don't we step into my office?"

Russ jumped out of his chair, desperate for an escape, but the only way out was through the lobby.

Ashley stepped through the doorway, her eyes on the floor. When she looked up, she froze. Her gaze locked with Russ' as her mouth opened, then closed. Rob stepped in behind her, escorting her to Russ' chair. Her gaze never left his.

Of all places. "Good morning, Ashley."

"Uh, hi. I didn't mean to interrupt. I can come back later."

"Nonsense," Rob said. "Having you both here will give us a chance to talk about your situation. Let me get you some coffee."

Russ sat in the chair beside her. She'd piled her hair on top of her head in a messy knot like his sisters wore, but everything else was perfectly put together—a pale-green sweater that brightened her eyes, jeans that fit in the best possible way, and a dab of pink on her cheeks. Regardless of whether she or the wind had done that, it suited her.

"I'm not sure what to say." She twisted her fingers. "I think I've reached my limit for shocking situations this month."

"Yeah, me too." He checked his watch. "It's nine a.m. and you're a functioning adult."

She gave a soft laugh as she relaxed into the chair.

Rob returned with a steaming mug. Before he set it down, Russ went to the kitchenette to fetch the cream. On his way back to the office, he bumped into Rob in the hallway. Rob raised an eyebrow.

"What?" Russ asked. "She's been at my house a couple of days. I know how she likes her coffee."

"How attentive of you." Rob escorted him back to the office. "Ashley, what can I do for you?"

Russ handed her the creamer. Her eyes sparkled as she smiled. Did Tom know that about her?

"I'm trying to figure out how to explain this," she said.

"The engagement, you mean?"

The world stopped spinning. Air ceased circulating. Only Russ' heart moved, beating a violent rhythm of disbelief and shock. "Rob!"

Ashley gasped. "Russ! Why did you tell him?"

"Because I needed advice. Isn't that why you're here?"

She snapped her jaw shut.

Rob chuckled. "Your secret's safe with me. I wouldn't have brought it up like that, but you're both here for the same reason.

We can avoid each other and be secretive about this, or we can get it out in the open and work through this together. Now, Ashley, what did you want to talk about?"

"I, um …" She set her coffee on the table. "I can't take the house."

"Legally it's yours, so you can do whatever you want with it."

Russ' gut wrenched.

"No, I can't. That house belongs to the Russell family. I can't take it from them."

"Thank you." Russ hadn't meant to say that out loud, but now that it was out there, he was glad he'd said it.

"You're welcome. Tom told me about Fourth of July picnics and Christmases there." Her face brightened. "I wanted to be a part of that, not end it. So, Rob, what are my options?"

"You can give the house back to the family."

"I would if I could, but"—she shifted in the chair, dropping her gaze—"I don't have any place else to go."

"She sold her house in Ohio," Russ said.

Rob scribbled on a notepad. "How much did you make on the sale?"

Ashley looked up, shifting her gaze between the two of them. "Enough to pay off my aunt and uncle's mortgage. Tom encouraged me to do it. When he asked me to marry him and move up here, we saw it as a chance to bless them."

"How much do you have left?"

"I invested some of the money and upgraded my camera and computer for my photography internship. I have a few thousand, but I also need a car. Mine died a few weeks ago, and Tom said he'd help me find a suitable vehicle for Michigan winters." She shook her head. "The internship is part time and doesn't start until after the New Year. I can keep doing the transcriptionist work, but I don't think it will be enough to cover rent *and* a car payment."

Russ considered the new information. She'd given up everything and gained nothing. If he took her to court for the house, she'd lose any bit of savings she had left. He wouldn't do that to her.

"You could sell the house back to the Russells."

Russ groaned.

His friend crossed his arms. "Care to elaborate on your enthusiastic response?"

Russ glared at him. "Who's she going to sell it to? I don't have that kind of money. Liz, Carrie, and Rachel have their own homes, and none of them make enough to take on a second mortgage. Mom's retired. There's no way I'm mentioning this to Tom's parents. They've been through enough."

"You can't afford to buy it, and I can't afford to give it away." Ashley sighed as she reached for her coffee.

"Even if you could, I wouldn't let you."

She stopped with the mug halfway to her mouth. "Excuse me?"

"Gentleman's honor. About a month after Dad died, Uncle Bill—Tom's dad—seriously considered selling the farm. He said it was too hard running it himself, but Tom and I talked him out of it. It took about a year before Bill told us how glad he was we convinced him not to sell. After that, Tom and I made a pact. If anything ever happened to one of us, we'd wait twelve months before doing anything with the house or farm. That's what Tom would want, so I'm holding you to it."

"You can't tell me—"

"What Tom would have wanted?"

Ashley flinched.

Too late. Now that he'd opened the valve, Russ' thoughts wouldn't be denied. She may have been engaged to Tom, but Russ grew up with him. "This is what he'd want you to do. He may not have told me about you, but he and I talked about everything else, including this type of situation. We lived through my grandpa's and my dad's deaths, so we knew how hard it would be. This is what he'd do if I—" But Russ couldn't say it. Didn't want to think about it.

A drawer scraped open. Rob handed Ashley a tissue. As she dabbed her eyes, Russ kicked himself. What kind of man didn't notice a beautiful woman's tears?

She crumpled the tissue. "You're right. Tom and I didn't talk about this, but he talked about you. All the time. If this is what you think Tom would want, then I want to honor it. I'll wait."

"And in the meantime?" Rob asked.

Ashley shrugged. "I guess Russ can stay at the house."

"What?" Russ' blood surged until he remembered the truth. "I almost forgot that I'm the homeless one, not her."

"No," Ashley said. "You're not homeless. There are four rooms in that house. I promise the rent will be reasonable."

Rob's laughter bounced through the office, knocking down the tension. The corner of Ashley's eye creased as her twitching lips struggled to hide her smile.

Russ let his frustration go as he leaned toward Ashley. "So witty before noon. You must be captivating after lunch."

"I think you're probably confusing sleep deprivation with wit. Whatever it is, I want you to know"—she covered his hand with hers—"I would never do anything to hurt you or your family. I wanted to be a part of it, not ruin it."

Rob said something, but Russ didn't pay attention. Ashley's words burned through his ears while her smile seared itself into his brain. From the moment he'd met her at the café, her compassion had shown in her face and through her actions. Despite everything she'd lost, *she* assured *him*. Comforted him. Her kindness wrapped itself around Russ like a down jacket.

Now he understood why Tom wanted Ashley in northern Michigan, but it was up to Russ to keep her there. For the family, of course.

CHAPTER 12

Ashley tugged at the hem of her skirt. The flowered purple material usually lightened her mood, but it didn't seem appropriate for the occasion. Of course, she hadn't planned for a funeral. Much like her senior year of high school when she swapped graduation parties for her parents' funeral. A shiver raced down her spine. Ashley hadn't attended many funerals since then. What would Tom's be like?

Her fiancé's funeral. The thought of it should make her cry, but it still didn't seem real. When her parents died, Ashley hadn't been able to stop the tears. Today, she wasn't sure what to feel. Could she lose what she never really had?

Someone knocked on the door. "Are you ready?"

Kathleen's warm voice calmed her nerves. Almost everything about the gentle woman calmed her. Ashley opened the door, smiling at her hostess. "I wish I had something better to wear. This seems too festive."

"Honey, you're lovely. No one will notice." Kathleen wore a yellow-and-green plaid jumper, a sunshine-yellow blouse, and Barbie-pink ballet flats. Ashley's clothes suddenly seemed tame. "This is a memorial service, not a funeral. We'll miss Tom, but he's with God now. Today we're going to celebrate his life, not mourn his death."

"I like that idea."

"Me too. Come on now. Russ left early to make a few stops, so it's just us. He'll meet us at the church."

After she plucked her coat off the bed, they were down the stairs and out of the house in no time. In less than an hour, Ashley would be surrounded by Tom's family and friends.

As anxiety ate at her insides, she barely noticed the drive into town. They arrived twenty minutes early, but a dozen cars already littered the parking lot. Despite the cold, kids ran around in the side yard of the one-story church as a few adults stood talking nearby. A white wooden cross hung above the front door of the L-shaped building. Like all of the other landscaping she'd seen since her arrival, the trees around the church stood bare. Naked shrubs lined the red, brick wall, except in open spots where Ashley assumed flowers grew in the summer.

Everyone waved at or hugged Kathleen as she and Ashley crossed the parking lot. Ashley smiled and nodded—she even accepted a few hugs—but no one struck up a conversation with Kathleen's surprise friend. Just as well. Ashley was still figuring out what to say when she met Tom's parents and sisters.

Inside the church, more people scurried around. Ashley followed Kathleen up four carpeted steps to a wide foyer. Flowers covered the tables and benches that lined both sides of the space, hiding bulletin boards and flyers behind a rainbow of petals. Unlike the school-sized contemporary church where she'd held her parents' funeral, the brown industrial carpet and white iron handrails of this church reminded her of Rose and John's midcentury house in Ohio.

A petite woman with long, gray hair and a sleek, navy pantsuit walked straight to Kathleen, who embraced the shorter woman. "You look lovely, Rita. The service will be wonderful."

Rita—Tom's mom. Ashley offered her hand. "Mrs. Russell, I'm Ashley Johnson."

"It's nice to meet you." Rita's warm hands enveloped hers.

Kathleen wrapped an arm around Ashley. "She's a friend of Tom's. She arrived this week and is staying with Russ and me. Excuse me for a moment, will you? Elizabeth's flagging me down." She walked away while Ashley admired Tom's mother. Despite the loss, Rita appeared fresh and lively even with her red-rimmed eyes.

Ashley gave Rita's hand an extra squeeze before letting go. "Is there anything I can do to help?"

"I think we're all set." She stepped back, a faint smile on her lips. "How did you know Tommy?"

Ashley's chest tightened. "He didn't mention me?"

"I don't think so, but I've been forgetting a lot of things this week."

Like her future daughter-in-law? Not likely. "We were … friends." The deception clogged her throat before forcing its way out through her stupid tear ducts. "Excuse me. I'm going to step outside for a moment."

Another couple greeted the grieving mother as Ashley walked into the crisp wind. It bit at her face as she replayed Rita's reaction. The woman had never heard of her!

Frustration welled up in Ashley's chest. Tom had promised her a family. How could she join a family who didn't know she existed? How could she make a home with strangers? She could handle the loneliness of his absence—she understood how to deal with that—but not the betrayal. Why hadn't he told anyone? She'd expected a warm welcome to Boyne Heights, not the cold hand of polite indifference.

Cars continued pulling into the parking lot, swerving around her. No one waved. No one cared about the stranger wandering between cars. They would embrace and comfort her if they knew who she was, but Ashley was too angry to say anything. She wouldn't add humiliation to the list of Tom-induced emotions.

None of it made sense. Tom had initiated the relationship. He proposed. He invited her to move north, all the while keeping his family in the dark. What was he thinking?

"Aren't you going the wrong way?" Great. Now someone cared. Pretending not to hear him, she kept moving. "Ashley?"

The sound of her name stopped her feet. "Russ?" He stepped out from behind his truck, his muscular frame easily recognizable, even with blurry vision. She blinked away the tears as he strode toward her. Sharp, clean slacks, a starched white shirt, and a jacket covered one of the broadest bodies she'd ever seen. Probably not the best time to notice that. At least it distracted her from her frustration.

"Are you okay?" he asked.

"I'm fine."

Russ pulled a tissue from his pocket and handed it to her. "Where are you going?"

Ashley inspected the edges of the tissue. "The park. We passed one on the way here."

"Shouldn't you be going inside?"

The tears had dried, so she stuffed the tissue in her coat pocket. "Thank you, but I need some air." She resumed her playground hunt. No one would miss her. They weren't expecting her.

She hadn't traveled this far into self-pity in a while. It wasn't someplace she liked to visit, but finding out she was Tom's dirty little secret cut into her determination.

She crossed the street and spotted the top of the slide behind a line of trees. As she made her way around the natural barrier, she found an empty swing. A few minutes to clear her mind, and she'd be ready to face the Russells. The chains creaked as she pushed herself back and forth watching the woodchips move beneath her feet.

Something crunched. Ashley froze. More crunching. Footsteps? As she glanced over her shoulder, Russ pulled up a swing.

"What are you doing here?" she asked.

"Swinging." He kept his eyes forward, rocking backward and forward. Heel to toe.

"You're going to miss the memorial."

"So will you."

"Yeah, but no one will notice." She started swinging again, the chain complaining. Russ' swing added a groaning harmony. What a sad duet. "How long are you planning to stay here?"

"As long as you, I suppose."

"Why?" Ashley twisted to face him.

"I think you should be at your fiancé's memorial, don't you? I can wait until you're ready."

"What if I'm never ready? No one knows who I am, not even Tom's mom. They won't care if I'm not there, and I don't feel like lying to them about why I'm here."

"My mom will care."

"Maybe, but she doesn't know who I am either." Ashley pulled the gold chain out from beneath the cover of her dress, the warm metal tickling her skin. Her engagement ring dangled securely from it. "They'd recognize this ring before they'd recognize me."

"Probably."

Not very comforting.

"Don't you at least want to meet the rest of the family?"

Her heart softened. "Tom talked about you and your sisters more than he did his own sisters. The first time I emailed him was because I read an article online about your family farm. He replied and told me about a winter vacation you took to Maine. His family, yours, your grandparents—all of you together for Christmas and New Year's. It sounded wonderful."

Russ chuckled. "It was chaos."

Ashley smiled. "You're trying to make it sound bad, but I wanted to see what having a big family was like. My mom had five older siblings, but I'm an only child. I loved the idea of becoming part of someone's family. That's why I came up here."

"I thought you came up here to get married."

"I did, but your family is why we agreed to get married."

Russ' swing stopped. "What are you talking about?"

How much should she tell him? He knew about the arrangement. Would it matter if she told him how they came to it?

"Ashley?"

"You have to promise not to think badly of Tom."

"I don't think I could."

"I mean it. I won't defend him because he doesn't need it. We made an informed, adult decision."

"I believe you."

But would he respect her? The handsome stranger in the swing watched her, his arms crossed, her own personal priest waiting for her to confess. With a deep breath, she sacrificed her pride.

"Yes, Tom and I both wanted to get married, but more than anything I wanted a family. I may not have loved him like I should have, but I fell in love with the idea of the Russells. After those first two emails, we stayed in touch. We kept emailing, then chatting." Ashley's thoughts drifted back to their first phone call, to the hours spent comparing their lives and interests. "Tom was easy to talk to. We talked every day, and one day we were discussing our futures. He wanted a wife. I didn't want to be alone anymore."

"So, you found a big family to marry into."

"No. I found a wonderful man who was willing to share his life and family with me. He just wasn't willing to talk about it." Ashley slouched against the chain, rocking on her heels. Russ swayed beside her as the church bells chimed. The service would start soon, but Ashley kept rocking.

Russ jumped up, moving in front of her and grabbing her swing's chains above her head. "Listen, I'm sorry Tom wasn't honest with us, but he had his reasons for giving you that ring. He wanted you to be part of our family. I'd like you to meet the rest of them."

"And I want to meet them, but what am I supposed to say?" The air thickened in her lungs. "I'm the weird stranger who showed up out of the blue. Now I'm stuck outside thinking I'd like to punch the man whose life we're supposed to be celebrating, but I'm angry and hurt and confused, and what am I supposed to do now?"

Russ blinked.

Deep breaths. One. Two. Three. Four—

"Are you done?"

"Give me six more seconds!" She shouldn't yell at Russ. The situation wasn't his fault, though he wasn't offering much help. "You know, you're not very comforting."

"I'm not trying to be comforting. I'm trying to get you into the church. It's cold."

Maybe she should go in for a while. Her fingers *were* getting stiff, and regardless if Tom's family knew her, Ashley had been counting the days until she could meet them. "You and your mom have been really nice. I *would* like to meet your sisters, but—"

"Listen, Tom's strategy stinks, I get it, but he gave you Grandma's ring. You were important to him, so that makes you important to us."

And she wanted to meet them, desperately. "If I go, will you … I mean, can we—"

"We don't have to explain anything to anyone. Besides, I doubt anyone will believe Tom was engaged if they don't see the ring."

"Not comforting."

"Forget comforting. You were important to him. That's all anyone cares about." Russ held out his hand. "Come inside. Meet the family. We'll figure out your next move later. Then we can get back to being mad at Tom."

"We?"

"He kept you a secret. He made me homeless. You're not the only one struggling right now, but today we're going to focus on the good stuff."

Ashley studied her brooding almost cousin-in-law. "He had his good moments." She slid her hand into his.

"I know. Come inside and we'll tell you stories."

CHAPTER 13

Children squealed. Adults laughed. Silverware and china clinked in the spacious hall, echoing off the cathedral ceilings. Sunlight streamed in through the wall of windows behind her as people mingled about. Two dozen round tables filled the center of the room, while long banquet tables held food along the opposite wall. At the far end of the room, men and women disappeared and reappeared through a swinging door that obviously led to the kitchen as every empty bowl they carried in came back out full of food. Ashley couldn't stop smiling from her seat at an empty table. Everywhere she looked, people in colorful outfits feasted and celebrated Thomas Russell.

A cold, wet hand landed on her arm. She jumped. The hand belonged to a little boy with curly white-blond hair and sky-blue eyes, red-rimmed and filled with tears. Her heart melted. "Hello. What's your name?"

"Mommy?" His bottom lip wobbled.

"Oh, sweetie, I'm not sure who your mommy is, but I'll bet Russ knows."

The lip stopped moving, and his eyes widened. "Wuss?"

"We can go find him together if you want."

"Find who?" A voice rumbled behind her.

The little boy ran around Ashley, his arms raised. "Wuuuuss!"

Russ picked up the kid, juggling him and a plate of food before dropping a kiss on his head. "Hey, bud, where's your mom?"

"Don't know."

"She can't be far." Russ gently shifted the child in his arms and sat next to her. "Phin, this is my friend Ashley."

"She not Mommy."

"I know. Ashley, this is my nephew, Phin. His mom is probably in the kitchen." Russ picked up a carrot and handed it to the boy. "Where's your dad, buddy?"

Phin pointed left then right as he gnawed on his treat. He cozied against Russ, who smiled—casual, friendly, and gorgeous. Ashley's insides melted at the mismatched pair.

"Oh good, you found him." A tall, broad man stepped up to the table, ruffling Phin's hair. "I figured he'd find his way to you or Rachel." The stranger turned to Ashley. "I'm Chad."

She accepted his extended hand. "Ashley."

"It's nice to meet you. Thanks for coming to the memorial."

"I'm glad I could make it."

"Chad married my sister Rachel," Russ said. "He also works with me on the farm."

Chad pulled out a chair and sat down. "How do you two know each other?"

Ashley shot a look at Russ, but his eyes were on Phin. She offered Chad a polite smile. "I'm a friend of Tom's. That's how I met Russ."

"I'm sorry about the circumstances, but it's nice to meet you."

A trim brunette set a plate of food in front of Chad before slipping an arm around his shoulders. She looked right at Ashley, her brown eyes intense. "I'm Rachel. Wife. Mom. Sister."

"I'm Ashley." Secret fiancée of the deceased.

Before self-pity could get ahold of her, an older, red-headed boy ran over, his shirt untucked and a clip-on tie in his hand. "Uncle Russ, can we go to the gym?"

Two more blond boys followed, as did a lanky teenage boy who maneuvered the room without looking up from his cell phone, thumbs flying across the screen. "I'll take 'em. Grandma unlocked it."

"Thank you." Rachel grabbed his face and smooshed a kiss to his cheek.

"Aunt Rachel!" He still didn't look up. "Jeff, fill a plate with cookies for everyone. Let's go." One boy ran for the dessert table as the rest ran after the teen. Phin shimmied off Russ' lap and plowed into the older boy, who—eyes on his phone—dropped a hand down and grabbed Phin's hand.

Chaos. Laughter. Family. Longing clutched Ashley's chest. As the family interacted around her, she spotted a thinner, feminine version of Russ. The young woman's eyebrows shot up when she locked eyes with Ashley, and she walked toward her. "Russ didn't tell us he was bringing a date to the memorial," the woman said.

Heat seared Ashley's cheeks. "I'm not his date."

"Carrie." Russ' tone held an unmistakable threat. "Ashley, this is my sister. Carrie, this is Ashley."

His sister's eyes narrowed. "You came in late together, sat together. I assumed—"

"You assumed wrong," he said. "What's with you?"

Her gaze never left Ashley's face. The people behind them chattered as Carrie took a seat at the table. She maintained eye contact, which gave Ashley time to notice the puffy circles under her eyes.

Ashley reached over and squeezed her hand. "It's an easy mistake to make. I'm actually a friend of Tom's. Russ was kind enough to escort me in. Can I get you anything?"

Carrie cocked her head to the side, then smiled. "Thank you, I'm fine. I think you'll fit right in."

If only.

"Has anyone seen Mom?" A trendy, young brunette walked up to the table with a well-dressed, well-groomed man by her side. "She walked off with Kristy almost half an hour ago."

Carrie pointed a thumb at the young couple. "This is our baby sister and her husband."

All of Tom's cousins present and accounted for. "I'm Ashley. It's nice to meet you."

"I'm Elizabeth. Listen, if anyone sees Mom before I do, will you tell her I need to get going? If we leave soon, Kristy will fall asleep in the car."

"I don't see Mom, but I see your baby," Rachel said. Ashley's eyes followed Rachel's finger until she spotted a woman cuddling a smiling baby girl.

"Perfect. We really should get home. I'll see you guys Sunday?"

The sisters chattered simultaneously as they took turns hugging Elizabeth. The men shook hands. Someone mentioned a potluck and a birthday cake. Their voices mingled together, a harmony of femininity accented by deep bursts of masculinity.

Ashley's heart ached. She'd be singing solo for a while longer.

Russ leaned forward. "Have you met Tom's sisters yet?"

More family. The ache deepened. "I don't think I can handle that right now."

"You should meet them eventually."

"Later, I promise." Maybe.

Without Tom there to bind her to his family, meeting them all seemed pointless. Living in his house didn't make her one of them, but she could watch and see what it was like. At least arriving with Russ gave her an excuse to sit with his siblings. Love radiated among them. They weren't simply family. They were friends. And they had no idea how close she'd come to joining them.

Russ nudged his plate toward her. "Tell me when you're ready to go."

* * * * * * *

Russ glanced at Ashley sitting gracefully beside him, her legs crossed as she leaned toward Rachel and looked at pictures on a phone. After she passed Carrie's inquisition, his sisters seemed ready to adopt Ashley. Their conversations would occupy Ashley's time for another hour or so, but then everyone would head home. What was he supposed to do with her then?

Ashley's laugh drew his attention. Her face glowed, all signs of her earlier stress gone. Phin had returned to sit on her lap, where he drove cars across the table as she talked with Rachel. Most of the guests had gone, leaving the family to mill around the church hall. The nephews came and went, interrupting the adults and creating a mess. Ashley took it all in stride, talking baseball with one boy and giving another tips on texting with girls. Everyone welcomed her, and she didn't shy away from anyone. If Russ didn't know better, he'd think she'd met the family before.

"How long are you staying?" Rachel asked, tucking away her phone. "Do you have to get on the road soon?"

Russ tuned in.

"I haven't figured that out yet," Ashley said. "I have a few things to take care of in town."

"Where are you staying? If you don't have a room yet, you shouldn't have a problem finding a place. This town is silent between golf and ski seasons."

Ashley scratched the side of her neck, glancing around without making eye contact. Time for Russ to step in. "She's actually been staying with me."

Every conversation stopped. All eyes turned toward him, including the stink eye Ashley shot his way.

"At your house?" Rachel asked.

Chad placed a hand on her back. "I didn't realize you knew each other that well."

"We don't. But she didn't know about Tom until she got here, so—"

Both sisters gasped as Phin smashed two cars together. Ashley looked like she wanted to send Russ to meet Tom in the afterlife.

"No one told you about the accident?" Rachel pressed her hand to her chest. Her lips trembled.

Oh no. Russ had two minutes to calm her down before she started crying, and no matter how tough Carrie pretended to be, she'd shed sympathy tears in no time. No more tears. He needed a distraction, fast. "Ashley's thinking about relocating here. Anybody know of anything for sale?"

Carrie and Rachel whipped out their phones.

"My receptionist's husband is a realtor—"

"I passed a few houses on the way here—"

They twittered and surfed. Ashley poked his side, leaning toward him, teeth clenched. "What are you doing?"

"Finding you a place to live."

"I have a place to live."

"They don't know that."

"I don't want to lie to them."

"You didn't lie to them. I asked if they knew of a place for sale. They don't need to know it's for me."

Ashley's pink lips parted as she leaned back. "You're not really giving up on your family's home, are you? You said to wait a year. You said—"

"I know. We'll figure this out together. In the meantime"— he nodded toward his sisters—"it keeps them busy, and they stop asking questions."

The frown eased from Ashley's face. She looked around the table, then smiled at Russ. "You're brilliant."

"I know."

"Oh! Here's a house near Boyne." Carrie moved closer, holding her phone out for Ashley. With Rachel sitting on Ashley's left side, Russ relinquished the seat on her right.

Someone smacked him on the back, nearly sending Russ toppling over Carrie. "That was a great service." Rob Kraft stepped up alongside him.

Russ considered hitting him back, but someone had to set a good example for the nephews. He clamped a hand around the back of Rob's neck, guiding him to another table, away from the women and children. "I'm glad you were able to make it. I thought about locking you out after the thing with Tom's will."

"Tom left a will?" Chad fell into step with them.

"He did." Rob slipped out of Russ' grip and faced him. "But it's not the will we need to talk about. It's the letter."

Russ rolled his eyes. "I know. I'm figuring it out."

"Well, there's more to figure out."

Perfect, because life wasn't complicated enough. "Chad, can you give us a minute?"

"He might as well stay," Rob said. "This affects both of you."

"How?" But as he said it, the lightbulb went off. "The farm. Tom willed away his share, didn't he?"

Rob nodded.

Russ wanted to hit someone.

"What do you mean he willed away the farm?" Chad crossed his arms over his chest. "When did he write a will?"

"It's not the will," Russ said. "It's the letter."

"Ashley emailed me a copy," Rob said. "I reviewed it more carefully at the office."

"What letter?" Chad looked between Rob and Russ.

Blood rushed to Russ' ears, running through his veins like fire and ice. Tom was lucky he was already in the ground, because Russ wanted to hit him.

Chad grabbed Russ' arm. "What am I missing?" His mountain of a brother-in-law stepped closer. "What happened?"

Russ scrubbed a hand over his face. "Tom left the farm to Ashley."

CHAPTER 14

The rushing heat from the dashboard slapped at Ashley's face. Russ sat behind the steering wheel, his eyes unwavering from the road ahead. "What do you mean, he left me the farm?" she asked.

"I don't have all of the details yet. Rob'll come by the house Monday."

"Good Lord." She shook her head, trying to straighten out the mess of information. "This is a disaster."

"Let's not worry about it until we have more facts."

"Easier said than done."

Colorful two-story buildings zipped past the window as they drove through Boyne Heights. Vibrant storefronts and historic office buildings filled the downtown area, which quickly gave way to quaint cottages and small, midcentury homes. Once they passed the town limits, acres of open land greeted them, dotted with taller, wider, and older farmhouses. Soon the trees outnumbered the buildings.

The setting sun cast long shadows across the road. Had they left the memorial that late? Russ and his sisters had sent Tom's family home, then stayed to help clean the hall. When Kathleen volunteered to escort Tom's parents home, Russ offered to drive Ashley, but now she wasn't ready to go home.

"Can we go someplace else?" she asked.

"Like where?"

"Anywhere. The hilltop maybe?"

"Okay." Russ took the next right, driving them down a tree-lined, two-lane path and away from the main road. Between the setting sun and the thickening trees, darkness closed in around them. How appropriate. Ashley gave up looking out the passenger window and focused on whatever she could see in the glowing beams of the headlights.

Within minutes the truck inclined, pulling them back up the country hill. Ashley looked out the window and sighed. "I don't suppose there's much to see in the darkness."

"Sure there is." Russ killed the lights. A dozen stars instantly appeared ahead of them. "Wait until the sun finishes setting. You can see galaxies from here." The truck took a few familiar turns before Russ parked and shut off the engine. He opened his door, and the heat rushed out into the crisp night air.

Ashley shivered as realization dawned. "We're sitting outside?"

"We can stay in the truck, but the windows will fog up in a few minutes. If you want to see the stars, the view's better out here."

She pulled her sweater close. "It's cold out there."

Russ rolled his eyes as he reached into the back seat. He tossed her a rumpled sweatshirt. "It's clean, I promise."

"Thank you." She stuffed her arms inside as Russ closed his door. He lowered the tailgate, which rocked the truck. Ashley slipped the sweatshirt over her head, settling its mass around her, wrapping her in warmth as well as the scent of woodchips and grass clippings. Burying her nose in the cotton, she inhaled.

It wasn't just a scent—it was Russ. The unexpected familiarity of it soothed her. The earthy tones had tickled her nostrils when he showed her around the farmhouse, and again at the memorial when she sat beside him. Drawing in another slow breath, she filled her lungs with the scent that comforted her achy heart and muddled mind. She didn't have any of those memories of Tom, but Russ had already crept into her life.

Opening her door, Ashley let the night air bite at her exposed legs as she walked to the back of the truck. The extra seat cushion waited for her. Beside it sat a pair of gloves, a stocking hat, and a thick gray blanket.

"Tom always told me you were the best guy that he knew." She pulled the hat over her hair. "Now I know why."

"I told you, I like to be prepared."

"You don't have to share." Ashley slid her hands into the gloves. "You could keep these for yourself."

His lips twisted. "What kind of man would let a woman in a dress freeze while he used the only blanket?"

She pushed her cushion toward him. When she hopped onto the truck, their legs brushed against each other. Ignoring the comfort of it, she unfolded the blanket and stretched it over both of their legs.

His fingers wrapped around her wrist. "What are you doing?"

When Ashley looked up, Russ' face hovered inches above hers. Woodchips and grass. She cleared her throat. "Sharing?"

"That's very kind of you, but I'll be fine." He took the blanket from her hand and draped it over her lap, tucking it under her leg.

Ashley's breath hitched at the intimacy of the simple gesture. Russ either heard her or felt the same thing because his hand froze, his fingers resting gently against her thigh. As if stung by a bee, he yanked his hand away and stuffed his hands into his pockets.

She forced her attention upward, watching as stars popped out against the ever-darkening sky. Crickets chirped. Branches popped. Russ breathed deeply. She mimicked him, releasing the tension of their awkward moment.

Not awkward. Unexpected. As strange as their new relationship was, nothing between Ashley and Russ felt awkward. If anything, the familiarity of his presence surprised her. She nudged his shoulder. "Thanks for today."

"What do you mean?"

"The playground. The memorial. After the memorial. You didn't have to drag me in or escort me through everything, but I appreciate it."

He shrugged. "It was nothing."

"No, it was everything. You went out of your way to make sure I was comfortable. Thank you."

Russ glanced at her before turning back to the night sky. "You're welcome."

"Why did you do it?"

He shrugged again.

"I don't believe you."

"What would you like me to say?"

"You could be honest."

Russ shook his head, but his lips curved slightly. "I didn't think I could be, but you changed that."

"What do you mean?"

"You were right about me not grieving after my dad died. There was too much to worry about—my mom, my sisters, the farm. When Tom died ..." Russ swallowed. "He was a brother to me and ..." He cleared his throat, but Ashley heard the pain he tried to cover.

She slid the glove off her right hand and reached into his left coat pocket, then pulled his hand out, threading her fingers with his. Everyone had expected her to cry when her parents died. They expected her to fall apart and need help. But Russ? A grown man, business owner, head of the family. What did people expect from him?

Covering their entwined fingers with her gloved hand, she leaned against him and waited. For whatever reason things had turned out the way they had, she was glad to sit on the back of a truck with Russ when he needed it.

* * * * * * *

The gentle weight of Ashley's head pressed against Russ' shoulder as he choked back the pain. The warmth of her soft fingers radiated through him, comforting the ache he'd tried to ignore. When he finally regained control of his breath, he cleared his throat again.

She pulled away and looked up at him. "Okay?"

He nodded, wishing he could see her more clearly. "I'm sorry about that."

"Don't ever apologize for your grief." Her tone reminded him of his mother's many scoldings.

Russ' muscles relaxed. "My mom and sisters have been trying to help since Tom died, but I've never been able to be honest with them. Why is it so easy with you?"

"Maybe because we're strangers. You're not trying to be the strong son or big brother with me. We don't have any expectations of each other."

"Maybe." Regardless of the reason, Russ silently gave thanks for it.

"Is that why you want me to stay?"

The sudden change in topic startled Russ. Why *did* he want her to stay? "I told you, it's nice having someone around."

"You have a lot of family here. You could probably have someone at your house every day of the week."

He groaned. "Don't give them any ideas. I don't mind most of the time, but it can be exhausting."

"How so?"

"They like having a protective older brother, but they don't want to feel pushed around, so I let them think they can manipulate me. Truth is, if I didn't want my mom staying with me this week, she wouldn't be. Sometimes I put up a fight to make them think they're winning, but no one's ever made me do anything I didn't want to do."

"And you don't have to play that game with me." Ashley's fingers wiggled between his. He squeezed without thinking, and her hand settled back into his.

"I didn't realize how tiring pretending was until I didn't have to do it." Another layer of guilt rolled off his back. "It's ... nice."

Ashley relaxed against him even more. For the first time in weeks, Russ felt like he could do the same.

CHAPTER 15

On Monday morning, Ashley again found herself in Tom's kitchen with Rob, Russ, and Tom's letter. Nothing made any more sense than it had the week before. She couldn't remember where in the letter Tom had mentioned any land. "How did I end up with Tom's share of the farm?"

"It's not that simple." Russ banged his coffee mug on the counter, animosity having replaced the gentleness she'd seen over the weekend. "It's a farm. It's been in the family for generations. We don't own stock like a company. We can't give Ashley the east acres or the MacIntosh trees." He glared at Rob. "Why would Tom leave anything to her, and without telling me?"

And how? Ashley sat a little taller. "The letter never said I could have the farm."

Rob waved the paper in his hand. "It's not as clear-cut as the house, but he did mention it. He talks about teaching you the business, working the land together. It's not as direct, but I looked at some case law. Depending on the judge, there's a real possibility that Ashley could inherit Tom's share of the farm. It's not absolute, but it's possible."

Russ scrubbed a hand over his face. "How would you determine what part of the farm is Tom's?"

"Did you buy the property from your parents?" Rob asked. "If we can show that he didn't have a legal right to give it away without your consent, we can save it."

"Tom kept track of that stuff."

Rob sighed. "Do you have *anything* in writing?"

"Tom made me sign things all the time. He was always asking for money and having me sign papers. Rental agreements, employee documents, something about an LLC and a scorp."

"You mean an *S* corp?"

Russ snapped his fingers and pointed at Rob. "Yes!"

"If he filed either of those with the state, I can look it up. I can also check at the courthouse to see who they have named as the legal property owner, but it will certainly help your case if you can find anything with your signature on it. It will definitely help if Ashley doesn't contest it." Rob winked at her.

"This is all so overwhelming." She searched Russ for emotional clues. His shoulders and face sagged. She didn't like doing that to him. "I won't fight you on this. I don't care what the letter says. The farm is yours."

"And any paperwork you have to support ownership would be great," Rob said. "You really should have your own copies of any legal documents you sign, anyway."

Russ leaned against the counter, his arms crossed. "Of course, but I always gave my copies to Tom for safekeeping."

Some of the weight left Ashley's shoulders. "That means there's proof someplace. All we have to do is find that paperwork and get this settled." Her stomach rumbled. "After lunch. Is anyone else hungry?"

Russ nodded. "I'll look through the office this week. Until then, do we have any of those little pickles left from the memorial?"

"I think so." Ashley hopped up and met him at the refrigerator. When she opened the door, he peeked over her shoulder. Spotting the little green bottle, she grabbed it and a few other jars, then stuffed them into Russ' hands. "Sandwiches?"

"Sure."

Rob cleared his throat. "I take it we're done with this conversation?"

Ashley turned back to the lawyer in time to see him packing up his briefcase. "We might as well be. Nothing really changes unless we have those papers, so we should probably find them first."

"And whenever we figure this out, there's the issue of Russ' one year waiting period."

Ashley sighed. "I'd almost forgotten."

"It's your house, so you can do whatever you want." Rob plucked an apple from the fruit bowl. "You enjoy your lunch. I'm going to go back to the office to pretend like Russ has a perfectly organized filing cabinet around here somewhere."

If only. Ashley returned to the refrigerator as Rob's footsteps faded away. Cheese, meat, bread, more cheese. She handed everything to Russ. Unlike his paperwork, he couldn't possibly lose the food between her hands and the kitchen counter.

But what if Russ couldn't find anything? What if they weren't good roommates? Could she get enough work in the next year to save up a down payment on a house? Panic squeezed her lungs. Ignoring the leftover veggie tray and fruit salad, she reached for the gelatin and set it on the island.

Russ handed her two slices of bread smashed around a pile of lunchmeat. "Looks like we can add the farm to our list of unexpected events." He threw together another sandwich, then stood beside her, both of them leaning against the counter, munching away. He tore through his food, staring at the floor. Ashley bit into her sandwich, but it gummed up in her mouth. She tossed it on the counter and grabbed the bowl of green, jiggly comfort instead.

Russ opened a drawer. "Spoon?"

"Thank you." She took the largest spoon and scooped out a mound of lime gelatin and whipped cream. "You know, as crazy as it's been since I got here, none of this should surprise me. Tom used to do this to me all the time. He'd start talking about things he forgot to tell me, then get mad that I couldn't follow the conversation. Of course he'd forget to tell you about me."

"You should've been his business partner. We always had stuff showing up at the farm without explanation. You're the first bride, though."

Ashley's laugh bubbled up, comfortable and relaxing. Nice. So was the dessert. And the company. In all honesty, grieving with Tom's family had been the friendliest, most enjoyable week she'd had in years, all things considered.

Russ reached behind her, brushing his arm across her back.

His nearness warmed her like hot coffee on a blustery day. She'd known nice men her whole life, but something about Russ … Ashley risked a peek at his rugged face. Firm jaw. Weathered tan. But she'd seen him cuddle with his nephew, and she'd held his hand while they gazed at the stars. Her pulse jumped.

This was what she had wanted with Tom—comfort, friendship, companionship. She had most of that with Russ, and then some. Her dreams of Tom had never affected her blood pressure the way Russ did. She knew from her conversations with Tom that Russ was older and had dated less often, but was he lonely? A spoonful of gelatin melted in Ashley's mouth as she sneaked sideways glances at him.

Russ seemed to like her. He certainly made her heart flutter. The more she thought about it, the more sense it made, but would Russ see it?

Only one way to find out. Ashley set the bowl on the counter before stepping in front of him. Inhaling deeply, she summoned her courage as her pulse quickened.

Russ' chewing slowed. "You okay?"

"I think we should get married."

* * * * * * *

Russ choked on salami and disbelief. Ashley shoved a glass of water at him, but he waved it away as he braced his hands on the counter. He struggled to breathe, his head spinning.

Ashley pounded on his back. Now she wanted to save him after nearly scaring him to death? She pounded again. The food finally dislodged itself, and air rushed into his lungs. He sucked in a deep, cleansing breath.

"Are you all right? Can I get you anything? What do you need?"

He needed a minute to think. Gasping for oxygen to clear his head, Russ walked to the sliding-glass doors and stared outside, looking at anything but Ashley's lovely face. What was he supposed to say? She'd just asked him to marry her. How did a man respond to that?

As he scanned the horizon, her reflection appeared in the glass. It came closer until a hand landed on his back. Small circles warmed his shoulder where she rubbed it, like his mom used to do when he got sick as a kid. His mom's actions always made him sleepy, though. Ashley's hand somehow triggered every nerve in his body. And she wanted to marry him.

"Russ?" She stepped closer, pressing her warmth against him. This was a bad idea, right? "Are you okay?"

"No, I'm hallucinating."

"I'm serious."

"So am I. It sounded like you proposed."

"It could solve our problems."

Russ watched their reflections, her arm partially wrapped around him as she continued to rub his back. Soft and warm. Trembling. Her eyes shifted. Her lips pursed. Unless he was mistaken, she was as nervous as he was shocked. "We should probably talk about this," he said.

"I know. It's sudden, but it fixes everything. We can both live here, the farm stays in your family. It's basically the same plan as before."

"Not quite." Russ returned to the kitchen to put some much-needed space between them. "You've prepared for marriage, and now you want to substitute me for Tom."

"That's not true, I thought—"

"That any Russell man would work?"

"No! Tom talked about you all the time, and I've spent a week with you, and I think you're a wonderful man. I wouldn't suggest spending the rest of my life with someone simply because he happened to be related to Tom. I'm not that—"

"I'm wonderful?"

"—shallow, I … what?" Ashley stopped, red-faced and wide-eyed.

"You think I'm wonderful? You barely know me."

"I know a lot about you."

"But you don't *know* me." They stared at each other from opposite sides of the room, the click of the furnace making the only sound.

She shifted her weight. "Maybe you're right." Finally, a moment of sanity. "Tom told me that you're Edgar James Russell the third, and you own a farm with your cousin. You grow apples, peaches, and cherries, but your favorite fruit is blueberries. You're thirty-eight, never been married, played football and basketball. You used to watch the History Channel with Tom because it reminds you of your grandpa."

A strange familiarity filled the room. "I didn't realize you knew all that."

"Tom liked to talk about you."

"I'm impressed that you remember so much, but that's not all there is to me."

"I know that too." Her gaze dropped to the floor. "You love your sisters, but you love their kids even more. You're a hard worker, but your family comes first, to the point that you'll drive a stranger around your farm to help out your mom. You were willing to miss your cousin's memorial to make sure a woman you just met was okay." She looked up, drawing his gaze back to the sincerity in her eyes. "You look like you stepped out of an Eddie Bauer catalog, you smell like a playground, and you're all the best parts of Tom."

Russ' throat tightened. No one had ever said anything so nice. Ashley's words, her eyes, her smile all made him want to know her the way she knew him, but he couldn't get sucked into her delusion. "I'm not a replacement."

"I'm not looking for a replacement. I'm looking to get on with my life. Our futures are linked now whether we like it or not, and I thought …" Her gaze dropped again.

Russ could practically hear the energy seep out of her. What he actually heard was a sniff. The tension melted off his shoulders as Tom's fiancée wilted. "I'm sorry."

"For what?"

"Whenever my sisters are upset, I apologize first and ask questions later."

Her chuckle lightened the mood. "That's smart, but you don't have anything to apologize for."

"I disagree."

Ashley peeked at him, her dark eyelashes framing those beautiful eyes. "Honestly, don't worry about it. I'm a little embarrassed, but I'll get over it."

"Don't be embarrassed."

"I asked a stranger to marry me, and after you said no, I tried to think of all the ways I could convince you, but it's just now occurring to me that maybe you're involved with someone else, or not interested, which would be understandable."

Her mouth kept moving as Russ watched uncertainty derail her confidence. He liked to think that he understood women better than a lot of guys, but this one confounded him. He heard "fat" and couldn't take it anymore. In two seconds, he stood in front of her, grabbed her arm with one hand, and clamped the other hand over her mouth.

Ashley's eyes bulged. "Whf?"

"I want to set the record straight. I like having you here."

"Yof duf?"

"I do."

Her cool fingers wrapped around his wrist and pulled his hand away. "But you don't want to get married, and I understand that. I shouldn't have suggested it."

"You were trying to help. Tom left us in a bad situation, and you want to fix it."

"I guess, but proposing was a dumb idea."

"Maybe, although I can see why you suggested it."

"You can?"

He shrugged. "You said it yourself. You're crazy about me."

"I said no such thing." Ashley pushed him away, her face twisted like he'd fed her lemons.

He smiled, tempted by her feigned disgust. He liked being able to get under her skin, even if it meant riling her up. He couldn't stop now. "Not that I blame you. I own a farm, live in a great house. My sisters tell me I'm pretty good looking. I can see why you fell for me."

Ashley's mouth opened, but no sound emerged. She waved a finger at him, her arms tense, face red. Cute, if it weren't for the bulging veins.

After a few more finger waves, she made a fist and slugged him on the shoulder. "You've got some nerve! I just humiliated myself. I'm trying to deal with Tom's death and your rejection, and you're standing there basking in your imaginary awesomeness. I'm actually trying to *fix* our problem."

"You did call me wonderful."

"I lied!" Ashley hit him again before storming out the patio door.

Good. Being upset might redirect her thoughts. No one married someone in a week. That was crazy. Only people in Bible times did that sort of thing. It might have worked for them, but that was a different era.

Besides, Russ didn't have time to think about marriage. Sure, it would be nice to have a family, but options were limited, and he was almost forty. Meeting someone, dating, hoping it worked. Nothing about that appealed to him. He'd wasted enough time with Jess. Never again. Every unattached woman he met was closer in age to his teenage nephew than to him. Russ shuddered. So he'd never have a family. He had a niece and nephews. That was enough.

Outside, Ashley paced the backyard. The wind tossed leaves across the lawn as the sun hid behind dark clouds. It was cold for November, and Ashley had to be freezing in her short-sleeved shirt. As if on cue, she rubbed her hands over her bare arms. When she spotted him standing in the doorway, her chin hitched up, and she walked farther away. She *must* be embarrassed if she was willing to freeze instead of facing him. He should take her a coat. And say what? *Here's your coat. Sorry I don't want to marry you.*

Ashley's hair danced around her face. She tucked a piece behind her ear, but it didn't contain the beautiful chaos.

Tom had amazing taste in women. If Russ had the time and energy to waste, he'd look for someone like Ashley—confident, strong, and compassionate.

The obviousness of the situation almost knocked him over. She wasn't asking him to date her or romance her or even buy her a ring. She got a family and a house. He kept the farm and stayed put. No unrealistic expectations. No games.

Could it really be that easy? Was he ready to ask a woman to stay with him, to sacrifice her life to accommodate his? Farming wasn't easy, even for a family who grew up with it. And Ashley saying she wanted a family didn't mean she understood what that meant. His sisters would grill her, Mom showed up whenever she felt like it, and holidays were an exercise in anarchy.

She faced the house, this time squaring her shoulders as she marched toward him.

Could it really work? Forgetting his family, forgetting the farm, could he commit himself to that woman? To that kind, intelligent, beautiful woman? The chaos in his mind settled. The panic in his heart faded. Thoughts of dating sapped his energy, but watching Ashley accelerated his pulse. Plucking his coat off the chair, Russ slid open the patio door.

Her eyes sparked. That kind of fire sure beat tears. Russ slowed his steps as she approached him. "I've been thinking about your proposal—"

"Me too." She stopped directly in front of him, toe to toe and completely oblivious to personal body space. Close enough that, even with the breeze moving around them, her spicy scent teased him.

Her hair blew up at him, tickling his cheek. He tucked it behind her shoulder, enjoying the soft strands. "You were?"

"Getting married is a good idea. Maybe I pitched it wrong. This isn't simply a business proposition."

"Then what is it?"

Her creamy skin went red, but she held her chin high, looking him in the eye. "It's a marriage, with everything that word implies." She sucked in a breath. "Everything." Ashley grabbed the front of his shirt. Pulled him close. And kissed him.

CHAPTER 16

Russ' breath warmed Ashley's cheek, but his unyielding lips chilled her straight through. That shouldn't be happening. He'd opened up to her. He seemed to like her. Her radar wasn't that far off, was it? Maybe she needed a different technique. Releasing his shirt, she slid her hands up to his broad, tense shoulders.

Strength and warmth wrapped around her waist, pulling her close. Russ tilted his head as his lips softened. The tang of dill clung to him. Strong fingers pressed into her back, guiding her against him, deepening the kiss. He held her—claimed her—and she let him.

"Ashley," he whispered against her lips.

"Shut up." She kissed him again. Unexpected emotions bubbled up. She didn't recognize them all, but she didn't fight them. When he kissed the skin beneath her ear, her knees melted.

"I'll marry you." His lips moved back to hers.

A million tingles raced up her spine. "What changed your mind?"

A deep chuckle rumbled in his chest. "You're a convincing woman." His lips brushed her ear, cheek, temple. She opened her eyes and found herself looking right at his lips. Desire coursed through her. "Up here." His finger tapped her chin up, shifting her gaze to his. The corner of his mouth lifted, crinkling the skin around his eyes. "You're also a surprising woman."

"You didn't say yes because I kissed you, did you?"

He raised his eyebrows. "I'm not that shallow."

Ouch. "I deserved that."

"You did."

But was it true?

"Don't look like that."

"Like what?"

"Like you found a worm in your apple. I came out here to talk about it when you kissed me." He dropped an arm from around her, and the wind bit at her skin. A heavy jacket settled on her shoulders. "See? I was bringing you a coat. I had a plan."

Ashley pulled the jacket close but still shivered. "What did you want to tell me?"

"I think your idea has merit."

"I noticed."

A full smile filled his face. "Not this part, the whole thing."

"Tom and I had a—"

Russ covered her mouth with his hand. "One thing I'd like to figure out is how *we* can do this, not you and Tom. If we get married, it's about us, not about what you planned with my cousin."

She pushed his hand away. "But it was a good plan."

"I'm sure it was, but I'm not Tom."

No, he wasn't. None of her interactions with Tom had ever startled her heart like Russ did, not to mention what his kisses did to her. His fingers squeezed the ticklish flesh at her waist. Despite the stiff brown coat between them, her skin sizzled.

"Then what do you want?" she asked.

"I want a wife, a family."

Her stomach rolled. She wanted a family too, but until kissing Russ, the act of creating one had merely been a theory. With her lips tingling from the memory of his, thoughts of that family nearly short-circuited her brain. "Me too. So … how do you want to do this?"

"We need time to get comfortable."

"How long does that take?"

"You tell me."

Blood rushed through Ashley's veins, pounding in her ears. "I have no idea."

"Three weeks?"

Three? "You want to have … you want … three weeks before we …" Start a family? Russ' kisses alone launched her heart into orbit, but the thought of more … when had it gotten so warm? "Three weeks?"

Russ' lips twitched.

Ashley's pulse relaxed. "You're teasing me, aren't you?"

"We don't need to mark the calendar."

She nodded. "We have plenty of time." Like decades. Decades with Russ. It was definitely getting warmer.

"Good." He wrapped his arms around her, pulling her close and brushing his lips across hers. "I hadn't really thought about this on my way out here, but since you started the kissing, it would be a shame to stop."

She liked kissing him too. Ashley smiled. "Okay."

"And I don't want to wait. If we're getting married, I want to go to the church and do it right away. If we wait, then one of us needs to move out."

"Why?"

"Call me old-fashioned, but I believe a man and woman need to be married before living together."

"Even if they're sleeping in separate bedrooms?"

Russ kissed her. Then again. And again. When he finally pulled back, Ashley clung to him. "I'm traditional, but I can only resist so much. I won't put you in a compromising situation."

Of course. "Tom and I talked about the same thing."

Russ cleared his throat.

"I'm sorry. I know, this is about you and me, but I'm glad you and Tom have the same values."

"We were raised in the same family." He grabbed her hands, twining his fingers with hers. "But as strong as my convictions are, I also don't want to wait because I don't want to explain this to my sisters."

"What would you have to explain?"

"If we tell my family, then try to plan a wedding, we're going to face the inquisition until we're actually married. When it comes to my sisters, it's best to act first, then ask for forgiveness. What about your family?"

"I have my aunt and uncle."

He cocked his head. "That's it?"

"My dad was an only child. My mom was born ten years after her youngest sibling. All of them have passed away except my aunt Rose and uncle John. They weren't comfortable with me moving up here to begin with, much less marrying someone I met online. You might be right about asking for forgiveness afterward."

"I'm okay with this, but are *you* sure? That means no big wedding. No reception."

"I've never been one of those girls who dreamed about her wedding. If I were, we wouldn't be having this conversation."

"So it's agreed. We'll do this tomorrow."

"Tomorrow?" Ashley stepped back.

"Why not? We said no waiting."

"But it takes three days to get a marriage license in Michigan. I looked it up when … you know."

"Maybe we can still make this work. What do we have to do?"

"Go to the courthouse with a photo ID and twenty bucks, then ask for a marriage license."

Russ pulled her back to himself. "If I can convince the clerk to rush the license, will you marry me tomorrow?"

Everything about him tempted her, but common sense forced its way back into her head. "No. We can't get married tomorrow."

"We agreed—"

"To get married as quickly as possible, but Tom's memorial was two days ago."

"Maybe you're right." Russ rubbed his thumb across the top of her hand. Such an innocent action, but so comforting. Ashley closed her eyes and soaked in the tenderness of his touch. She hadn't enjoyed someone's company that completely in a long time. A kiss brushed her cheek and sent a tremble rippling through her.

"What's wrong?" His whisper warmed her neck.

"Are we crazy?"

"Maybe. What are you thinking?" He kissed her jaw.

Ashley shuddered. "It's hard to think when you kiss me."

"What were you thinking before I started kissing you?"

Before his arms and lips and the tingling? "That this could work."

His stubbly face pressed against hers. "And now?"

"That I've never felt like this before."

He smiled against her cheek. "Sounds like a yes." He shifted her in his embrace, his lips moving back toward hers. Her pulse throbbed, threatening to deafen her.

Ignore the high blood pressure. Think. John and Rose would freak out. Russ' sisters might interrogate her. Kathleen would be oddly thrilled. And Russ. He held her, cradled her, cared for her.

Maybe she was crazy. What would her mother think? But it wasn't insanity or the memory of her mom that touched her heart. "Peace." Ashley inhaled. "I can't explain it, but when I imagine living here with you, I simply have peace."

"Perfect." His lips captured hers, comforting yet exciting her, then pulled away. "The courthouse is open for two more hours. Plenty of time to convince the clerk."

CHAPTER 17

Russ sat beside Ashley in the cab of his truck. She stared out her window with a Mona Lisa-type smile. Tomorrow they'd be married. After nearly four decades of bachelorhood, he'd have a partner. He'd let a pair of pretty eyes seduce him.

Well, maybe more than pretty eyes. Ashley understood him. She appreciated him. Not to mention her lips. One taste and he was hooked.

Nothing had prepared him for Ashley's touch. Russ had tried to resist her, but she'd opened the door and invited him in. Only a fool would've said no. He could've pulled away, tried to be reasonable, but her tenderness was as addictive as potato chips. Truth be told, he wasn't sure he wanted to resist.

"Are you sure?" Ashley's gentle voice pulled him out of his reverie.

"About what?"

"Getting married."

He rolled his eyes. "If you ask me that one more time, I'm going to think you've changed your mind."

"I don't want to force you into anything."

Russ laughed. "Ashley, I can tell you're a tough, independent woman, but not even you could force me into something I don't want to do. Especially getting married."

"Good." She exhaled, leaning back into the seat. "I appreciate your honesty."

"You should expect it. Contrary to popular television, not all men lie."

"That's refreshing."

He hoped the same was true for Ashley. Not all women could be trusted, but he'd give her the benefit of the doubt. Tom had.

"Why did you say yes? Honestly."

"You're kind of cute."

"You said you'd be honest."

Russ shrugged. "I don't know."

"You can turn around now."

"What?" Something clawed at his throat. Panic? "Why do you want to go back?"

"You're holding out. If you can't tell me why you agreed to marry me, then we need to seriously reconsider what we're about to do."

Reconsider and hope another intelligent, considerate, beautiful woman moved to town wanting to get married without dating? It would never happen. Russ could barely believe it was happening now. He wasn't the smartest kid in the family, but he wasn't an idiot either. He wouldn't let her get away. "I don't believe in dating." There. Honesty.

"Why?" Ashley twisted toward him in the seat.

"Did Tom tell you about his sister?"

"Yes. She's divorced, like one of your sisters."

"Carrie. My grandparents met in high school, had a small family wedding, and were married for over sixty years. Carrie and my cousin are smart, amazing women who wanted the same thing, but they got caught up in the romance and wedding, then couldn't figure out how to make a marriage work. Whatever my grandparents did worked, but today's relationships don't last. I want a partnership that will last."

"Lots of people are realizing that, but why do *you* want to do this?"

Maybe she had more in common with his sisters than he thought. "I've had some bad experiences. The last one was a doozy."

"Everyone has bad experiences. I went on a blind date with a guy who referred to himself in the third person all night. That doesn't mean you should give up, though."

"I could handle third person. This was worse." He glanced at her. "The last girl I dated wanted more than I did. She sort of ..." How could he say it without sounding judgmental?

"What, she stalked you?"

That would do. "Basically."

Ashley slid closer. "Really? I was kidding."

"Well, I'm not. She moved north a year ago, and I decided I was done dating."

"How can you be sure I'm not a stalker?"

"You've been vetted."

She relaxed into the passenger seat. "By Tom. I feel the same way about you."

The closer they got to town, the darker the clouds. Russ flipped on his headlights and turned up the heat. "Have you ever been in northern Michigan in the winter?"

"We visited in the summer, and I was too young to remember."

"Where did you grow up?"

"Near Cincinnati."

"Isn't that in the southern part of the state?"

"Closer to Kentucky than to Michigan."

And a completely different climate. She'd get used to the weather eventually. Until then, "Do you have winter tires for your car?"

"I don't have a car, remember? I'm still driving a rental."

"That's right."

"I haven't exactly had time to go car shopping. And I don't care to drive, so when my car died, Tom suggested I wait until he could help me find a good one. Will I need winter tires? What's the difference?"

"They keep you on the road and out of the ditch."

Ashley chuckled. "Don't all tires do that?"

"Yes, but winter tires are designed for snow and ice. I never drive without them."

"I suppose I'll consider it."

He'd heard similar things from his sisters, but he'd convinced them. Convincing Ashley would be tougher. Maybe he needed a different approach. "Then it's settled. We'll get you a car *and* winter tires."

"You can't make decisions for me. It's my car. I can handle—"

"A car in Cincinnati. If you buy anything like that little clown car you rented, it isn't going to get you thirty feet down the driveway unless you put some extra traction on it."

"I don't—"

Russ pressed a hand over her mouth. "Not an option. I'm the winter-driving expert. Trust me."

Ashley's lips tensed. He preferred when they were softer, when they were next to his lips instead of his hand, but he wasn't about to compromise on his soon-to-be-wife's safety. He pulled his hand away. "Are we agreed?"

"Fine. I'll buy new tires."

"It's not always going to be this easy, is it?"

"What?"

"Our fights."

Light laughter floated through the cab. "Our first fight."

"At least we got that out of the way."

Russ glanced over and caught her smiling at him. Her eyes twinkled. Those soft lips parted. He couldn't wait to touch her again, and she didn't seem like she would protest.

The truck vibrated. Snapping out of his thoughts, he pulled back into his lane. Not even the best winter tires could keep a truck on the road if he couldn't.

Twenty minutes later, he stood in front of the courthouse staring through the glass double doors. Somewhere in that building was a marriage license that would soon have his name on it. And Ashley's.

Her hand slid around his bicep. "Ready?"

He took a deep breath and opened the door for her. Musty, hot air blasted his face as they entered. A brown, plastic sign hung on a brick wall pointing the way to several offices. The only one he cared about was in the back. They followed the arrows, linoleum, and fluorescent lights around a corner and to the office of Willa Jones, County Clerk.

Russ walked up to the counter. A salt-and-pepper-haired woman sat at the nearest desk typing intently, barely visible behind a computer monitor and vertical file holder. Behind her sat another desk, cleaner and tidier than anything at the farm office, but the dents and scratches suggested it might be as old. Vases of flowers on the far table and the counter added some much-needed color to the industrial cream-and-brown interior. Clearing his throat, he smiled at the woman. "Is Mrs. Jones here?"

She finished typing, then stood and smiled. "She's in the back. Can I help you with anything?"

"I need a marriage license, but I'd like to talk to Mrs. Jones, please."

"I'll get her for you."

After she disappeared into an office in the back, Ashley leaned close. "She probably could've helped us."

"Probably, but Willa and I have history."

"Are you planning on charming her into speeding up our license?"

"I won't have to charm her. Watch."

Salt and Pepper returned with a petite peroxide blonde wearing cherry-red lipstick and a giant, beaded necklace. "Edgar, how are you, honey?"

Ashley squeezed his arm and chuckled. "Edgar."

He resisted the urge to roll his eyes. "I'm fine, Mrs. Jones, how are you?"

"Your mother beat me at gin again last week, but I'm due for a win. And it's Willa, please. I'm sorry I couldn't make it to the service this weekend. How was it?"

"Not how I wanted to spend the day, but the memorial was good. Tom would have been happy with it."

"I'm glad to hear that. Now, what can I do for you?"

Russ braced his feet, taking a deep breath. "I'd like to get a marriage license, please."

Willa's eyebrows shot up. "You're getting married? Your mom never said a word! I didn't think she could keep a secret, especially one this big. Congratulations, honey."

"Thank you. This is my fiancée, Ashley."

Ashley offered Willa a hand. "It's nice to meet you."

"A pleasure. When's the big day?"

He cleared his throat. "That's why I wanted to talk with you. We'd like to get married tomorrow."

Salt and Pepper's jaw dropped. Willa's eyes widened, but she cleared her throat, and her clerk face reappeared. "There's a three-day waiting period on marriage licenses. I can put through the application today, but you'll have to wait until Thursday before you can get married."

"I understand that's the standard, but don't you have the ability to speed up the process? Something about …" He glanced at Ashley.

"Good and sufficient cause," she said.

Willa clasped her hands in front of her. "That's true, but what's your cause?"

"Tom's memorial made me realize that we never know what tomorrow's going to bring." Russ slipped an arm around Ashley and pulled her close, surprised at how much her nearness comforted him. "He would have been the best man at my wedding. Without him here …" Emotions burned behind Russ' eyes as the words clogged his throat.

Ashley rubbed circles across his back. "We don't want to risk anything keeping us apart."

Like a horde of angry sisters.

"Oh, honey, I understand that, but there's nothing I can do."

Ashley leaned over the counter. "Sure there is. You can agree that we have a good and sufficient cause. There's no set definition online, so it's completely up to your discretion." She sandwiched Russ' hand between hers. "Every year on our anniversary, we can remember Tom and how important he was to all of us."

He should have let her do all the talking. If Russ was the clerk, he would have given Ashley the license already. One look at Willa's twisted lips, however, told him she wasn't buying it.

"What will convince you that we're worth the loophole?" he asked.

"I'm not sure this is one of those situations. The only time I've ever sped up the process was when the groom forgot to apply for the license."

141

His chance had arrived. "Isn't that technically what I've done? I would have been here earlier, but we've been busy with the funeral arrangements. Isn't this another case of a forgetful groom?"

Willa's lips twitched. "I can't imagine how hard this must be for you. Your mom said Rita's still numb from the shock of it all."

Time to pull that last heartstring. "First my dad, now Tom …"

The clerk laid a hand over her heart. "It certainly has been a rough few years for you, hasn't it?" She reached across the counter and covered his and Ashley's hands. "Give me a sec." She winked before heading back into her office.

Ashley bumped her shoulder against his. "You really know how to work the ladies, don't you?"

"Only when they're my mom's friends. You're not so bad yourself."

"Excuse me." Salt and Pepper approached them. "You're Edgar Russell, Tom Russell's cousin, right?"

"That's right."

"I'm sorry to hear about your loss."

"Thank you." The woman smiled pleasantly enough, but the hair on his arms stood up. "You are?"

"Sue Whitley. I've talked with your mom when she's called for Willa."

As if on cue, Willa burst from the office and walked right between Sue and the counter. "I wanted to double-check a few things before I made a decision. I'll let you pick up your license tomorrow." She slapped a piece of paper on the counter. "You know I love you, but I still need to see a photo ID. Fill out this information, and it'll be twenty dollars."

Ashley hugged his arm, leaning fully against him. The smile she flashed him lit up her face and pulled him in. He hadn't seen that smile before. If he had, he might have said yes to her proposal sooner.

"Edgar." Willa cleared her throat. "If you want to get married, you need to fill out this paperwork."

He did. He would. But first, Russ leaned across the counter and planted a kiss on Willa's cheek. "You're a gem."

She waved him off, but her cheeks matched her lipstick. "Now stop it. Hurry up and sign this so you can get to kissing your girl instead."

"Yes, ma'am."

CHAPTER 18

Ashley snuggled into the corner of the couch. Heat from the fireplace radiated through her. With Russ at the other end of the couch, her senses were on high alert. She looked at the book in her hands but couldn't concentrate. Kathleen sat in the nearby chair with her feet propped up on the coffee table and a puzzle book in her hands. Tomorrow, Ashley would pick up a marriage license, and Kathleen had no idea.

Guilt gnawed at Ashley's conscience. She should be giddy. A measure of excitement did bubble up, but so did the weight of hiding from their families. Was this really what her mom would have wanted for her?

Kathleen huffed. "What is going on?"

Ashley set down her book, trying to maintain a neutral expression while her heart pounded. "What do you mean?"

"This." She waved her book in the air. "This is supposed to be fun? I remember when these used to keep me busy for hours, but this one." She shook her head. "I've finished four crossword puzzles since dinner. Where's the challenge?"

Russ set down his magazine and reached for his mother's book. "Where did you find this?"

"In your basket over there. I guess I shouldn't complain. Wisdom comes with age. I've collected plenty of knowledge over the years."

"This is for kids, Mom. Rachel left it here for when the boys visit." Russ tossed the book back at her, laughing. "What were you saying about age and wisdom?"

Ashley bit back a smile.

Kathleen tossed her pencil at Russ. "I'm going home tomorrow."

"It's an honest mistake." Ashley slid to the edge of her cushion. "You don't have to leave."

The Russells laughed. "I wouldn't leave over anything that silly," Kathleen said. "It's time I headed back to my place. Russ knows where to find me if he needs me, but what about you? What are you going to do?"

"You don't need to worry. I'm not going to sell your family's house or anything."

"I'm glad to hear that, but I didn't ask about the house. What are *you* going to do?"

Kathleen's eyes shone with such compassion that Ashley's determination wavered. How could she hold the truth back from her future mother-in-law? She caught Russ' eye. "Well, I ..."

"Ashley's going to stay here for a while," he said.

"I see." Kathleen shifted in her seat, crossing her legs and resting her hands on her lap. "I've enjoyed getting to know you, Ashley. You're a wonderful young woman, but are you sure this is a good idea?"

"It is." Russ took Ashley's hand. "We're getting married tomorrow."

The air whooshed out of the room, or maybe Ashley and Kathleen sucked it all out when they gasped. Russ moved closer to Ashley but never took his eyes off his mom. Ashley couldn't pull her gaze from Russ' handsome, traitorous face. What happened to not telling anyone until after the wedding?

"Why didn't you tell me you two were dating? How long have you known each other? What—"

"We didn't want to talk about it because there was so much going on." Russ dropped his free hand onto Kathleen's knee. "We hadn't planned on getting married so soon, but we decided not to wait."

Technically true. Ashley could support the story thus far, as long as she didn't have to answer any questions about their history. The possibility of lying made her cringe. Then again, the thought of admitting the truth didn't make her feel any better. Russ leaned back, wrapped an arm around her, and lightly massaged her shoulders. She hadn't realized how tense she'd become until he started soothing her muscles.

"I don't know what to say." Kathleen rubbed a shaky hand across her forehead. "Will the girls be able to make it on such short notice? And tomorrow's a school day. Maybe if you wait until the evening they can come after work."

Ashley leaned back, Russ' nearness supporting her in more ways than one. "Please don't go to any trouble. The family has been through enough. We don't want anyone to sacrifice more time for us."

"Sacrifice?" Kathleen practically bounced out of her chair. "Honey, this is a miracle! Edgar James Russell, your sisters have been trying to marry you off for years. They won't want to miss it. This is our chance to celebrate!"

"I know, Mom, but we want to do this privately. The last two weeks have been, well …" He shook his head. "Nothing has been this hard for me since Dad died. I appreciate that you've been here for me, but I need time to deal with Tom's death." Russ' arm slipped lower, wrapping around Ashley's waist and securing her against his side. "And I want to have Ashley with me."

The tightness in her chest eased. Did he really? Even if he didn't completely mean it, it was nice to hear.

"Oh, Russ." Kathleen's eyes glistened. "Are you sure? This is a wonderful thing. Your family wants to celebrate it with you."

Family. Tomorrow Ashley would finally have one, but she wasn't going to have them with her? How contradictory. "We will celebrate," she said, "but after the wedding."

Kathleen sat a little straighter. "This weekend?"

"That's quick," Russ said.

"Is that enough time to plan a party?" Ashley asked.

"Of course. The girls have been secretly planning his wedding for years."

Russ turned to Ashley. "I don't mind, but we won't do this unless you want to."

"I do. Your mom's right. This has been a hard time for all of us. Everyone could use a reason to celebrate."

"Oh, yes!" Kathleen clapped her hands. "I'll call the girls and tell them to clear their schedules. I'm sure we can find a place in town this weekend. Maybe the church rec room is available."

"Don't bother, Mom. We can have it here."

"Don't be silly. You don't need to worry about hosting a party. You have other things to take care of."

"I'd prefer it," he said. "But only family."

"Fine, we'll wait until Saturday." His mom pulled a cell phone out of her pocket. "You should tell Liz first."

Russ swiped her phone. "Not yet. Not until after the wedding."

"Russ—"

"Mom, if we tell Liz, she'll keep me on the phone all night. Then she'll call Carrie and Rachel. I don't have the energy to explain our decision to them, and you know Carrie. If I don't give her the answers she wants to hear, she'll harass me until the minute I say 'I do.' I don't need to explain this, and I don't need their permission. We'll call them after the wedding."

Kathleen chuckled. "You're right. My girls are a determined bunch."

"Exactly. Give us twenty-four hours. Then you can start the phone tree."

Ashley waited as the Russells stared at each other.

Kathleen's eyes watered, then she cried. Then laughed. "I have waited thirty-eight years for you to find a good woman. I almost gave up hope, but it's finally going to happen, isn't it?"

Russ squeezed Ashley. "Yes, it's going to happen."

"I'll wait." His mom clasped her hands together. "I can't believe this is finally happening!" She jumped up, grabbed Ashley's hands, and pulled her into her arms. "Welcome to the family, honey."

Ashley sank into Kathleen's embrace, savoring the comfort of a mother's hug. John and Rose had given Ashley so much, hugged her so many times, but Kathleen's embrace filled a long-empty hole in her heart. "Thank you for understanding."

"Are you kidding me?" She leaned back, shaking her head. "I don't understand a thing about this, but I've seen the two of you this week. I could tell there was something there."

She could? Ashley blushed. "And you're okay with it? I mean, you're not trying to talk us out of it?"

"This little old mama isn't going to stop her son from doing anything. I can't even convince him to shave that beard. Besides, you two are adults. I'll support you in whatever way I can, including waiting until tomorrow to call the girls."

"Tomorrow night, Mom." Russ patted her shoulder. "After the ceremony."

"Fine, after the ceremony. Will you call me when it's over?"

"I can, but I was hoping you'd be there with us."

She pressed her hands to her lips. "Don't tease me. Do I really get to come?"

Russ hugged her. "I know you've been waiting for this longer than anyone else. I wouldn't dream of not having you there. Besides, we need a witness."

She smacked his back but didn't let go. "Where should I meet you?"

"Let me confirm everything with Pastor Stanford, then I'll let you know. Sometime in the afternoon, but we need to double-check everything."

"Of course." Kathleen stepped away, wiping the back of her hand across her cheeks. "I'm going upstairs to plan the menu. I'll let the two of you have some alone time." She wrapped them in a tight hug before padding through the living room and up the stairs.

Ashley's anxiety faded with each step. They'd survived telling the first family member. Tomorrow, while Kathleen called her daughters, Ashley would call John and Rose. Rose would be sad to miss the ceremony, but she'd understand. Maybe. At the very least, she'd forgive Ashley. Eventually.

The bedroom door whined and clicked, then Russ dropped onto the couch.

Ashley plopped down beside him. "My heart almost popped out of my chest. You handled that really well."

"I'm glad you think so. I hardly remember what I said. I just started talking and prayed for the best."

"You're good on your feet. And your mom is wonderful. She won't call anyone, will she?"

"Nah. Mom's word is good." He tipped his head back and draped an arm along the back of the couch, closing his eyes as he inhaled deeply. "There's no turning back now. I doubt my mom will sleep tonight, and she'll hog-tie and carry me to the wedding tomorrow if she has to."

Excellent. Ashley didn't have to worry about Russ changing his mind at the last minute. She shifted in her seat, turning so she could watch him. Light from the fire flicked across his face as the logs crackled in the fireplace. He may have exaggerated what he told his mom, but nothing about his posture suggested any anxiety. If he hadn't just been talking with Ashley, she might think he was asleep.

Lucky him. She doubted she'd get much sleep. "Is there anything else we should consider before tomorrow?" she asked. "Is it possible your sisters will randomly drop by the house? Should we have a backup plan?"

"They live too far away. They won't come back until there's a reason to, especially now that winter's coming." Russ' voice trailed off, his breaths getting deeper and slower.

While she listened to him breathe, her thoughts swirled. Tomorrow he'd be her husband. Eventually he'd relax in bed beside her, fall asleep next to her. Warm shivers ran across her arms. Her husband. Memories of their kiss tickled her lips. The crook of his arm invited her to scoot over.

A snore echoed through the room.

Ashley hopped up and ran upstairs. No sense tempting fate. Tomorrow would arrive soon enough.

CHAPTER 19

Russ tightened another bolt, confident the lawn mower was finally winterized and ready for storage, as were the weed whip and chain saw. No signs of snow yet, but he could feel it coming. He didn't need to tune up the snowplow. Snow shovels leaned against the house on the porch and back deck, waiting for the first flurry. Finding the ice scrapers for the cars wouldn't take long. That left him—he checked his watch—ninety minutes before he and Ashley needed to leave for the wedding. Ten minutes to shower, five minutes to get dressed. Seventy-five minutes to kill. Russ looked around the barn. What else could he tinker with?

HONK! HONK-HONK-HONK!

Perfect. A distraction. He tossed his wrench in the toolbox and headed to the driveway, willing to sit through any sales pitch today. The sharp air outside refreshed his spirit.

Rachel's van barreled toward him. It had barely stopped moving before the doors popped open. His nephews jumped out, the older boys helping the younger ones, while Rachel and Carrie charged at Russ.

They knew. Mom had promised not to tell anyone, so how did they know?

"You're getting *married?*" Rachel spewed the last word like spoiled milk.

"Why are you all here? Don't your kids go to school?"

Carrie reached him first. "Teacher training day. And don't try to change the subject. You told us she was a friend of Tom's. Why didn't you tell us you were engaged?" She wore the same face she used when disciplining the kids. Just what he needed. A lecture.

"Ashley and I didn't want to talk about it in light of the funeral. How did you—"

Rachel grabbed his arm and spun him toward her. "You've never talked about her. You didn't look like you were even interested in her, much less engaged. What happened? Why are you getting married?"

He wrenched his arm away, surprised at her grip. "You've been bugging me about getting married for decades."

"We want you to be happy, to find someone to settle down with, but this?" Rachel waved an arm toward the house. "How long have you known her?"

"Why does that matter? Saturday you all loved her. You were ready to sell her a house."

"We do like her." Carrie's voice softened a fraction. "She's nice, but we didn't realize we were going to be related to her in less than a week."

"Maybe we should have told you, but there was a lot going on, and we didn't want to distract from Tom's memorial. You're obviously upset, but why did you drive all this way?"

"Because Rachel's crazy, and she had to find out if it was true."

"You could have called."

Carrie rolled her eyes. "And you would have ignored us."

True. "So now you're here, and you know the truth, and your sons are digging up my driveway."

Rachel turned in time to see Phin throw a fistful of dirt in the air. "Leo, I told you to watch him!"

While she stormed toward them, Carrie slipped her arm around Russ. "She's freaking out."

"Why?"

"Why do you think? She thought you'd meet a girl, they would become friends, Rachel would be a bridesmaid. They'd organize a bridal shower and bachelorette party. She had plans, and you ruined them." Carrie tugged his arm, guiding him toward the house.

"And what do you think?"

She shook her head. "I don't think I believe it yet."

"It's happening."

Her grip tightened. "You're sure about this?"

"Yes, I'm sure. I made the arrangements myself. We head into town in an hour and a half."

She jabbed him with her elbow. "Not about the wedding, about the marriage. Do you really want to spend the rest of your life with this woman? You don't have any doubts?"

"Of course I have doubts."

"Then don't do it."

"And you didn't have any doubts about Paul? Come on, Carrie. No one's perfect. If I concentrate on all the things wrong with women, I'll never get married. I need to focus on the right things. Ashley's kind, intelligent, devoted to the marriage, and ..." Tom.

"And what?"

"Tom really liked her. He'd approve."

Rachel met them at the porch steps, a squirming Phin under one arm. "Who'd approve of what?"

Russ wrapped his free arm around her, steering her up the stairs. "I'm getting married. It'll be fine."

"You weren't going to tell us, were you?"

He shook his head. "I can't believe Mom called you. She promised not to."

"Oh, Mom didn't call me."

Every fiber in his body stiffened. "We didn't tell anyone else."

"Laney's mom, Sue, works at the clerk's office, and she told Laney last night at dinner." Rachel sat Phin on her hip. "They probably weren't supposed to talk about it, huh?"

A thousand pounds of frustration dropped onto Russ' shoulders. Maybe not a thousand, but at least one hundred twenty pounds of Laney Whitley. "Did she tell anyone else?"

"Probably her family, but she has four siblings."

If only the porch would swallow him now. So much for keeping it a private affair. "I don't suppose they'll keep it to themselves?"

"Don't know. Laney called me first thing this morning to find out if it was true. I felt like such an idiot, so I said yes and made up a bunch of stuff. It's kind of big news. A few years ago, the women at Mom's salon started a betting pool to guess when you'd get married. I wonder who's going to win."

"Are you serious?"

"What does it matter now? The big news is that you were one of the most eligible bachelors in the county, and now you're not. Those ladies have been waiting."

The mob of boys rushed the stairs. Phin kicked, but Rachel adjusted her grip. "Can we move this thing inside before I drop my son?"

Russ took his nephew, then tossed him in the air. As the little guy giggled, Russ tried to figure out how to warn Ashley about the mob.

Carrie opened the door, but it stopped abruptly.

"Ouch."

He cringed. "Ashley?" She peeked around the edge of the door. Her eyes widened. Russ cleared the frustration out of his throat. "So, my sisters are here."

She held onto the door, inching it open as she backed away. "What brings you both back to town?"

"They know about the wedding."

Ashley's jaw clenched. "I thought we were going to call them later."

"We forgot to tell the assistant clerk that. Apparently she's Rachel's best friend's mom."

As Rachel and Carrie moved inside, they stripped dirty coats and boots off the boys. Russ stepped between them and Ashley. "I'm sorry," he whispered. "They just showed up." She nodded, but the color had faded from her face. "What do you want to do? Tell me and we'll do it."

"Do we really have any options?"

"We can leave the house right now if you want. Let my sisters wait here for us."

"You would run away from your sisters?"

"Absolutely."

Her eyes shifted, her lips in a tight line. Was she thinking? Angry? He'd have the next few decades to figure out her expressions, but right now he'd kill for Cliffs Notes.

Rachel appeared beside him, glaring at Ashley. "You're really going to marry him?"

Carrie smacked Rachel's arm. "I think my sister means congratulations."

Ashley sighed. "I'm sorry we didn't tell you. It's not that we didn't want you to know, but—"

"We didn't want to tell you until this afternoon." Russ released Phin before sliding an arm around Ashley and escorting her into the living room. Aiden and Leo dumped blocks on the floor as Phin ran toward them. His sisters' shoes clicked as they followed him to the couch. Not wishing his sisters' interrogation upon his worst enemy, he sat beside Ashley. She deserved his support in whatever way he could provide it.

Carrie sat on the chair closest to them. Her face was relaxed, but she picked at her fingernails. Never a good sign. "Where are you getting married?"

"At the Lakeside Inn," he said. "Pastor Stanford is meeting us there."

Rachel plopped herself onto the coffee table. "Why the Lakeside? Why not the church?"

"We don't need the whole building for four people. Besides, the inn has a great view."

"The owner was nice when we called," Ashley said. "They were happy to let us have a small spot for a wedding."

"How long have you two been dating?" Rachel crossed her arms. "Why didn't you mention anything about it at the funeral?"

Ashley shifted, sliding deeper into the couch. Russ covered her hand with his and said, "We weren't trying to keep it from you. It was a recent decision."

"How do you know each other?" Rachel asked.

"We met through Tom," Ashley said. "We honestly haven't known each other that long, but it's been long enough."

Carrie picked. Rachel narrowed her eyes. Ashley sat still as the room filled with tension.

He should say something, try to comfort the women in his life, but he wasn't an idiot. He'd grown up with this interrogation technique. Silence was his friend.

Ashley hopped off the couch. "Does anyone want a drink?"

"That's it?" Rachel straightened, her eyes wide. "You're going to bring me a soda and pretend like this is normal? We haven't gotten to know each other yet. Where are you from? Do you have a job? Where's your family? Won't your friends—"

Carrie threw a pillow at Rachel. "Forgive my sister. She's a bit of a control freak. She needs to know all of the details and figure everything out before she's comfortable with a new situation."

Ashley picked up the pillow. "But you're okay with this?"

"Carrie inherited my mom's sensibility," Russ said. "Even if she doesn't agree with me, she knows she'll never change my mind. Besides, you passed her test at the memorial."

"There was a test?"

"Have you considered all of the outcomes?" Rachel asked, never deterred. "How long have you known each other?"

Russ crossed his arms. "How long did Carrie and Ben know each other before they got married?"

His sisters' jaws dropped.

"I thought your husband was Paul," Ashley said.

"Ben was my first husband. It lasted six months."

"Oh."

Russ wrapped his hand around Ashley's. "I'm not trying to be mean or suggest that we know better than you did, but we've thought this through, and we're committed to each other and this marriage."

"Though we appreciate your concern," Ashley said. "It's nice to know you care."

"But you're not going to talk us out of this." Russ squeezed her hand.

DING-DONG! Now who?

"It's probably Liz." Carrie stood. "We called her on our way here."

Of course they did. "How is it that none of you have to work today?"

Carrie's laugh carried into the living room. "That's the joy of working for yourself." She opened the door, and cold air blew through the house. The smile dropped off her face.

Every protective nerve in Russ fired. "Carrie?" She looked at him, her eyes wide, then back at the door. He headed toward her, ready to shoot, hit, or tackle. "What is it? Who's here?" He pulled the door open wide, and the breath stopped in his lungs. "Jess?"

"Who's this?" Ashley stepped up next to him.

Russ couldn't speak. What was happening?

His past stood on the porch, smiling. "I'm Jess, Russ' ex-girlfriend."

CHAPTER 20

Ashley stared at the strawberry blonde on the porch, blinking twice to make the vision disappear. It didn't. Russ didn't like dating. He didn't have ex-girlfriends, except … "Excuse me, you're who?"

"Jessica Miller, but everyone calls me Jess."

"My ex-girlfriend." Russ crossed his arms. "What are you doing here?"

Carrie spun around. "Rachel, why don't we get the kids a snack? I'll bet Russ has chocolate around here somewhere."

"Chocolate!" The kids squealed.

Russ' family disappeared as Ashley stepped closer to *her* boyfriend—no, her fiancé—ready to defend her claim. A bitter wind tossed Jess' shoulder-length curls around her face. A brown leather jacket and dark jeans hugged her body, flattering her curves. The green scarf fluttering around her neck popped against the neutral palette. She smiled at Ashley, but her lips looked stiff, forced. Probably a reflection of Ashley's own awkward smile.

"Why don't you come in? It's pretty cold out today." Ashley grabbed the back of Russ' shirt and pulled him out of the way.

"Thank you," Jess said. She stepped inside and closed the door. "It's been a while since I was here. Not much has changed."

"A lot has changed. Tom's dead. This is Ashley." A hard, cold arm wrapped around her. "My fiancée."

Ashley's stomach rolled at the harsh tone of his voice. If this was his "bad experience," she could understand, but that didn't explain why Jess was here. Ashley glanced up at Russ. He clenched his jaw.

Jess unzipped her coat. "I'm sorry to hear about Tom. My dad told me. I would have come to the funeral, but I wasn't sure what to say."

"Yet you figured it would be okay to show up now?" Russ' fingers squeezed Ashley's waist, pinching her skin.

"Can I get you a drink?" she asked, stepping away from his vice-like grip.

"I'm fine, but I would like to speak to Russ privately for a few minutes if that's okay with you."

Ashley nodded, welcoming yet dreading the opportunity to leave. "I'll go to the kitchen and see about that chocolate." She glanced at Russ, hoping for some guidance. The return of Stone Face didn't help her figure out what to do next, but it did give her comfort knowing he wasn't pleased with the newest arrival. "Did you want that drink?" she asked him.

Russ shook his head. "We won't be long." He motioned toward the living room. "Jess?"

The couple walked one way as Ashley went the other. They looked good together. Jess was almost as tall as Russ, and their jean-clad legs fell into step with each other. He shoved his hands into his back pockets while she sat on the edge of the loveseat. Was she trying to force him to sit near her? Was she trying to win Russ back? It would make sense. Why else would an ex-girlfriend show up today, and how did she know?

A thousand more questions raced through her head. Carrie had recognized Jess. That seemed like a good place to start asking. Ashley marched into the kitchen, ready to get answers.

Rachel met her at the doorway, a bowl of M&M's in hand. "What did she say? Why's she here? You left them alone?"

"She wants to talk to Russ." Ashley took the bowl. "What can you tell me about her?"

"I'll answer your questions if you'll answer mine."

"Okay. What do you want to know?"

"How long have you known Russ?"

"Mommy, I want Ms." Phin hustled over, reaching for Ashley's bowl. "Peas?"

Rachel patted his head. "Mommy and Miss Ashley need to have a talk. Can you and Leo play in the family room together?"

Carrie, the shorter, friendlier sibling, came over and scooped out a handful of candies. "Why doesn't Aunt Carrie put in a movie? I'll be back in a minute. Rachel promises to play nice."

"I'm always nice."

"Come on, munchkins." Carrie passed out M&M's as she led the boys away.

Too bad. Ashley would rather talk to Carrie. Or Phin. Rachel gave the impression that there wasn't a right answer for why Russ and Ashley were getting married, and the woman talking to Russ in the living room made Ashley wonder if Rachel was right.

Rachel grabbed some candy. "So, how long have you known each other?"

Ashley sucked in a deep breath. "We met at Pearl's Diner."

"You've been to Boyne Heights before?"

"No. We met last week."

Rachel stared.

"I know. It's fast. Do you want peanut butter?" Ashley searched the cupboards until she found a jar. "When did Jess and Russ date?"

"A couple of years ago. Are you serious? You and Russ met last week?"

Ashley pulled out a spoon and sat at the island. "Yes, I'm serious. Why would Jess show up today?"

"Because my brother attracts crazy women."

Rachel stood on the other side of the island as Ashley opened the jar and dumped in a handful of candy. She dug out a spoonful of peanut butter and chocolate bits. As the salty sweetness soothed her frazzled nerves, Rachel's statement hit its target. Crazy women. Jess *and* Ashley.

"Why do you want to marry him?" Rachel asked.

"It makes sense. Is Jess the stalker?"

"You aren't in love with him?"

"I've only known him a week, and you didn't answer my question."

"Jess is a nonissue. Why would you marry a man you just met?"

"That's three questions, and you still haven't answered mine." Ashley poured more M&M's into the jar.

Rachel pulled out her own spoon. "He doesn't talk about it."

"What do other people say about it?"

"According to what Laney's mom heard, Russ got cold feet. He says it never got that far. All I know is he seemed more relieved than upset after the breakup. A year ago Jess relocated to Marquette, and I haven't seen her until today."

Ashley stopped the next spoonful before it reached her mouth. "That's it?"

"I'm sure there's more, but I only believe what I hear from Russ and Laney." Rachel scooped out her first helping as Carrie returned to the kitchen.

"What did I miss?" she asked.

"Ashley and Russ have known each other for a week, and now they're getting married because *that* makes sense." Rachel stuffed her spoon in her mouth, then smiled around the peanut butter.

"It doesn't sound good when you say it that way," Ashley said.

Carrie whistled. "Russ finally snapped."

"Excuse me?" She'd expected that kind of response from Rachel, but Carrie?

"The pressure finally got to him. It's like when he bought his truck. He kept fixing up his old one, refusing to accept that he needed a new one. Then, one day he got pulled over for a burned-out taillight, and he snapped. Instead of changing the bulb, he went out and bought a new truck." Carrie shrugged. "That's the way Russ works. You might be his new truck."

His dad's death, a complicated ex-girlfriend, Tom's death. That could create some pressure. Ashley sighed. "Great. My engagement is the result of an emotional overload."

"That's not a bad thing, though. He *loves* that truck, but why in the world would you want to marry Russ after a week, especially after this week?" Carrie shook her head. "I don't get it. Paul and I dated for four years before we got married."

Ashley set down her spoon, too confused to indulge. "You were so supportive of us a few minutes ago. What happened?"

"I'm supportive of my brother because I know I can't talk him out of anything, but you seem relatively intelligent. Maybe I can convince you to save yourself and take things slow. I'd be happy to drive you around this weekend and go house hunting. You and Russ could date for a while, get to know each other better."

"We were planning on having a reception this weekend." Ashley looked at the clock. "Of course, we're supposed to leave in seventy-five minutes to get married. If we don't get out by then, I may have some free time."

It made sense that she'd miss her own wedding. Nothing else had worked out the way she'd expected. The thick peanut butter clung to her throat.

Rachel helped herself to another scoop. "You still haven't told us *why* you're getting married. How do you start that conversation with a person? And what do your parents think of this?"

"My parents are dead."

Both sisters stopped moving. They didn't even blink. Ashley looked between the two women, unsure how to convince the life-sized statues to move. "It's okay, I promise. They died a long time ago."

Carrie walked over and pulled Ashley into a hug. Nearly two decades later, and people still felt the need to do that.

"I'm so sorry," Rachel said, her voice low and sad.

Ashley leaned away from Carrie. "It's fine. It happened seventeen years ago."

Carrie held Ashley at arm's length. "You must have been a kid."

"I was eighteen. It was a car accident. They didn't suffer."

"Do you have any siblings?"

"It's just me."

Carrie cocked her head to the side as she gave a half-smile. Ashley swallowed a sigh. Someday she'd be able to tell this story without people getting all weepy. Russ hadn't turned to mush when she talked about her parents. That was one thing she liked about him, not that it mattered much. One hour and fifteen minutes until departure, and Jess still had him cornered. Ashley couldn't decide if she should panic or cheer. Yesterday everything had seemed so clear. Today three more sets of lenses blurred everything.

DING-DONG!

Great.

****

Russ recognized Liz's car as soon as it popped through the trees. Would this day never end? Before he could answer the door, snappy steps pounded on the hardwood. Steeling himself for his baby sister's assault, he stood by the loveseat and watched Carrie open the door.

Liz burst through and wrapped one arm around Carrie as the other cradled Kristy. And then they looked at him. It was hard to decide which was wider, Liz's eyes or mouth. Carrie elbowed her.

"I'm sorry, that was rude." Liz hustled over. "Jess. It's nice to see you again."

"You too. This must be your daughter." Jess' eyes brightened. Russ groaned. No woman alive could resist the maternal instincts Kristy inspired.

Liz smiled. "She'll be eight months next week."

"That's amazing. It's really been—"

"We'd love to stay and chat, but we have chocolate in the kitchen." Carrie swooped in and took the baby. "I'll put her in with the boys, and we can join Rachel and Ashley."

Liz walked right up to Russ and leaned into his personal space. "Is it true?"

"Yes."

She stared at him, wrenching his heart with the sadness in her eyes.

"Can we talk about this in a few minutes?"

She nodded and walked away, taking all of the warmth out of the room. In the kitchen, his sisters and Ashley were no doubt enjoying girl talk, strengthening their bonds and friendships. He still had to deal with Jess.

He summoned every ounce of his manners. "You've had me in here for five minutes. It's nice that your job is going well, but let's skip the small talk. Why are you here?"

"Emily called me."

"How did Emily ... Brian. Her husband is Sue Whitley's son, isn't he?"

"She called Emily last night," Jess said. "Emily called me."

"Isn't this an invasion of privacy? Aren't they sworn to secrecy?"

"Maybe she shouldn't have said anything, but I'm glad she did. So the rumors are true? You're getting married?"

"In about an hour."

"A year ago you told me you weren't ready to get married. You said maybe a different time, but now you're marrying someone else?"

"You're twisting my words. I wasn't ready then, but it wasn't just the timing. We weren't good together. You know that."

"We were good at the beginning, but then everything in my life went wrong. I'm sorry about how things ended between us. After my dad left my mom, I got a little clingy, but I always thought we'd get another chance. I didn't realize you were ending it for good."

"Even if it was bad timing, you moved to Marquette."

"Not forever."

"How was I supposed to know that? Not that it matters. We'd never work."

Jess stepped into the space Liz had vacated. "Emily didn't even know you were dating anyone. No one in town has ever seen Ashley before. Does she understand what life on the farm will be like?"

"I don't care what Emily knows about Ashley and me. I'm sorry you don't like my explanation, but that's all I have for you."

"Is everything okay out here?" The quiet voice drowned out everything else. Ashley stood in the kitchen doorway, hands clasped in front of her as her shoulders rose and fell with deep breaths. Her eyes moved between Russ and Jess.

Great. Russ pressed a finger to his throbbing temple. Between his ex and sisters, maybe he'd make it to his wedding in two or three hours. Why were there so many women?

"I think I'll give you some space." Ashley walked through the room and toward the front door.

Russ' sisters stepped out of the kitchen as she strode away. He could let her leave—he'd already let one woman walk away, but letting Jess go had been freeing. As Ashley put her coat on, something inside him broke. When she stepped outside, he lurched.

"Ashley!" He took four steps to get outside. Another three to catch up to her beside her car. "Please don't leave."

She stopped at the driver's door, hands in her pockets, her back to him. Russ braced himself for an argument. Tears. A slap. He could take it. He probably deserved it. But when she turned around, bright eyes shone up at him. "I'm not leaving you. I'm leaving the house," she said.

Hope threatened. "How is that not leaving?"

"Listen, I understand that you have a past. I have a past. This isn't a conventional arrangement, so I have no expectations of normalcy, but things have gotten a little crazy in there." She crossed her arms, rubbing her hands over her sleeves as she looked up at the house. "I've been dreaming about being part of a family for years, but the reality is more than I expected."

Russ couldn't stop his smile. "They can be a little overwhelming."

"They can, but it's not enough to scare me away."

If it wasn't his sisters, then … "Is it Jess?"

Ashley shivered. "Sort of." Her hazel eyes turned back to him. "It's kind of surprising. A little disturbing, maybe." Her cold white hand landed on his arm, and Russ wrapped it in his hands. "You don't need to tell me everything that happened between you, but I need time to think without an audience."

Russ rubbed his palms over her warming skin. "Then you're not mad at me?"

"I'm a little frustrated. Maybe disappointed." She looked at his hands. "Confused."

"I'm sorry about all of this. With the exception of Jess, the rest of them come with me. Can you handle that?"

She puckered her lips then wiggled them back and forth, the same way she had yesterday. Without looking at him, she nodded.

He wanted to see those eyes again, see if he could figure out what she was thinking. Russ tucked a finger under her chin and lifted her gaze to his.

Ashley sucked in a sharp breath. "I can't think when I'm this close to you."

He released her hand and stepped back. "Better?"

"Not really, but it'll have to do." She stuffed her hands in her pockets. "I need to know … do you want to get married? Not just to me, but in general. Do you even want a wife?"

His heart boomed. "Yes."

"Then why me? Why not Jess?"

"It's a long story."

"Give me the short version."

He sighed. "We met at an agriculture expo three years ago. Two years ago we started dating. She brought up marriage, and I couldn't see it. I tried to break up with her for weeks, but she kept calling and showing up. Twelve months ago she moved."

"And she's here because she thinks you two have a chance?"

"No, she misunderstood why we had problems, and she thought I might change my mind. You know, she stormed out of my house a dozen times when we were together, and I never wanted to follow her." He inched closer to Ashley.

She shifted her balance. "You wanted to follow me?"

"Looks like it."

Her gaze flickered down to his lips. "But this is still about—"

"Practicality and commitment. I remember."

She inhaled, her breath shaky. "You and me. I won't be alone anymore."

He chuckled. "Even if I'm gone, there's a house full of people behind us who will make sure you're never alone, whether you want to be or not."

"Like when we're trying to plan a secret wedding?"

"Exactly."

The edge of her mouth twitched. Finally, a smile.

"We're still on for this afternoon?" he asked.

"Yes. I gave you my word, and I won't take that back."

"I expected as much. We did kiss on it." And that kiss haunted him more than he cared to admit.

"I remember," she whispered. "I'll meet you in town, I promise, but I'd like to drive around to clear my head."

Russ checked his watch. "We need to be there in sixty-five minutes. Do you remember how to get to the inn?"

"Take Copper Trail into town, then follow the signs?"

"Good. I'll stop at the courthouse to get the license."

Her posture relaxed. "I'd like that."

"Do you have a dress you want to wear?"

"No, I'm fine. I can wear it Saturday. I'd like to get going."

Sensible. Confident. Russ liked her more every day. "Drive safe."

She flashed him a full, breathtaking smile. "I promise."

His sisters and Jess were undoubtedly watching through the front window, but Russ couldn't resist Ashley's magnetism. He leaned down and pressed his lips to hers. "I'll see you at the inn."

CHAPTER 21

As soon as Russ stepped onto the porch, Liz opened the door. Everyone gathered around her in the foyer, their gazes pressing on him like a lead dental apron. "I don't have time for this," he said. "You're going to have to wait until this weekend. I need a shower."

Jess pushed her way to the front, zipping her coat. "I didn't believe Emily when she called me, but I had to see it for myself." His ex managed a tight smile. "I really do wish you the best, and I'll be here for you if anything goes wrong."

He grabbed her arm as she walked past. "Did you get whatever you came here looking for?"

"I wasn't looking for anything, but that"—she pointed down the driveway—"does not make sense."

Neither did the fact that he was still having this conversation. Russ released her arm and stepped inside. "I'm okay with that. Like I said, I need a shower."

She shook her head as she hurried away. One down, three to go. Russ closed the door and headed straight for the steps.

"No you don't!" Liz ran in front of him, her skinny arms stretched out as if she could hold him back. "You weren't going to tell me?" Kristy whined in the other room.

"Don't you need to answer that?"

"The boys can handle it."

Russ sighed. "Don't take it personally. I wasn't going to tell any of you."

Liz scrunched up her lips.

"Don't manipulate me with that pouty face. I hate it."

"Do it, Lizzie." Rachel stepped up beside her. "He hasn't answered any of our questions yet. What are we supposed to think about any of this? Do we get to come to the wedding? How are we supposed to handle this?"

"Ewww! Mommy!" Phin ran into Rachel and latched onto her leg. Laughter erupted from the other room. "Kisty 'ploded!"

Liz raced into the living room. Before Russ could take another step, Carrie wrapped her arm around his. "Come on, Russ. We want to support you, but we don't understand. The least you could do is give us a bit of comfort in knowing you haven't lost your mind."

Russ sat on the stairs, kicked his feet out, and leaned back on his elbows. Why had God given him sisters? Carrie sat on his left, Rachel on his right. The same way they'd sat after Dad's funeral. He patted their knees. "This isn't a sad day, you know. It's my wedding day."

Rachel leaned against the arm rail. "How long before you need to leave?"

"About forty minutes."

"Then start talking."

* * * * * * *

Ashley threw the map on the passenger seat. She remembered exactly how to find the inn once she was in town—turn right at the light, follow Main Street around the big curve, left at the bowling alley, and up the hill. First building on the right. Russ had shown her pictures and made her commit the map to memory. Why hadn't he been as insistent with the directions to get into town?

There weren't that many roads in the area. Why did they all have the same name? How was she supposed to know Copper

Trail South and Copper Trail North weren't two sides of the same road? Looked like it was time for another U-turn, then she'd like to have a talk with the road commissioner.

Shifting the car into reverse again, Ashley started her multi-point turn on the narrow dirt road. Her tires spun in the mud until finally grabbing hold and throwing the car backward. Mud spewed everywhere, even splattering the windshield. So much for time alone to relax. What a nightmare.

She checked the clock again. 3:50. Ashley's chest tightened. Russ would be picking up the license now. She had ten minutes to get to the inn, and she had no idea how long it would take to get there.

She needed to call Russ. By the time she dug her phone out of her purse, she had the car heading the right direction. Raindrops plopped on the windshield. Maybe the rain would wash off the mud. She flipped on the wipers as she dialed information.

Silence, except for the tinkling raindrops and screeching wiper blades. Ashley held the phone up in front of her. No signal.

The car fishtailed. Ashley dropped the phone, white-knuckling the wheel. She swerved to the right. Rain and mud covered the windshield. She tapped the breaks. Steered left. Held on. The car kept moving, moving, moving. The front end dropped.

Ashley gasped.

WHUMP!

The seatbelt cut into her shoulder, pinching her skin but holding her tight against the seat. Her pulse pounded in her ears as her lungs inhaled and exhaled with gale-force breaths. At least the car had stopped moving.

She sucked in a slow, deep breath, her chest expanding against the tight seatbelt as her heart calmed down. Then reality set in. A car accident, but she'd survived. Relief and terror ripped through her. Rain continued to pelt the windshield, sliding left across the glass. That couldn't be good. Ashley sped up the wipers. After a few swipes, she identified grass and dirt in front of her. Definitely not good. She stuffed the map and phone into her purse. With a shaky breath, Ashley opened her door.

Ice-cold raindrops assaulted her as the wind howled through the trees. She slammed the door. Only an idiot would go out in that weather. An idiot or a desperate woman. She could wait for the rain to pass, but without reception she couldn't check the weather to see how long that would take. She wasn't going to get reception sitting in her car. Hoping for anything she could wrap around herself, she searched the backseat. Nothing. Maybe the trunk.

Sliding between the front seats, she pushed herself over the center console, then dropped onto the back seat. She pulled down the passenger-side backrest and reached into the dark trunk. Carpet. Carpet. Towel. Ashley yanked on the fabric. About the size of a newspaper and covered with the rental company's logo, it wouldn't offer much protection, but she wrapped it around her shoulders anyway. She only needed to walk until she had cell-phone coverage, however long that would take.

****

The door at the inn remained closed. Russ checked his watch. 4:30.

Mom touched his arm. "Maybe you should call her."

"No, she'll be here."

"I know what she said, but—"

"She'll be here."

"Honey, at least call to see if she's okay."

Rain blurred the inn's view. Most cars could handle the freezing rain on the main roads, but he didn't live on the main roads, and Ashley could have taken any number of routes to town. And she was driving that ridiculous car. He wanted to make sure she was safe, but … he sighed. "I don't have her number."

Pastor Stanford slapped him on the back. "Son, how long do you want to wait?"

The front door opened—finally! One second of relief died a quick death when a group of strangers walked in.

Annoyed, Russ faced the pastor. "I don't know how long to wait. I just got used to the idea of being married. I hadn't considered it not happening."

"I can give you ten more minutes, but then I need to head home. The grandkids are coming over for dinner, and Mary would be disappointed if I showed up late."

Russ understood the disappointment of being stood up, and he wouldn't burden Mary with it. "Why don't you head home now?"

"Are you sure?"

"I'm sure. Regardless of what happened, we won't be able to do this today. I'll call you to reschedule after I touch base with Ashley."

The pastor offered his hand. "Call me if you need to talk. Anytime."

Russ shook his hand. "Thank you." As the pastor walked away, Russ pulled out a chair for his mom and took the seat next to her. Now what? She produced a phone and started dialing.

His throat tightened. "I told you, I don't have Ashley's number."

"I'm calling your sisters. They'll want to know what happened."

"No." He stole the phone. "They've harassed us enough today. Now Ashley's AWOL. I doubt it's a coincidence."

Mom's jaw tightened. "You don't really think they scared her off, do you?"

How should he know? She said it didn't bother her, but she also said she'd be there. Russ tossed the phone on the table, but abusing technology didn't make him feel any better. "Maybe I should go look for her."

"Where would you go?" She tucked a piece of hair behind her ear, her hand trembling.

"Don't get yourself worked up. I don't actually think this has anything to do with the girls."

"I'm not worried about that. Ashley doesn't seem like the kind of woman who scares easily." Mom gave a tight smile. "My mother's instincts are kicking in. I've already imagined a dozen reasons why she's not here, and none of them are pleasant."

Neither were the ideas fighting in Russ' imagination. He wouldn't give in to fear, though. Not now. "Did you see her tiny car? It's not even hers. It's a rental. Who knows how well that thing handles?"

"What do you want to do?"

"Excuse me, Mr. Russell?" A young woman wearing black pants and a long white apron stepped toward them. "You have a phone call."

His stomach flipped. "Should I follow—"

The girl handed him a wireless phone.

Anxiety coursed through him, shaking him to the core, but he stilled his hand enough to take the phone. "Hello?"

"Russ?"

Ashley! He jumped to his feet. "Thank God. Are you okay?"

"I'm fine. I'm so sorry. I—"

"Where are you? I'll come get you."

"I'm in a tow truck on my way back to your house."

"A tow truck? What happened?"

"I forgot how to get to town, then I got stuck in the mud, and there was no cell service, so I had to walk about a mile, but then I didn't have your phone number, so I called information and—"

"It's okay. Don't worry about it." Mom stood in front of Russ, her eyes wide. "It's Ashley, she's fine. She got lost, then stuck in the mud. She's on the way home right now."

The creases of Mom's face relaxed, and she gave him a genuine smile. "*Now* I'm going to call the girls."

"Thanks." Russ let his mom hug him, absorbing some of her relief. Ashley's voice wasn't enough to push the weight off his back, though. He needed to see her. Touch her. Know she was safe. "Do you remember how to get to my house?"

"Yeah. The driver's name is Pete. He said he knows you."

Pete Hanson, Russ' high-school classmate. "He's a good guy. Ask him to wait with you until I get there."

"That's not necessary. I'm wet but fine."

"You might be, but I'm not. I'll be there in twenty minutes."

"Drive slow. It's slick out."

Outside, the gray sky hid the sun, muting nature's glory as a herd of emotions trampled through Russ. Relief. Frustration. Terror. He wasn't sure which feeling to wrangle first.

Mom stepped beside him and leaned her head against his arm. "I knew it would be okay."

"You did?"

She shrugged. "I hoped. Why don't you head home? I'll talk to the manager for you. Give Ashley a hug for me."

"Sure." A hug, or something else.

CHAPTER 22

Russ twisted his fists around the steering wheel, his eyes on the wrecker. Frustration rose again, but he wrestled it down. In the past few days, he'd let down his guard, and no matter how many times he reminded himself it was a marriage of convenience, his emotions fought to confuse and control him. As he approached Pete's wrecker, common sense told him to say thank you and pay the man, but his tumultuous emotions told him to grab Ashley and hold on.

Russ pulled alongside the house where Ashley's mud-streaked car sat. Relief chased common sense down the driveway. He jumped from the truck and jogged inside to see for himself that she was okay. Shoving the front door open, his heart calmed as laughter greeted him. A fire crackled.

"Ashley?" He stepped into the living room. She sat on one end of the couch, smiling.

She pointed at the fireplace. "Pete made a fire to help me warm up."

Pete raised a hand. "It's looking a little sad, but it'll catch. Good to see you."

"Thanks for taking care of Ashley." Russ tossed his coat on the rack, then kicked his wet shoes in the corner.

"There wasn't much taking care of. She made the coffee and brought me the kindling, but I'm happy to help however I can."

"Still, it's appreciated."

Pete met Russ halfway between the couch and the door. "I'd love to wait for the coffee, but I need to get going. I was on my way to another stop when Ashley called. As soon as she said your name, I figured I should get to her first. I couldn't justify letting your girl stand in the rain while I hauled a dead truck to the scrapyard."

"You're a good man, Hanson." Russ shook Pete's hand.

"Remember that when you get my bill."

He started to ask about Pete's family, but Ashley shifted and he recognized his faded blue hoodie. Liz hated that sweatshirt, called it old and ratty. On Ashley it looked amazing.

The door closed, snapping him out of the daze. "You look okay," he said, struggling to control his voice.

"I told you I was fine."

Better than fine. Beautiful. Long wet hair framed her pink cheeks and sparkling eyes. She inspired thoughts that had nothing to do with convenience, and he couldn't look away. The coffee maker beeped. She moved, but Russ held up a hand. "Let me get it for you."

"Thank you. With cream, please."

"I'm familiar." He walked to the kitchen, the vision of her burned into his mind. Another night at home, engaged but strangers, and her wearing his clothes. That didn't seem like something strangers would do, yet he didn't mind. Should he? *Don't overthink it. Just pour the coffee and enjoy the night.*

When he returned to the living room, Ashley stood in front of the fireplace stoking the wood. The sweatshirt covered her to midthigh. She wore those black, skin-tight pants that Rachel liked and a pair of his wool socks. Maybe they were hers, but he liked thinking they were his. "Nice sweatshirt."

She turned and smiled at him. "I found it in the laundry room when I tossed my clothes in the dryer. I hope you don't mind." Her skin glowed in the orange firelight. Nothing about her said stranded city girl. Of course, he didn't honestly know if she was a city girl.

He set her mug on the end table and sank into the far end of the couch. "Where are you from, anyway?"

"Caperton, Ohio. Population five thousand eighty-four."

"Exactly eighty-four?"

"Close enough, but it sounds more official when I say it that way." She returned to the couch, closer to him than to the other end.

Russ cleared his throat. "You don't have dirt roads and rain in Caperton?"

"We do, but we give all the roads different names so it doesn't confuse people." She cradled her coffee in her hands. "This feels great, thank you. I hope I didn't scare you this afternoon. Everything was okay, but I didn't have your number, and then all I could think of was getting out of the rain."

"I'm glad you're all right. You don't need to keep explaining."

"But I do. I don't want you to think I was looking for a way out. I sincerely thought I knew my way back into town."

"I'll take you in tomorrow and let you drive so you get used to it." And then he'd let her drive to the dealership so they could look for a reasonable vehicle. Just thinking about that death trap spiked his blood pressure, so Russ turned his attention back to the fireplace. Focus on the fire.

He couldn't look at Ashley. The emotions in her eyes tugged at and confused him. They were both grieving, both working through massive life changes. How could they flirt and enjoy themselves in the middle of so much turmoil?

"Do you think this might be a sign?"

"What?" He glanced at her, looking for a quiver of humor. She sipped her coffee, hiding her mouth behind the mug, but her eyes didn't flinch. "Are you serious?"

"Kind of, but I'm more curious about what you think. First your sisters freak out, then your ex-girlfriend shows up. Now this." She lowered her cup revealing the tight line of her lips. "Maybe they're signs that we shouldn't do this."

"Or maybe they're obstacles we need to overcome. The right way isn't usually the easy way. Still, we aren't married yet, so you can change your mind."

Even as he said those last words, Russ hated them, but they needed to be said. As Ashley processed them, her lips shifted back and forth. Her thinking face. One expression down, four million to figure out. And, despite what he'd said, he wanted the chance to do that.

Her expression relaxed. "Do you think it's a chance to persevere?"

"It makes sense. I remember when my dad and uncle were considering these new apple varieties for the farm. They read the research, visited other farms, and talked with experts."

"What happened?"

"They went for it. Then our equipment broke. The supplier nearly doubled the price of the trees. The township showed up to investigate some bogus allegations."

"That's horrible."

Russ nodded. "It was rough. One night I overheard my parents talking, and my mom sounded like you, asking if it might be a sign. I'll never forget my dad's answer. He said the circumstances of our lives shouldn't dictate what we do. Right is right and wrong is wrong. Circumstances don't change that. My dad and uncle believed they were doing the right thing, and they weren't going to let anything get in their way. They fought through a lot of stuff, but they added the new apples."

"Was it worth the hassle?"

"Everything's worth the hassle if you're doing the right thing." Russ smiled. "But it did feel good when those trees flourished. They became some of our most productive varieties." Wanting to reassure her, he looked Ashley in the eye. "I still think getting married is the right decision."

The warm glow of the fire softened her features, but softness could be deceiving. He liked that she hadn't tried to hide anything, and he liked having her around, even looked forward to seeing her. Look how crazy he'd been, needing to see her after the accident. Was that what he wanted? Irrationality and nerves? Absolutely not. But for Ashley ...

"I'm not just marrying you because I told you I would," he said. "I'm looking forward to it."

"You are?" Her eyes widened. She didn't say another word, but her face communicated everything. Uncertainty, doubt, hope, tenderness.

He set down his coffee. "When do you want to try this again?"

"I suppose now that your sisters know, they'll want to be at the wedding."

"They wouldn't forgive us if they weren't. How about this weekend?"

"That's three days away. A lot can happen in three days."

"At this rate, one of us might lose a limb before Saturday. I don't need my little toe, though, so I'll risk it."

"Speak for yourself. I'm rather fond of my extremities."

"It's almost winter, so the farm is slowing down. I could keep an eye on you and your extremities until then." Russ winked. "Make sure nothing bad happens. You might have to go to the office with me, though."

"Won't I get in the way?"

"Nah. Things calm down for me when the ground starts to freeze. Besides, Chad told me to take the rest of the week off."

Ashley took another sip of coffee as she turned her attention to the fire.

Russ waited for her to say something, but she kept staring at the flames. Her cheeks glowed even more. Was she blushing?

She raised her mug, paused, lowered the mug. Up, down. Up, down. It didn't take a man with three sisters to realize Ashley had something on her mind. He should ask her about it, but he didn't want to spoil the moment.

Instead, he turned to watch the fire with her. A gust of wind whistled around the corner of the house, a whisper of it sneaking down the chimney. The flames shivered. A puff of sharp, hearty wood scent flowed through the room.

"What are we going to do until Saturday?" Ashley asked.

"Huh?" He started to turn, but she'd moved to the middle of the couch—less than half a cushion away. Close enough to touch. "Uh, hi. What were you asking?"

"What are we going to do about our living situation until Saturday?"

What indeed. "I could stay with my mom for a couple nights."

"Is that necessary? We're both adults."

But their age wasn't the issue. They couldn't even get a marriage license without the town gossiping. How long would it take for everyone to find out they were living together? He couldn't compromise his convictions, and he wouldn't sacrifice Ashley's reputation.

Besides, when Ashley sat that close, with her lips smiling and inviting, common sense washed away with the cold rain. He had to get out of the house to protect them. Three nights alone were too tempting. It hadn't been an hour, and he couldn't resist moving the damp hair from her face. Or letting his finger trace the warm curve of her jaw. Leaning in close enough to smell the spice and orange and rain in her hair. Their breath mingled. "This is why I should stay with my mom."

"You don't want to be this close to me?"

"Completely the opposite."

She pressed her cheek against his palm. Her long lashes lowered, touching her cheeks as she sighed. Russ slid his hand into the hair at the base of her neck. Her head tilted. He surrendered. He remembered those lips, and he wanted to taste them again.

"I'm home!"

* * * * * * *

Ashley jumped. Russ' hand tangled in her hair as the blood raged through her veins. Temptation avoided.

Kathleen stood in the foyer smiling, a suitcase by her feet. "Ashley, I'm so glad you're okay." She tracked water into the living room as she walked to the couch, arms open. "We were so worried."

Ashley pushed herself up to wrap her arms around the woman. "I'm sorry about that."

"I'm wet, so I'll make this quick." She pounded twice on Ashley's back, then held her at arm's length. "Don't beat yourself up about it. There's not a person in this family who hasn't gotten their car stuck at one point in time. Of course, you're the first to do it on your wedding day. It doesn't smell like you've cooked dinner yet. Why don't I get that started?"

Russ stood, pulling his mother in for a quick hug. "I'm not going to say no to one of your dinners, but what are you doing here?"

"Call me old-fashioned, but I'm chaperoning."

A smile split Russ' face. "Old-fashioned and God-fearing. I'm okay with that."

"Just until the wedding. It wouldn't be right to leave you two here unsupervised. Imagine what your father would say. You obviously can't be left alone. Who knows what would have happened if I hadn't walked in just now?" She winked at Ashley.

"I'll be in the kitchen if you need me. Russ, will you take my bag upstairs when you have a second? No need to rush." She whistled as she tromped through the house.

Russ chuckled.

Heat consumed Ashley's face, and it had nothing to do with the fire. "I guess you don't need to move out now."

"Guess not."

"Properly chaperoned."

"Yep."

Wonderful.

"I should see if my mom needs anything." He walked away, taking his lips with him.

Where had those urges come from? She'd dated a couple of guys, had one serious boyfriend. While the cuddling and kisses were nice, she'd never craved them as she did with Russ, with the intensity of a starving child craving food. Maybe that was a bit much, but she'd never experienced such chemistry or anticipation. Somehow those crazy urges surprised yet calmed her.

Her fiancé and soon-to-be mother-in-law chatted in the kitchen while Ashley's mind calculated. Kathleen's arrival gave her two whole days to get to know her intended. He could show her around. They could talk, date, do whatever would be appropriate—and normal—to do with your mother in the house.

Russ rounded the corner, a dishtowel in his hands. "Hey, Ash, do you care if we have broccoli or green beans?"

The thought of a real date night produced a smile. With the other guys, it had been stressful and awkward, putting on a good show while trying to figure out if he was the one, but with Russ she knew. She could relax. "I want to go out on a date."

Every inch of him froze. Not even the towel moved as it dangled from his fingers.

"Not tonight, since your mom's here, but maybe tomorrow? We can go out and get to know each other better?" His silence wrapped around her. "What is it?"

He shook his head. "I hadn't thought about dating."

"We have two nights before the wedding. It would be fun to try something a little more traditional."

"Traditional?" He tossed the towel over his shoulder and crossed his arms. "Are you sure you want to do that?"

A rotten ball of reality rolled around in her stomach. "Yes, because someday it's also going to be a regular marriage, I hope. Why not start with a date?"

Russ scrubbed a hand over his face, smoothing out subtle lines that sank back into his face the second he pulled his hand away.

She was losing him. Ashley's feet hit the floor, target in her sights. She stepped once, twice—right into his personal space— wrapped her arms around his neck and kissed him.

This time he didn't hesitate to pull her close and kiss her dizzy. His lips ministered his strength and passion and kindness. Every second deepened her need for more. Ashley held on, wooing him with her kisses. How had she lived so long without them?

Russ tore his lips away and pressed his fuzzy cheek against her temple, his raspy breaths moving her hair. He chuckled. "I'm still trying to decide what to think about you."

"Think good things."

"I suppose this means I need to take you on a date."

Ashley shook her head, enjoying the light scratch of his whiskers on her skin. "No, I wanted to kiss you, not manipulate you."

"Then you wouldn't care if I said no to tomorrow?"

That nasty ball in her stomach soured. "I would care, but I'll respect your decision."

As Russ leaned away, the wall pressed against her back. How had she gotten there?

He looked at her as she tried to slow her breathing. No need to lose her head over something as ridiculous as a make-out session with her fiancé.

"Every now and then you get this look on your face that I can't figure out." He traced a rough finger along her cheekbone. Down her nose. Along her upper lip. "I want to know what this means. I guess I'll need to spend some more time with you to figure it out."

Her heart fluttered. "O-okay."

"You decide what you want to do tomorrow, and we'll do it."

She smiled.

"That look I recognize." He let her go and stepped back, grabbing the towel from her shoulder and tossing it over his. "Give it a few minutes before you come into the kitchen. Not that it will matter. There's no way my mom will believe it took this long to discuss vegetables."

CHAPTER 23

Russ groaned. How had Tom known where to find anything? The emptiness of the office closed in around him. Tom would have known what to do if Russ died, but Russ needed his cousin to walk him through the books. He didn't want to imagine running the farm without Tom. They had picked up the slack from their fathers, but could Russ do the work of four people?

Chad burst through the front door. "I knew you couldn't stay away. Thanks for showing up today. I win the family pool."

"How much?"

"Hundred bucks."

"That's it?"

"Hey, the economy's tight." Chad stripped off his winter layers and dumped them on a chair near the door. "As happy as I am to see you, what are you doing here?"

"Still looking for paperwork."

"While you're at it, see if you can find your sanity. Rachel said you and Ashley are getting married. What are you thinking?"

Russ leaned back, teetered, then braced himself as the wheeled chair slid beneath him. "I'm thinking this paperwork doesn't exist. If it doesn't, marrying Ashley will solve a lot of problems."

"Yeah, that's a great reason to get married." Chad wandered over to the coffeepot and poured a cup. "You know that's crazy, right? You don't marry a complete stranger to get her house. This isn't the Dark Ages."

"I don't need a lecture. Besides, we won't be complete strangers when we get married. The wedding didn't happen, so we have a couple more days to spend with each other."

"Rachel mentioned that. What's the plan?"

"To get married Saturday, but if our luck keeps up, there's a good chance the church will burn down before we get there."

"Maybe God's trying to tell you something."

"And maybe it's bad luck."

"Well, I don't want to add to your troubles, but sometime soon we need to figure out what to do about the farm."

How was that not adding to his troubles? Russ smothered a growl. "Look, whether I find the paperwork or get married, the farm is secure."

"That's great, but that's not what I mean. The township called again. They're still interested in using the farm for that preservation thing. There's an envelope on your desk from the extension office. I think they want you to teach."

Teach? As in children? Exactly what he didn't need—more chaos. "That can wait."

"It can't." Chad took a deep breath and adjusted the cap on his head. "We need to decide what we're going to do with this farm because it's only us now, and ..."

And Russ had always known this day would come. "You want out."

"I might. I think we need to seriously consider our options. I love working with you, it's been a blessing to be part of this family and part of your history, but I never wanted to run a farm. I just couldn't seem to get away from it."

This was the time to get away? Where would that leave Russ? "You think we should sell the farm?"

"I'm not saying that." His linebacker of a brother-in-law practically folded up on himself as he sat down. "I *am* saying we should consider our options. Maybe partnering with the college will lessen our burden."

Russ' spine tightened. What could he say? "Let's talk about this later."

"We need to *act* later. We need to talk about this now."

"No." Russ jumped out of his seat, knocking the chair to the ground. He needed to think, away from the clutter of death and abandonment.

Chad stood, towering over him. "You can't avoid this forever."

"I won't, but I'm not doing this now. This isn't the right time to talk about selling the farm."

"I'm not talking about that either, but you're clearly too stubborn to be sensible. Find me when you're ready to listen, but you need to know I'm considering my options."

Perfect. He might as well sell everything and move to Detroit. Russ couldn't do that, though. Ashley owned the house. The tension climbed up his spine, tightening around his neck like a noose. "I need to get out of here."

"Take the rest of the week off. Seriously, don't come back until Monday. Think about what I said."

"Fine." Russ yanked his coat off the floor and righted the chair. "If you happen to find any legal-looking documents from Tom saying he was crazy and didn't mean anything he said in his letter to Ashley, give me a call." He crossed the room, ready to get out of the stifling office.

"Russ?"

"Yeah."

"Congratulations."

"Huh?" He looked back at Chad.

"The wedding. Congratulations, man."

"Thanks. We'll talk later." After he talked to Ashley. The township's proposal affected her now too. What would she think about it? The idea of discussing his future with her eased the tension.

Clear blue skies and frosty air greeted Russ outside, the morning sun blinding him. He dug the phone out of his pocket, his bare fingers stiffening in the cold as he dialed. Almost nine. Ashley had to be up by now, though he'd left her asleep on the couch again.

"Hello?" Her soft voice moaned the word into his ear, stirring his heart and easing the morning's pressure.

"Did I wake you?"

"Um ... yeah. Who is this?"

Of course she wouldn't recognize his voice yet. That reality chilled him more thoroughly than the wind. "Russ."

"Oh, hi." She yawned into the phone. "What's up?"

"What are you doing this morning?"

"I've been awake for five seconds. I haven't made plans yet."

"How about we start our date early? I'll pick you up in fifteen minutes and take you out for breakfast."

"No."

So much for that idea.

"I can't be ready in fifteen minutes."

"How long do you need?"

She yawned again. "Half an hour? Coffee first. Then we'll talk. Uh ... how did I end up on the couch?"

"I'll pick you up in half an hour and tell you all about it."

* * * * * * *

At 10 a.m., Russ paced the kitchen, lecturing himself about falling for Ashley's thirty-minute estimate. They'd shared a house for a week. He knew how long she took in the bathroom, but what could possibly take so long?

Footsteps clicked on the hardwood. "Okay, I'm ready." She walked into the kitchen and stole his breath away. Black heels and jeans. Long, dark waves and a fire-engine-red sweater. Her pink cheeks creased with a relaxed smile that was worth the wait. He couldn't look away.

She'd looked comfortable last night, but today pushed her out of the comfortable zone and right up to beautiful. Russ fought to control his expression, not wanting to let her see how much she'd affected him.

"Are you okay? You look sick."

Maybe he was trying too hard. He smiled instead. "I'm fine. You look amazing."

"Thanks. Where are we going?"

"That depends on what you want to see. We can go to Traverse City and see where Liz lives, or go up to Cheboygan to visit Rachel. She's always happy to have company."

"Do we have to visit anyone today?"

"Not if you don't want to."

"I'd like to drive around, but I'm not ready to face your sisters again so soon."

Russ laughed. "I can understand that."

"Thank you. What are my other options?"

He pressed a hand against the soft material on the small of her back as he ushered her to the door, then pulled her coat off the rack and helped her into it. "Let's go to Petoskey. It's far enough from everyone that you can see northern Michigan without having to explain to anyone why we didn't stop by to say hi."

"Perfect."

* * * * * *

Ashley clung to the door handle, straining to see the edge of the road through the rain-streaked windshield. The wipers thwapped across the glass, but the world blurred around her. "Are Novembers always this rainy?"

Russ barely held the steering wheel with his right hand as his arm rested on his leg. "Not often. A little colder and it'd be snowing. Don't you like the rain?"

"Not particularly."

"It's not usually this bad here. It's the freezing rain that makes things tricky."

"How often does that happen?"

"There's no way to know. What's with you and rain?"

A car whizzed by, throwing a wave of water into Ashley's sightline and testing her nerves. Russ didn't seem to mind, but she couldn't tell without taking her eyes off the road. While her ability to see through the windshield wouldn't change the driving conditions, knowing where they were going alleviated some of her anxiety. She'd been so focused on the wedding yesterday that she hadn't considered the weather before going out. Today, however, every raindrop pounded on her heart.

Risking a quick look to her left, she made eye contact. Her pulse spiked. "Shouldn't you be watching the road?" The truck slowed, and they coasted to a stop along the shoulder. "What's wrong? Why did we stop?"

"Why do you hate the rain?"

"What?"

Russ slouched in the driver's seat, watching her. His eyebrows pinched together above his nose as the corners of his mouth folded down.

Her blood simmered. "Don't pity me. It was raining when my parents crashed. I know it was an accident, but it could happen to anyone."

"But it was raining?"

A chill rippled through her. "Yes."

"How did it happen?"

"Another driver lost control and hit them. The police said he was speeding and spun out. He had a head injury, so he doesn't remember the accident. He got to walk away with no memory of killing my parents." Someday that injustice wouldn't hurt so much.

"I'm sorry. I shouldn't have asked."

"Why not?"

"It obviously still upsets you."

"I don't mind talking about my parents." Ashley crossed her arms. "It's the look."

"What look?"

"The 'poor you' look, as if I'm the only person who's ever lost a loved one, like I'm a pity case because I'm alone. I don't want people feeling sorry for me. I'm not—"

"I don't feel sorry for you."

Their breath fogged the windows as his reaction fogged her head. "You don't?"

"Not at all. I'm impressed."

She wasn't sure how to take that. "Why?"

"Aside from the whole driving-in-the-rain thing, you seem to have things together. You've lost a lot of people in your life, but that hasn't stopped you. I was wondering how you do it."

"I didn't handle it well at first, but it's been almost twenty years. The time helps." A gentle swell of concern for Russ warmed her heart. "I remember nights when my head hurt from all the crying and thinking during the day. It fades, though."

He nodded, but his expression didn't change.

She turned to face him completely. "I didn't realize you were struggling so much. I should have noticed."

"There's no way you'd know." He unlatched his seatbelt, letting it slide back into the panel. "Come on, slide over."

"What?"

He reached over and unlatched her belt. "Slide on over." He tapped the steering wheel, and every ounce of her strength melted away.

The rain pounded in time with her heart. "No."

"You can do this." His fingers wrapped around hers, pulling her toward the center console.

She pulled away toward the comfort of her door. Russ gently tugged her arm. She shook her head, but somehow her body moved closer to the center. "Why are you making me do this?"

"I would never make you do anything. You drove in the rain yesterday. Why does today scare you?"

Rivers rolled down the windshield, captivating her. "I never leave while it's raining."

"And the weather was clear when you left the house yesterday."

She focused on the rivulets. The same substance she needed to survive had killed her parents. Children laughed and danced in the rain. Ashley shivered.

Russ' warm hand covered hers, entwining their fingers. He pressed a soft kiss to the inside of her wrist. "You're trembling." He loosened his grip but didn't let go.

She admired their hands together—his large and tan, hers smaller and pale. His free hand cupped her cheek, his thumb brushing across it, spreading a trail of moisture. Tears?

Breaking contact, she looked away and wiped her face. "I'm not usually a crier."

Russ chuckled. "Are you sure?"

Between the nightmares and the rain, she'd cried more in the last week than she had in the last year. "I promise, I don't usually cry this much, not even when I talk about my parents."

"I don't mind."

"I do."

Russ exhaled loudly. "Good, because I lied. I wouldn't mind a few less tears."

His honesty tricked a smile out of her. "I'll see what I can do."

He cupped her face again, then slid his fingers into her hair, tickling a tender spot on the back of her neck. Her eyelids fluttered down. The closeness soothed her. Tom had promised her friendship. With Russ she had understanding. Support. A tenderness that surprised her.

And chemistry. Goose bumps popped up on her arms as he wove his fingers deeper into her hair. Man, did they have chemistry. She'd given up on that fairy tale years ago, but being with Russ changed her mind. He changed everything.

"Thank you," he said.

She looked at him. "For what?"

"For being here."

But she hadn't done anything. Of course, John and Rose hadn't done much after her parents' funeral, but they made themselves available, and that eased worries she hadn't even identified. "I'm glad I could be here. I remember what those days were like."

"How did you deal with it?"

"Sometimes I laughed. Sometimes I cried. I'm a girl, so I talked a lot."

Russ wrapped his other arm around her. "I'm not much of a talker."

"Don't try to force it. You'll work through your grief when you're ready." She leaned back, smiling at him. "Have you met that person yet who swears he knows exactly how you feel because he lost his dog once? Or because his eighty-nine-year-old great aunt died, he completely understands what you're going through?"

Russ' lips twitched. "Not this time, but I remember that from my dad's funeral. People kept trying to tell me what to expect next. I hated it."

"I'll never forget, at my parents' funeral, this guy who used to work with my dad walked up and hugged me, then started talking about how his mom had recently died peacefully in her sleep, so he understood exactly how I felt. I know he meant well, but I wanted to punch him."

Russ' laugh reverberated through the cab, relieving the heaviness of their shared grief. Before she could talk herself out of it, Ashley touched his beard. "I like hearing you laugh. My aunt says a cheerful heart is good medicine, and I've found that to be rather accurate."

He wrapped his arms around her. The butterflies in Ashley's stomach fluttered. His grip tightened, inviting her in as his eyes darkened.

"Russ?"

His lips captured hers, fierce and passionate, as if his next breath depended on the touch of her lips. Ashley locked her arms around his neck. Each kiss pulled at her heart, drawing her closer to him, urging her to let go. She surrendered, kissing him back, matching his passion and eagerness.

His lips left hers, caressing her cheek, jaw, the soft spot beneath her ear. She trembled. A warm breath washed over her neck.

"We might not make it to Petoskey in time for breakfast," he said.

She kissed his temple, then the crow's feet at the corner of his eyes. He sighed against her, and she chuckled. "I don't mind. This is the best drive I've ever taken in the rain."

CHAPTER 24

Dusk covered Boyne Heights as Russ navigated the streets, Ashley sleeping beside him. He scrubbed a hand across his face as he replayed their day in his mind. One full day with her, and their relationship definitely wasn't about convenience anymore. Convenience didn't explain how she affected him.

Each time they touched, his brain shut down. When she held him, everything seemed okay. He almost forgot about the stress of the farm and his family, but how long could that last? He and Jess had had physical chemistry, and look how that turned out. What if Ashley was as crazy as Jess?

No, Tom had never liked Jess and had tried to warn Russ, but Tom picked Ashley. She couldn't be nuts. Then again, Tom kept his engagement a secret, so maybe it wasn't Ashley's sanity Russ should be questioning.

She seemed normal enough. She had smiled as they explored Petoskey, spoken intelligently without talking his ear off. He'd enjoyed the afternoon, but now they were heading back to the farmhouse. Back to reality. What would happen after the wedding when Mom went home, and life started again?

"Where are we?" Sleeping Beauty yawned as she ran her fingers through her hair, rustling the already-messy mass.

"Almost home."

"Darn it. The sun's setting."

"Is that a problem?"

"I wanted to take pictures of the house and barn, but the light will be gone by the time we get there. That's okay, though. I can take pictures tomorrow."

Russ turned the truck onto the main street, rolling along the quiet stretch of road.

"Wait!" She squeezed his knee. "The courthouse. The sun's perfect against the brick. Can we go over there?"

"Don't you need your camera?"

She reached into the back seat, then produced a rectangular blue bag.

"Where did that come from?"

"I'm sneaky. I would have taken pictures in Petoskey, but I didn't want to ruin the mood. Oh!" She pointed across him. "Over there."

Russ turned left, jumping the curb as he pulled into the courthouse parking lot. As he drove toward a vacant spot, he spotted her.

Ashley leaned toward the windshield. "Isn't that Jess?"

"Yes." His ex skipped down the front steps of the courthouse.

"I thought she lived in Marquette. Why is she still in town?"

"I have no idea." But he could guess.

Ashley opened her door before he stopped the truck. She hopped out, the camera pressed to her face, and snapped pictures as she walked. Why was she taking pictures of Jess?

His shoulders tightened as he climbed out. The two women greeted each other. His gut told him to run, but his brain kicked into gear—nothing good could come from those two talking.

Jess raised a hand, smiling. "Hi, Russ."

He tipped his head. "Jess."

"Your fiancée promised to send me copies of these pictures."

"Ashley. Her name's Ashley."

"Yes, I know." She tucked a piece of hair behind her ear, tilting her head toward him. He'd once thought she looked cute doing that. Today he cringed.

"I'd like to get a few pictures while the light is good. Do you mind?" Ashley looked between Russ and Jess, who took a step closer to him.

"Russ and I can catch up while we wait," she said.

Great. Ashley headed toward the far side of the building.

"She seems nice."

"I like her."

"I figured since you're marrying her."

"Yep." A cold wind blew between them. "Why are you still in town? Don't you have to work?"

"You're really going to marry her?"

"Haven't we had this conversation?"

"I thought maybe you had come to your senses."

"And decided to marry you instead?"

Jess stepped in front of him, arms crossed and icy-blue eyes narrowed. "That's not what I meant. You just lost your best friend, and your farm is in trouble—"

"No, it's not."

"You're emotional, and she's pretty, but I know you. We have history."

"Not a good history."

"Those weren't my best days. I get that."

"Not your best days? That's like calling a hurricane inclement weather."

Jess winced, taking half a step backward.

Guilt rammed into Russ. "I didn't mean it like that."

"No." She stared at the ground. "You're right. That was a hard time. My job was a mess, we moved Nana to a nursing home, and my little brother went into rehab. And the thing with my parents. It was a lot to handle, and I didn't do it well."

"You wouldn't let me break up with you."

An unnatural shade of red seeped into her face, all the way to her hairline.

His stupid, big mouth. "I'm sorry, I'm—"

"Don't be." She snapped to attention, straightening her coat and looking him in the eye. "It was bad—embarrassing—and not just with you. I basically got myself fired, but you'd already broken up with me, twice I think, so I never mentioned it."

"Fired? I thought you left the credit union because of the job in Marquette."

"Hardly. I applied for a promotion and tanked the interview. I kept telling them I needed the job and how it fit into my five-year plan." She shook her head, blonde hair swinging around her shoulders. "I rambled for half an hour. By the time I left the office, I was bawling. It was too embarrassing to stay after that, so I told everyone there was a job, but I needed to get away. I lucked out when the agricultural extension had an opening."

And Russ had thought the meltdown was about him. "I don't know what to say."

She waved a hand as if to dismiss his misunderstanding. "I probably deserve whatever it is you think about me, but regardless of what that is, I'm worried about you. She's a stranger."

"I appreciate your concern, but I'm sure about this."

Jess' eyebrows pinched together, shadowing her eyes. If she started crying, he might actually run.

Instead, she sighed, her face sinking into a half-pout, half-frown. "I wish we'd met a year later, when my life wasn't such a mess, and I wasn't so ..."

"Crazy?"

To his relief, she smiled. "I've always appreciated your honesty."

"Then you should believe me when I say I know what I'm doing." As if on cue, Ashley stepped around the corner of the courthouse. Beautiful salvation. "Excuse me, Jess. I'm going to see my fiancé."

* * * * * * *

Ashley snapped another picture of the cracked brick, careful to keep Jess and Russ out of the shot. Jess smiled. She could have been in a toothpaste commercial. Russ said something, then looked at Ashley. His chest expanded, and he headed toward her. She might not have a Hollywood smile, but at least he was walking in her direction.

"Russ!" Jess said. He looked back at her. "I'll be in town for a while." He tipped his chin at her before continuing toward Ashley.

She put the camera to her eye and zoomed in on a tree branch before panning the lens across Jess' face. No one should be that beautiful without discernable make-up. She waved at Ashley, then headed toward the parking lot. The camera nearly slipped out of her hands. Good thing she wasn't scheduled for any stakeouts.

Refocusing her attention on Russ, she tried to ignore the puffs of breath that crystalized in front of her. She should have brought gloves and a hat.

Russ sauntered toward her.

"How's Jess?" she asked.

"Good, I guess. Apparently she's in town for a while."

"Is everything okay between you two?"

"There's not anything between us."

"Do you think you'll see her again while she's here?"

"I'm not planning to, but it's a small town."

True. Whatever Jess was planning, Ashley wouldn't worry about it. After all, Russ was standing with her, not the catalog-ready model.

The aroma of grilled beef wafted over from the nearby bar, and Ashley's mouth watered. "Do you want to get dinner?"

"Sure. Where can I take you?"

"I asked you. My treat."

Russ offered his arm. "I'm afraid I can't allow that."

"Keeping chivalry alive?"

"That, and my mom would never stop lecturing me if she found out."

"Do you think she'd find out?"

"After everything that's happened, you have to ask?" His phone dinged. "That's probably her now."

"I'll get it." Ashley reached into his coat pocket and pulled out his phone. She slid her finger across the screen.

Just checking to see if this number still works. Jess

CHAPTER 25

Ashley pulled Russ' sweatshirt over her head as she shuffled down the hall. Light slipped out from beneath the bathroom door, accompanied by the muffled rush of water. She skipped down the stairs as laughter and applause sounded from the family room.

Kathleen sat on the couch knitting while a classic rerun filled the TV screen. "You look comfy. Going to join me for a little late-night TV?"

Ashley looked at the clock. "I don't think nine o'clock qualifies as late night, but I'd love to." She settled on the far end of the couch and draped a blanket over her lap.

Kathleen chuckled. "My husband slept with the sun during the summer, but in the winter he was in bed by nine. It was a rare evening when that man saw double digits."

"Wasn't that hard with kids?"

"Not at all. When they were little, they were in bed before he was, and if anyone ever woke up early, he'd take them out to do chores with him."

"Did they like it?"

"Carrie and Liz didn't care for it, but Rachel enjoyed working in the barn." The gentle clack of her knitting needles slowed. "Then there was Russ. He would get so mad when he missed going out with his dad. You know you've got a farmer on your hands when a seven-year-old gets up at six a.m. to catch a ride to the orchard."

"Russ always wanted to run the farm?"

"I wouldn't say that. He was more fascinated by the trees than the production and selling." Kathleen dropped her hands in her lap and stared out the front window. "Tom loved going to the markets, working with the local restaurant and business owners. I'm not sure what Russ will do without him."

"What about your daughters? Don't any of them work the farm?"

"Carrie and Liz didn't get the bug, I'm afraid. For a while, I thought Rachel might stick with it."

"Isn't that unusual?"

"Sometimes. Carrie's my planner, and she never liked the financial uncertainty of the farm. We were older when Liz was born, and my husband adored having a little princess. He'd take her out to work with him, but he loved going to her dance recitals and taking her to see shows. As much as he loved the farm, it can be a hard life, and he wanted something easier for her."

"What happened with Rachel?"

"Kids." Kathleen shook her head, but she smiled. "Rachel loves the farm, but she and Chad started their family when she was nineteen. She wanted to stay home with them. Chad has worked with us since he and Rachel started dating in high school, but that boy is wasting his talent."

"How's that?"

"He has a master's degree in journalism."

"Really?"

Kathleen swiveled toward Ashley. "That boy is brilliant. He started taking college classes in high school and has been taking online classes ever since. He's a fantastic writer, but he's also crazy in love with my daughter. He moved to town his freshman year in high school and waited about a week to ask her out. My husband wouldn't let the girls date until they were sixteen, so Chad applied to work on the farm." She laughed. "It worked. My husband offered Chad full-time work as soon as they graduated. Then the kids got married, started having their own kids, and Chad never left."

"He got stuck in a rut and couldn't get out." Ashley could relate.

"He's given everything to help save our farm. Have you met Jay yet?"

Ashley shook her head.

"He went to school with Carrie, and for a while, we thought he might join the family, but he only joined us in the orchards. The thing is, he doesn't need to work if he doesn't want to. His wife is an attorney, and she could take care of them. But he's like Russ and Tom. He has the trees in his blood."

Would that be enough to keep the farm running, though? Maybe Ashley could learn to love the farm, to make it her own. She could help with the books. She wouldn't need to be up before dawn for that.

Footsteps thundered in the foyer, and Russ walked into the family room, his wet hair brushing the collar of his flannel shirt. "Can I get you two anything before bed?"

Ashley waited for the punch line, but Russ' serious expression didn't crack. A nine o'clock bedtime for her nearly-forty-year-old fiancé? The realization made her laugh. "I'm not going to bed anytime soon. Would you like me to get *you* anything?"

"I'll grab myself a snack, then I'll see you in the morning."

Kathleen set her yarn and needles in a bag on the floor. "I should probably head up. I'm leaving early tomorrow to babysit Kristy. A whole day with her Maw-Maw. I can hardly wait." She dropped a kiss on Ashley's head on her way out. "Don't make too much noise down here."

"Good night, Kathleen."

"Night, Mom." As soon as she disappeared around the corner, Russ tousled Ashley's hair. "She must like you."

"How do you know?"

"She's leaving you alone with her son. That's basically her stamp of approval."

"No, she has to get up early—"

"Trust me. That woman will sit up in her bed reading until midnight. You're good."

He strolled into the kitchen. Ashley craned her neck to follow his tall, lean frame. So handsome, so put together—he did a great job hiding the stress of Tom's death, but she knew it was there. It pressed on her too. Maybe she could help. She kicked off the blanket and followed him. "Have you had any luck finding the documents Rob needs?" she asked.

"I haven't found anything at the office yet."

"Did Tom keep any paperwork at the house?"

Russ shut the refrigerator, a carton of orange juice in his hand. "Maybe. There are some boxes in his closet."

"Would it be okay if I looked through them? Maybe I can find something that will help."

He leaned against the counter, swigging from the container. "It would be nice to have copies of everything to give to Rob. It shouldn't matter after we're married, but I'd like to get all of this legal stuff sorted out in case anything else happens."

"Then let me help. I'll look through his boxes and see what I can find." She waited for an okay, but Russ simply stared at her. Nervous willies crawled over her skin. "What?"

"You look good in my sweatshirt." He took another long drink, then tossed the empty carton in the sink. "I'll get the boxes, and we can get to work."

* * * * * * *

A thin layer of paperwork covered the dining-room table—folders, envelopes, receipts, napkins, and Post-its. Ashley's head hurt. Tom was the organized one?

Something tickled her thigh. She jumped, brushing off her leg. "You okay?"

Her pocket buzzed again. "I forgot my phone was on vibrate."

"It's kind of late for a phone call."

Ashley checked the clock and frowned. "It's only ten, but even I don't call people this late." She didn't recognize the number, but it was from her aunt and uncle's area code. "Hello?"

"Hi, sweetheart, it's Aunt Rose."

Warm memories wrapped around Ashley. "It's good to hear your voice. I almost didn't answer the phone. Where are you calling from?"

"Now, I don't want you to worry, but I'm at the hospital—"

Icy teeth bit into Ashley's spine. "What happened? Are you okay? Is it Uncle John? Which hospital? I'll fly out first thing in the morning."

"Calm down. We're okay. That's why I started with 'I don't want you to worry.' "

As if that would keep the fear away. "Aunt Rose?"

"Your uncle had a small accident, but he's fine."

"He's obviously not fine, or you wouldn't be calling from the hospital!" What kind of accident? How small was small? Ashley's hand shook as she held the phone to her ear.

A warm hand covered hers, and the phone slid out from her grip. Russ pressed a button, then set the phone on the table. "Is this Rose?" he asked.

"Oh, uh, yes. Who's this?"

"I'm Ashley's friend, Russ. She's a little shaken up, so I put you on speaker phone."

"Oh, thank you. Now, everything's okay, so calm down. John was out walking tonight, and he stepped off the curb wrong and broke his ankle. We're at the hospital getting him fitted for a walking cast."

"He's eighty years old. Why was he out walking by himself?"

"Ashley Elaine Johnson, we are old, not decrepit."

Russ snorted.

Ashley glared at him.

"I'll go get us something to drink." He squeezed Ashley's shoulder and headed toward the kitchen. The silent gesture pulled a bit of the tension out of the situation.

"Are you still there, sweetheart?"

"Yes, I'm here. I'm trying to recover from a near heart attack."

"Well, don't you blame that on me. I told you everything was fine."

"After you told me you were at the hospital!" She sucked in a crazed breath. "I love you, Aunt Rose, but sometimes I think you and Uncle John are trying to age me."

"Pish posh. I wanted to let you know what's going on, that's all."

"Which ankle did he break?"

"Oh, I'm not sure."

Wait a minute. "How did you get to the hospital?"

"I should probably go see how—"

"Aunt Rose! Your license was revoked. You're not supposed to be driving, especially at night!" The thought of the two of them driving through town made Ashley's eye twitch. "How long will he be in the cast?"

"Four weeks. The doctor says it's a hairline fracture. If John would agree to stay off his foot, he wouldn't need the cast, but you know your uncle."

"How are you going to get around until then?"

"We'll be fine. I can still drive during the day."

"You're not supposed to."

"There are plenty of people in the community who can take us around."

That was probably true, but Ashley didn't trust her independent aunt and uncle to conform to someone else's schedule. Besides, she couldn't leave her family in the hands of strangers. "I'll fly down there as soon as I can."

"You'll do no such thing."

"You don't have a choice. You and Uncle John have always taken care of me. Let me take care of you for a while."

Rose sniffled. "Oh, Ashley." No doubt she would've figured out how to survive for the next month, but she couldn't hide the relief in her voice.

"Let me find a flight. I'll leave a message at your house with all the details."

"It won't be any trouble for you, will it?"

"Not at all. I can help you around the house and be back before I start working with the photographer. I have some transcribing to do, but I can bring that with me."

"Sweetheart, we'll get to spend Thanksgiving together."

Ashley smiled. "When the doctor discharges Uncle John, take a cab home. We'll pick up your car when I get there. Got it?"

"I promise. I can't wait to see you again."

"Me too. I'll call you as soon as I book my flight." As Ashley hung up, Russ returned with a steaming mug of hot cocoa. "Thank you."

"My mom always made it for my sisters when they had bad break-ups. I thought it might work in this situation too."

"Good instincts." She wrapped her fingers around the mug, holding it close and savoring the sweet aroma.

Russ pulled out the chair beside her. "Do you think they'll need your help?"

"It wouldn't be such a big deal if my aunt could drive, but her eyes are bad, so her driver's license was revoked. My uncle takes her everywhere. I don't care what she says, I know they won't sit still."

Russ leaned back into the chair. "I'll drive you to the airport in the morning."

"But the wedding."

"We'll postpone it."

The tension in her spine eased. "You're okay with that?"

"They're your family. You have to go."

"I could leave right after the wedding."

He shook his head. "Not unless you want to leave a day or two later. My family won't want to miss it, and if they show up, there'll be food and a party, and they usually have this brunch the next day. My sisters' weddings took days. You should go tomorrow. Your family needs you."

She should've been grateful, but his ease with the situation unnerved her. "I'll agree to postpone if you tell me why you're not concerned about it. What if I go to Florida and change my mind?"

His eyebrows popped up. "Are you going to change your mind?"

"Four weeks is a long time. Anything could happen."

"Yep, but we're committed, my mom likes you, and we told my sisters. Besides, this is a practical decision, remember? Convenience."

"True." But it sounded cold when he said it out loud. Ashley sipped her cocoa, hoping it would warm her nerves. Was she flattered or annoyed by his confidence?

Russ took the mug from her hands, gazing into it as he set it on the table. When he looked back at her, he smiled. "Sometimes, in the right light, the centers of your eyes are the same color as the hot chocolate." The smile brightened his face, highlighting his strong jawline and deep eyes. She'd never had a man so handsome stare at her with such intensity.

"I'm not worried about you coming back," he said, holding her hands in his. The callouses on his fingers rubbed across her soft palms, tickling her skin and heart. "And don't worry about me. I'll be here when you get back."

"But will you still feel the same way?"

"This isn't about feelings."

"I mean, will you feel the same way about the arrangement?"

The corner of his mouth twitched. "I know what you mean."

"So we're good?"

"Yes."

That single syllable made her want to stay. Everything about him—his eyes, his honesty, his gentleness—pulled at her heart. "I promise I'll come back if you want me to."

He cupped her cheek with his hand, brushing his thumb across her bottom lip. As Russ leaned forward, Ashley held her breath until his lips touched hers. Soft, gentle. She melted, pressing his hand against her face and holding onto his confidence.

He pulled away slowly, breaking the kiss, but staying close. "I want you to come back." Her lips curled up, unable to hide her relief. He quickly kissed her smiling lips. "I'll get my laptop, and we can find you a flight. I'll take care of my family. You take care of yours."

"You're amazing."

"I want you to remember that in four weeks."

"I will."

He kissed her again before slipping away. She missed him already. How would she survive the next month?

Something dinged. Ashley lifted stacks of papers until she found Russ' phone. Who would be texting him that late? The teeth returned to her spine. It had to be another emergency.

She checked his phone, ready for bad news.

Good news. Will b in town thru Xmas. Hope 2 c u. Jess

Worse.

CHAPTER 26

A large, sweaty body bumped into Ashley, knocking her off balance and into the seat in front of her. Readjusting her bag, she righted herself and continued down the aisle, ready to be off the plane. Four hours ago, Russ had wrapped his arms around her, holding her near the security line at the airport. He didn't mention Jess' text message, and she didn't ask. She simply held on, loving the way she fit against him.

Now, two cranky senior citizens sandwiched her as they tried to force their way past her. Ashley pulled her purse over her shoulder and let the crowd herd her onto the walkway. As soon as she spotted an opening, she wove her way through the people, easily passing small groups of travelers.

By the time she reached the luggage claim, she'd broken away from the pack. Her suitcase slid along the edge of the moving carousel, right past her aunt and uncle.

"Aunt Rose, what are you doing here?"

"Don't fuss. Our neighbors dropped us off with the car." Rose rushed toward her, laughing as she hugged Ashley around her puffy white coat. Her aunt wore white capris and flip flops with a light jacket. A definite contrast to Ashley's jeans and boots. "You could have left this at home, sweetheart. It's supposed to be eighty degrees this week." She helped Ashley out of the coat.

"Don't worry. I brought a ton of clothes, just to be safe." John hobbled over, a cane in his right hand and a cast on his foot. Ashley's heart ached, but she put on a smile. "You look good for an old man."

"You're more beautiful than you were when you left."

"That was two weeks ago." She hugged him quickly, inhaling the familiar licorice scent. "Seriously, I can't leave you alone for fourteen days without supervision."

"It's not me that needs supervision. You need to find that kid on the bike who ran me off the sidewalk."

Ashley's suitcase came back around, so she passed her purse off to Rose while grabbing the ragged, flowered case. John tried to take it, but she smacked his hand away. "You've got a cast and cane."

"A gentleman always offers." He dropped a kiss on her cheek. "I'm going to head for the car. It'll take me a while to get there."

Ashley lagged behind him with Rose, happy to have a minute with her alone. "He seems to be doing okay this morning. How's he handling the break?"

"It's been less than twenty-four hours, and he's taking painkillers, so he's fine for now. Ask again next week."

"How are you doing?"

Rose inhaled, her breath trembling. "I was so scared when he didn't come back. I knew something must have happened, but I didn't know if I should look for him or call the police."

Ashley glanced at Rose, whose tears clung to her lower lashes. "It wasn't your fault."

"I know, but I was so worried. John and I take such good care of ourselves that I haven't thought much about how to get to the hospital without him. I'd call 9-1-1 for an emergency, but is a broken foot considered an emergency? The whole thing took me by surprise."

"A broken foot would surprise anyone. The important thing is that you handled it, and you have a better idea of what to do next time."

"I don't want to think about a next time."

Ashley bit back a smile as she draped an arm over her aunt's shoulders. "That's why you didn't know what to do yesterday. We'll come up with a good plan for you, in case anything like this happens again."

Jingling from inside Ashley's purse interrupted them. Rose managed to find the phone immediately and handed it over. "Who's Russ?"

Ashley's heart tingled at his name. "A friend." She took the phone and stepped away. "Hello?"

"Hey. I wanted to make sure you made it."

"I just got here. My aunt and uncle met me at the airport, and we're on our way to the car now."

"Good to hear. Pearl's here with my lunch, so I should go."

"Say hi for me. And thanks again for the ride this morning."

"My pleasure. Why don't you call me tonight, fill me in on how things are going?"

The tingles intensified. "Sure. And you can tell me how things went with your sisters."

"I'll tell you everything later."

"And by later tonight you mean before nine, right?"

His chuckle washed over her, warmer than any winter coat she'd ever owned. "Call as late as you want."

"Okay. I'd better go. My aunt's giving me the evil eye."

"Have fun."

Ashley slipped the phone into her pocket, but the lift of her aunt's eyebrow told her the conversation was far from over.

"Who is Russ, and why are you blushing?"

How was she supposed to tell them about Tom's accident, the funeral, and the engagement? The airport didn't seem like the right place to have that conversation, especially the part about Russ.

"Sweetheart, are you okay?"

"Yeah. Russ is Tom's cousin. And I'm not blushing. It's a lot warmer here, that's all. Come on, Uncle John should be to the car by now." Ashley wheeled her suitcase away. "Why don't we figure out how to spend the next month?"

Rose slipped her hand around Ashley's arm. "We can, but you're going to tell me about Russ sooner than you think."

Great.

****

Rachel and Carrie talked, shaking their heads as Russ wove through the crowded restaurant toward his family. He didn't normally eat out twice in one day, but there was no rush to get home now that Ashley was gone. Instead, he looked around the table as he dropped onto the hard seat. "What happened to the boys?"

Chad motioned behind him. "Paul took them to play video games so your sisters could talk."

Rachel smacked Russ' arm. "Why are you still talking to Ashley? She left you at the altar. Again."

Liz leaned her shoulder against his, her blue eyes wide. "Did she change her mind?"

"No."

"Then why did she leave?"

Frustration tightened his shoulders. "I told her to go. She went to take care of her eighty-year-old uncle with a broken foot. Ashley didn't leave me at the altar again. She hasn't done it once."

"You could have at least called and saved us another trip into Boyne," Chad said. "This is costing me a fortune in gas money." Rachel elbowed her husband.

Russ chuckled. "And miss another opportunity for the Sister Inquisition?"

Chad shook his head. "You're nuts."

Three sets of eyes turned on him. Russ couldn't see his sisters' faces, but he suspected they weren't friendly. He raised a glass to his brother-in-law. Taking one for the team.

Carrie refocused on Russ. "Where's Mom?"

"We explained what was going on, so she decided to move back home. She was awake this morning when I took Ashley to the airport."

"How did she handle the news?"

Russ shrugged. "She seemed happy to see Ashley taking care of her family, and she believed me that we're not calling off the wedding."

"Are you certain she's not coming back for four weeks?" Chad said. "I'd like to plan ahead if possible, so I can adjust the budget for another trip to town."

"Four weeks is enough time to plan a proper wedding," Liz said, her voice perking up. "It shouldn't be hard to find a banquet room in December. We won't have many choices for flowers this time of year, but we can at least decorate and have some music. If I can find a place, who do we want to cater?"

Rachel huffed. "Why would you want to do that?"

Liz crossed her arms. "Ashley's going to be family, whether we like it or not. Instead of making her and Russ feel like they need to sneak around, maybe we should open the door and welcome her in."

"If she actually shows up."

Russ rolled his eyes. "She'll be here."

Liz pulled a pen out of her purse and brushed off a napkin. "Then let's give her a proper welcome. We could get poinsettias, go with a Christmas theme."

All three women talked simultaneously. Russ didn't understand most of it, but he understood "invitations" and "guest list." Warning bells sounded. "Hold on a second. We don't want anything big."

Carrie waved him off. "This isn't about you."

"How can it not be about me?" He looked among his sisters' faces, waiting for one of them to smile, but they'd never seemed so serious. "You're planning *my* wedding."

"No, we're planning Ashley's wedding," Rachel said. "I don't care what she told you. Every woman has expectations for her wedding day, even if it's small." She swiped his phone off the table. "I'll ask her myself."

Fear clenched at his heart as he reached for the phone, but Rachel shielded herself behind Chad. Russ' eye began to twitch. "Don't bother Ashley. Let her have some time with her aunt and uncle before you start harassing her."

"I'm not calling her this second. I'm just getting her number."

"I thought you didn't like Ashley. Why are you suddenly so helpful?"

Rachel passed his phone back to him. "I like her well enough. It's this whole situation that's ridiculous, but Liz has a point. Regardless of how much I dislike it, I'm not willing to let you mess it up even more by having a horrible wedding reception. We all know I plan the best parties. I'll call her in a few days and find out what she wants."

The thought of Rachel calling Ashley didn't do anything to calm Russ' nerves. When Carrie pulled out her phone, all-out panic grabbed him by the throat.

"Does Mrs. Hicks still cater?" Carrie asked. "She always had the best food."

"Too greasy," Rachel said. "Besides, she's probably a hundred years old by now."

Liz tapped the pen against her lips. "Russ, how can we reach Ashley's family?"

"She's with her family."

"No, how do we get ahold of everyone else?"

"She doesn't have anyone else. Just her aunt and uncle."

Liz's eyes widened, but Rachel and Carrie shook their heads, so she put pen to napkin, then faced Russ. "Okay then. We need to do whatever it takes to get them here. Who else should we invite?"

That was one detail Russ wanted a say in. "*Only* family." All eyes turned on him like he'd suggested they have the wedding at a nudist colony, but he wouldn't cave. "I'm serious. Uncle Bill, Aunt Rita, and the cousins. That's it."

Carrie cocked her head. "You know I'm not a fan of big parties, but even I think that's small for a wedding."

Russ pointed at each sister. "The three of you alone practically overwhelmed Ashley. She should enjoy her wedding, not be looking for an escape route. If you want to be there, then it's family only."

Their waitress showed up then, unloading trays full of sandwiches, chicken strips, and French fries. Chad headed toward the video games. The dinner pandemonium would give Russ at least thirty minutes of peace.

"Hi, Russ."

Or God could continue to test him. He turned to face the death of his reprieve. "Jess. I didn't realize you were still in town."

"Didn't you get my text?"

"I must have missed it."

She flashed an easy smile. "I'm glad I ran into you then. I'm going to be training employees in the area, so I'll be around for a while. Between that and vacation days, I should be here until Christmas."

Russ could feel the burn of his sisters' eyes on the back of his neck. Maybe he could get his meal to go.

"Unca Wuss!"

God bless toddlers. Phin ran straight for him.

"It's nice to see you, Jess." Russ picked up his nephew and plopped him onto his lap. "Maybe we'll run into each other again before you leave."

"I hope so." She squeezed his shoulder.

When he turned back to his family, Carrie raised a finger, her mouth open. Russ grabbed a fistful of French fries and gave them to Phin. "Dessert for anyone who keeps their mom and aunts too busy to talk to Uncle Russ!"

"Yeah!"

Blessed chaos.

CHAPTER 27

Ashley tossed her purse on the table, rolling her eyes as her uncle huffed behind her.

"All I'm saying is I've seen Mrs. Miner drive these streets. Pretty hypocritical of her to criticize anyone else's driving." He passed his cane to Rose, then shrugged out of his jacket. "Last week, I saw her—"

"There's a new winter cooking show starting tonight." Rose passed the cane back. "Why don't you find the channel while I make tea."

John snorted, but he hobbled into the living room.

Ashley slipped out of her coat. "Before I hang these up, are you sure we're done for the day? Uncle John's not going to think of another errand that can't wait until tomorrow?"

"Not with his cooking shows on."

"Then I'm going to disappear for the rest of the night."

Rose kissed Ashley's cheek as she handed over her and John's jackets. "You deserve a break. Thank you for playing chauffeur."

After hanging the coats in the hall closet, Ashley retreated to the guest room. She chuckled as she pulled the rainbow afghan off the bed and around her shoulders. It had been in the donation pile when she left Florida, but the blanket—as well as a few other colorful remnants from her childhood—had somehow made their way into the tan-and-cream bedroom. The fuzzy, blue pillows could stay with her aunt when she left, but she might take the blanket with her.

She grabbed her transcribing equipment from the dresser, then settled herself on the bed and got to work. The dining-room table would have been more comfortable, but also more distracting. John would have insisted she watch TV with them, and she rarely had a good enough reason to say no. Plus, if she finished her projects before Thanksgiving, she'd earn a small bonus that would help her buy toys for her soon-to-be nephews and niece.

PING!

Ashley jumped. Her back protested as she reached across the bed for her phone. Nine o'clock already? How had that happened?

R u awake?

Russ? Ashley rubbed her eyes. *Yes. Y r u?*

The phone rang, and she almost dropped it. She hadn't been that nervous since introducing her freshman homecoming date to her dad. With shaky fingers, she answered the call. "Hello?"

"I figured you'd still be up."

"Of course, but you're rubbing off on me. I'm already in bed. How did it go with your family?"

"Better than I expected."

"Have you been on the phone all day?"

"I didn't call anyone. I met them at the church."

Ashley gasped. "Why would you do that? They must think I'm—"

"They think *I'm* a jerk for not calling them, but I couldn't have the same conversation three times. They would have kept calling or texting me all day, and then I'd have to change my number. It's a hassle."

A tremor flittered through Ashley's chest. "I can't imagine they're too happy with me."

"Accidents happen. It wasn't your fault, and they know that. They did, um—" He cleared his throat. Something brushed against his phone, sending static through the receiver. She pictured him looking at the floor, avoiding imaginary eye contact. Finally, he sighed. "They decided to plan a wedding for you."

"They what? I didn't think they'd want to see me again."

"Why?"

"This is the second wedding I've missed."

"For good reason. Don't worry about it. I'll try to talk them out of it, but—"

"Don't do that!"

Silence.

"Are you there?"

"I thought you didn't want a wedding."

"I do, but considering our circumstances, I didn't want to be fighting with our families through the whole process. There's something nice about your sisters wanting to plan this for us, though." Ashley pictured her parents' wedding photos. Her mom in the beaded, puffy-sleeved dress. The crisp black tux her dad wore. "Can I break our agreement for a few minutes?"

"Which part?"

"Talking about Tom."

Russ sucked in a deep breath, blowing it into the phone. "I'll hear your argument, then decide if we should break procedure."

Ashley smiled. "Thank you. When Tom and I talked about our wedding, he was incredibly vague. He kept coming up with ideas, but we never settled on anything."

"That sounds like him."

"And now that I've met you all and realize he didn't tell anyone about me, well …"

"You're wondering if he ever really planned anything."

Ashley tucked the soft, Downy-fresh blanket under her chin. "Is that wrong?"

"No. That's Tom's way. He always had great ideas, but he never followed through. He probably thought up a dozen different ways to marry you and tell us about you, but he never did."

"That's a nice thought, but the truth is, I sort of stopped dreaming of a wedding when I realized he hadn't done anything."

"Why would you ever let him plan it, anyway?"

"It seemed like a good idea at the time. He knew the prettiest locations and the tastiest food, and I didn't know anything about Boyne Heights. Now that I say it out loud, it does sound pretty stupid, doesn't it?"

Russ laughed. "Don't be too hard on yourself. No one warned you not to ask Tom to plan anything. Especially a wedding."

"But now your sisters want to plan one, and that's kind of exciting. Running off by ourselves made me think of a shotgun wedding or two people sneaking off to do something forbidden. I like the idea of your family being there like they want to celebrate with us."

"I'm glad you feel that way because they've picked a reception site and they want to fly your aunt and uncle up. How did they take the news?"

The truth curdled in her stomach. "I haven't told them yet."

Russ cleared his throat. "Excuse me?"

"It's been a busy day. We've run a million errands, and Aunt Rose wanted to know all about Michigan. There hasn't been a good time to tell them about Tom."

"You haven't even told them about Tom yet?"

Ashley pulled the blanket closer, trying to block the sudden chill. "I haven't had a chance."

Another deep breath on the other end of the line. "Ashley, you're doing the same thing to your aunt and uncle that Tom did to us. Rachel wants to buy them plane tickets for the wedding, and they don't even know who you're marrying. I can tell you exactly how they're going to feel when they get the call and have no idea what she's talking about."

The weight of reality pushed her deeper onto the bed. "I didn't think about it that way."

"You need to tell them."

"I will."

"Tomorrow."

Ugh. "Fine."

"Rip off the Band-Aid."

"Yeah, yeah, yeah."

"Are you pouting?"

"I don't pout."

"It sounds like a pout." His voice stayed even, but Ashley could hear the smile in his voice.

"I promise I'll talk to them."

"Thank you. Did you want to talk about your day?"

"Are you sure? It's getting late."

"I don't mind."

That's right. He received late-night text messages too. "I don't want to bore you with details about the pharmacy and my uncle's fourteen trips to the grocery store. I'm actually working on a transcription right now. I was hoping to finish it tonight."

"I'll let you get back to it then. I'll talk to you tomorrow?"

She hoped so.

* * * * * * *

Russ handed another file to Chad. "Why do we have so many useless files?"

"Employee records aren't useless."

"They aren't helping."

"If you'd keep track of everything you signed, this wouldn't be an issue."

"I never had to worry about it before. Then again, I never thought Tom would will away the family house, so ..." The ancient heater growled, then hissed, blowing musty air through the office.

Chad flipped through another folder before tossing it on the growing pile on the floor. "How many more drawers do we have to go through?"

"This is the last drawer in this cabinet."

"How many more cabinets?"

Russ looked up from the papers in his hand. "Two, but I think one of those has my paperwork in it."

"You don't even know where you keep *your* files?" Chad shook his head. "I can't believe we're still in business."

The front door opened, blasting the small space with cold air. Wayne Dunville. Great. "Councilman," Russ said, "it's nice to see you."

The stocky, curly-haired man walked toward the desks, the top of his head level with Chad's shoulder. "It's Wayne, please. I'm sorry to stop by without an appointment, but I haven't been able to reach you by phone."

For a reason. Russ tapped into his manners and motioned toward the kitchenette. "Can I get you some coffee? Water?"

"I'm fine, thank you. I would like a few minutes of your time, though."

Chad picked up a stack of manila folders and made his way across the office. Russ motioned toward the vacant chair. "What can I do for you?"

When Wayne sat, he practically disappeared behind the desk. "I wanted to talk to you about the farmland preservation effort."

"I'm not selling the farm."

"I'm not asking you to. I need to know if you're interested in turning part of it into a learning and preservation area."

"Chad told me about that. You want to let college kids come in and farm the land. There isn't a formula they can learn in one semester. I don't want kids coming and going, destroying the land and my trees."

"It wouldn't be like that." Wayne picked up a bag Russ hadn't noticed him carrying. He pulled out a shiny yellow folder and set it in front of Russ. "Central Northern Michigan College contacted me about a program they're trying to set up. They want to develop a hands-on, multicurricular program that will teach all aspects of farm management, not just the agriculture or business side."

"What does that have to do with me?"

"They need a farm. They aren't expecting large numbers in the program, so the farm can't be too big, but it needs to be big enough for the students to get experience outside and in the office."

In the office? Russ glanced at the tower of files. "What kind of office work?"

"Students will be required to learn all aspects of farm management. That includes accounting, employee records, and general office management."

Interesting, but "I don't want a bunch of kids accessing my accounts and legal affairs. And I won't be able to teach them anything about it anyway. This was Tom's thing. You can see what's happened since I took over, and it's only been two weeks."

Wayne pointed at the yellow folder. "If you'll read through the information, you'll see how the school plans to make it work. This is an inclusive, interactive program. The business department is involved for office management and accounting. Natural sciences will offer the agricultural studies."

"Why my farm? There are hundreds of farms in the area."

"But not many are the right size *and* have your family's history attached." Wayne flipped through the folder. "Somewhere in here is a history tract. They would like to work on a centennial farm so the history department has the option to get involved and do genealogy work. All of the students would work here as interns."

Russ picked up the folder. Growing up on the farm, he'd never needed an internship, but he'd heard good things from others about their experiences. Maybe he could provide that opportunity to someone else. Besides, even if it didn't work out, a business professor couldn't possibly make the office situation any worse.

The idea had merit. He dropped the folder on the desk. "I suppose I could talk to the dean about it. Why did he send you, anyway? What does any of this have to do with the township?"

"If the history department gets involved, we can apply for farmland preservation status and assistance from the state. You may qualify for funding."

Funding? Russ' shoulders tensed. "You think I need grant money to run my farm?"

Wayne leaned back, his tired eyes trained on Russ. "It's no secret that things have been hard since your dad died. I can't imagine things will be any easier now. I'm not trying to be coldhearted. I'm trying to help. This was a good idea last month when I first called you about it. It's still a good idea, and it might make the transition easier."

Anger rolled through Russ. "I'm not walking away from my farm—from my family—because you think I can't run the business without Tom."

"That's not what I—"

"This farm has supported my family for four generations. I'm not turning it over to a bunch of eighteen-year-olds who want to pick cherries one year and design video games the next because farm work is too hard, and the township doesn't think I can handle it!"

"Russ, I didn't mean—"

"I don't care." But the pain and frustration rushed to the surface. "The Russell family farm is not for sale, it's not for consideration, and it's not going to be a stomping ground for kids! I think you'd better—"

"Leave that folder here, and we'll take a look at it." Chad walked over and pushed Russ back down onto his chair.

Wayne offered his hand to Chad. "I realize the timing isn't great, and I'm sorry about the circumstances, but I wanted to give you the information. I've always respected your family and all you do for the community. I think this is a good opportunity for all of us. I don't need an answer until the end of the year, but the school needs to plan, and I'll need to start paperwork for the state historical society."

Chad pumped Wayne's arm. "We'll get back to you."

"I'd appreciate it. And please, read the paperwork. It should answer most of your questions."

Russ shifted in his seat, but Chad's hand anchored him to the chair. Fine. Russ nodded once. "Thanks for the information. You can leave now." Vice-like fingers crushed his shoulder before Chad escorted the councilman from the building.

The nerve. Insulting Russ' abilities. Butting in on family business. Russ scrubbed a hand over his face, trying to erase the image of the township official.

Normalcy. That was all he wanted. Why couldn't anyone leave him alone and let things get back to normal?

When Russ slid his hands down his face, his gaze landed on the ugly yellow folder staining the crowded desk. He tossed it on the table behind him. He would read through it after finishing the documents already in front of him.

Chad reclaimed the seat across from him. "Now what?"

"I haven't got a clue. Rob's supposed to be looking into this too. Maybe he's had some luck." Russ picked up the office phone and dialed.

"Rob Kraft."

"It's Russ. How's it going with the document search? Have you found anything yet?"

"Hi, Russ, I'm fine thanks. How are things with you?"

"Sorry. How's the family?"

"They're good. How's Ashley?"

"She's good."

"I hear she's in Florida."

"Word travels fast. She had to go take care of her uncle."

"So I heard. You two still planning on getting married?"

Apparently he'd heard everything. "We are."

"Then there's no rush on the paperwork, right? I mean the farm isn't in any jeopardy. You'll share the house. Nothing to worry about."

"I guess, but I need to take care of this. If anything ever happened to me, I wouldn't want to leave my sisters with this kind of mess."

"I'll keep digging around, but I haven't found anything yet. I'll call you if that changes."

"I'd appreciate it."

Russ hung up as Chad closed another file. At their current rate of speed, the rest of their week might revolve around those stupid files. The piles weren't going anywhere, and Rob had a point. What was the rush? Russ smacked the desk. "I'm done for the day. How about you?"

"Leo's having listening issues lately. Rachel would probably appreciate it if I gave her a break."

"Then let's get out of here and take tomorrow off too. Our brains need a break. Nothing's going to change while we're gone."

"I'm glad you're finally taking time off."

"Only because I don't want to do paperwork." Russ didn't bother straightening the desk. It would be easier to pick up where he left off if he left everything where it was, open folder and all.

"What are you going to do with your free time?" Chad shrugged into his coat, heading for the door. "If you want to spend some quality time with your nephews, I can arrange for babysitting at my house."

"Not going to happen." Russ slid into his coat as he followed Chad outside. The phone buzzed in his pocket. "I'd better check this. Say hi to Rachel."

Chad climbed into his truck.

Hi Russ. Going 2 TC tonite for errands. Join me for dinner? Jess

He didn't have time for this. Stuffing the phone back into his pocket, he ran to Chad's truck. "How would you and Rachel like to go out to dinner tonight?"

CHAPTER 28

Ashley held her mother's journal as she rocked herself in the wicker rocking chair on Rose and John's porch. Nearly identical houses lined the quiet street. White-trimmed porches, windows, and rooflines accented various shades of tan siding. Young palm trees dotted the yards. A white-haired man waved at her as he drove his golf cart down the wide, winding street.

Rose walked along the sidewalk toward the house, her skin glistening in the afternoon sun. "What are you up to today?" she asked, skipping up the front steps.

"Enjoying the Florida sun. How was your walk?"

Her aunt adjusted the hem of her pink velour jacket. "Lonely without John. Where is the old coot?"

"I lost track of him. He's probably retiling the kitchen."

"That man doesn't understand how to rest." Rose sat on the matching rocker beside Ashley. "Speaking of men, how's Tom? And tell me about Russ."

Ashley's foot slipped across the decking. Even though she'd promised Russ that she'd tell them, she had managed to avoid the subject for a few days. Apparently her time was up. "What would you like to know?"

"You haven't told us much. If you aren't driving us around, you're out taking pictures or transcribing something. I want to hear about this new family of yours. Russ sounded nice on the phone. Why was he there with you?"

"Russ is Tom's cousin."

"So you mentioned. His name seems to make you blush."

Ashley pressed her hands to her cheeks. "I didn't realize."

"Why does he make you blush?"

"I don't know." Liar.

"Do you like him?"

"Yes."

Her aunt stopped rocking. "What about Tom?"

Ashley drew in a calming breath. Now or never. "There was an accident, and Tom was killed three weeks ago—"

"Sweetheart!" Rose covered her mouth with her hands. "Why didn't you call? Are you okay?"

Ashley squeezed her aunt's knee. "I didn't find out until I got to Boyne Heights. That's why he didn't call me before I left. I thought maybe he'd extended his trip, but"—sorrow weighed on her shoulders—"he died in a hiking accident."

"Why didn't someone call you?"

Embarrassment warmed Ashley from the inside. She leaned back in the rocker, turning her attention to a couple walking on the other side of the street. "He didn't tell anyone I was coming."

"But they could have called—"

"No one knew about me. He never told them."

The blades of the chairs creaked against the composite decking. Muted chatter floated through the air. The woman beside Ashley, however, didn't make a sound.

"It's not as bad as it sounds."

"It sounds like you avoided an awful mistake."

Ashley's jaw dropped. "Aunt Rose! Tom is dead. That's hardly appropriate."

"What's inappropriate is a man asking you to give up your life, to relocate for him, then treating you like some awful secret. Why wouldn't he tell anyone?" Rose crossed her arms, her face tight. The corner of her eye twitched like it had when she found the neighbor's dog digging up her flower bed.

Ashley sandwiched her aunt's hand between hers. "Please don't be upset for me. The last couple of weeks have been hard for everyone. My discomfort hardly matters compared to everyone else's loss."

"But that doesn't mean it hasn't been hard on you too. Why didn't you tell me? I would have come up to see you. How are you doing with all of this? It can't be easy, especially all by yourself."

Ashley leaned back and resumed rocking. "I cried the first two nights, and I started sleepwalking again."

"Oh, sweetheart, are you sure you're okay?"

"I am, mostly. It's all so surreal."

"Is this how you met Russ? Because of Tom's accident?"

"Yes. Russ and Tom were roommates."

"Did *he* at least know about you?"

"Russ and I have spent a lot of time together. It's been nice to have someone to talk to and mourn with. He really has been a godsend. I don't know what I would have done without his friendship."

"I'm glad he was there for you, but what are you going to do now? I don't think it would be a problem for you to live here for a few months, or did you want to go back to Cincinnati?"

"It's too late for that. The new owners closed on the house before we got you and Uncle John settled here for the winter."

"Maybe our Ohio rental is available. We can call the landlord and see if he has space."

"Actually, I sort of have a place."

"Thank goodness." Rose exhaled, relaxing into a synchronized rhythm with Ashley. "Where are you staying?"

"Tom left me his house."

"In Michigan? You want to stay there after everything that happened?"

"There's more." Ashley focused on the view ahead of her, careful not to look directly at her aunt. "Russ has agreed to marry me."

The rocking stopped. Out of the corner of her eye, Ashley watched Rose stand. She braced herself for whatever her aunt had to say. It couldn't be worse than anything Russ' sisters had said. Instead, she stepped in front of Ashley, her face blank and eyes staring into space. Then she walked past her and into the house.

"Aunt Rose?"

The screen door clicked shut, creating the largest barrier that had separated them in nearly two decades. Of all the scenarios Ashley had imagined, silence hadn't been one of them.

As her nerves trembled, she rubbed her hand across the soft, worn cover of her mother's journal. Mom would have liked Russ and had always wanted to see Ashley get married. It shouldn't matter how she got there, right? So why was Rose so upset? A mixture of guilt and panic gripped Ashley's chest. She hadn't expected her aunt and uncle to fully embrace the quick engagement, but to turn their backs on her? Tears filled her eyes, but she willed them to stay in place. She had to fix this.

The door swished.

"Aunt Rose?" Ashley jumped up but met the tired eyes of her uncle.

"Why don't you come inside and talk to your aunt and me?" He held the door open, but his gaze went back inside.

Would neither of them look at her? Ashley's heart ached in a way she'd never experienced, in a way worse than loss.

She picked up the journal and shuffled across the deck as one of the tears escaped. John opened the door wider for her to slip past his extra-large foot and cane. She couldn't look at him as she made her way to Rose sitting at the dining-room table.

"Let me explain. I didn't mean to upset you." Ashley sat across from her. "The situation is unusual, but please trust me."

The soft thump of John's cast set a somber tempo as he joined them. "Your aunt didn't tell me everything, but when I see my sweetheart this upset, it's time to step in. Do you want to tell me what's going on?"

Ashley rehashed the conversation. Rose didn't look any happier. John's face wrinkled even more, his normally cheerful eyes darkening. "You're going to marry this man?" he asked.

"We were supposed to get married Saturday but agreed to postpone the wedding so I could be with you. We're planning on getting married when I go back next month."

Only the ceiling fan dared speak. The silence pounded in Ashley's ears. "He's a great guy. You'd like him. I'm sure Mom would have."

"You've known him for two weeks." Rose shook her head. "This is a lifetime commitment. You can't change your mind in a year or two."

"I understand that, but I'm not worried. Mom had her doubts about Dad, but—"

"Your mom and dad knew each other for years before they started dating." She twisted the wedding ring around her finger. "This isn't the same. Your mother wanted you to fall in love and start a family, not marry some random man so you could say that you're married. She wanted you to have a good life, not simply go through the motions. I can't." Shaking her head again, she pushed her chair back, then headed to the kitchen.

Drawers and cupboards pounded out an unsteady beat. Ashley had to make this right. "I'm sorry I didn't tell you sooner, but I didn't know *how* to tell you," she said. "Then I thought forgiveness would be easier than permission." Obviously not.

Rose sniffled. "You were going to get married without us. If John hadn't tripped … you weren't going to tell us? I would have missed your wedding."

"What can I do to help you feel better about this?" Ashley turned so she could see her aunt. "I didn't expect you to be thrilled about the situation, but I don't want to do this without your blessing either."

"Then you may need to give us time to get used to the idea," John said. "Why do you want to do this, anyway? Why not move back to Ohio? You have friends there."

"Because I don't want to move backward. Yes, Russ and I just met, but Tom told me so much about him that it feels like I've known him for months. When Russ told me Tom had died …" Ashley sighed, propping her elbows on the table and leaning forward. "When I told Russ about me and Tom, he didn't pity me. He didn't try to cheer me up. Instead, he invited me to join the family and introduced me to everyone. He welcomed me."

Rose returned and set three mugs on the table. "Do you love Russ?"

"It's been two weeks."

"You're blushing again."

Ashley covered her cheeks.

John grunted. "If you're going to marry this man when you go back, then I suppose that gives you four weeks to get to know him first. You can do the computer thing again. It worked for you and Tom."

"But they spent six months dating, or whatever you want to call it." Rose sat beside her husband. "Six weeks isn't enough time."

"It's better than two weeks, Rosie."

A flicker of hope sparked in Ashley's heart. "Are you giving me your blessing?"

John shook his head. "I can't honestly tell you that I'm happy about this, or that I want you to go through with it, but you've got a month to figure out if this is what you really want."

"It is. I've thought—"

He held up his hand. "I don't doubt you've thought about this, but I want you to be confident in your decision. If you're still sure at the end of the month, then I'll bless it."

The teakettle whistled, but Rose didn't move. "You can't be serious. This is crazier than the online dating."

"She's a grown woman. We can't ground her."

"What if he's taking advantage of her and her situation? She's beautiful and vulnerable. That's no way to start a relationship, much less a marriage."

"I didn't say it was, but what do you want to do, forbid it?"

"We don't have to encourage it!"

Ashley's heart deflated. It was bad enough that they worried about her. Now they were fighting because of her. Was it worth it? Her hand instinctively went to the journal.

Grief clung to her like the humidity clung to her skin. Russ had a large family to console him, but she only had her aunt and uncle. She couldn't please Russ *and* them, but she couldn't do something that would hurt them either. Regret clawed at Ashley's throat. "I won't do it."

Rose and John stopped arguing.

Ashley swallowed. "If it upsets you this much, I won't do it. Russ and I tried to make this a practical decision, to do what we thought was right, but it's upsetting everyone. I don't know how he moved past his family's reaction to the news, but I can't. I don't want you fighting because of me. I won't do this if it upsets you this much. I'll call it off."

Her aunt's eyebrows pressed together. "You would do that?"

She offered a weak smile. "I'd do anything for you. I never wanted to upset you."

John whacked his cane on the ground. "You can't *not* marry the boy to make Rosie happy any more than you should marry him for your mom. What do *you* want, Ashley?"

"I want a family, and you *are* my family. It would be stupid to hurt my relationship with you to start another family with someone else." The words sounded good, but her heart wasn't convinced.

Rose finally rushed to the kitchen and silenced the whistling kettle. Ashley didn't need to see her to know that she would come back with peppermint tea, and they would have apple pie for her uncle's birthday, sweet-potato pie for Thanksgiving, roast lamb at Easter, and every other tradition Ashley grew up with. She didn't need kids around the Christmas tree or a house full of siblings on the Fourth of July. Rose and John had always been enough. They would be again.

Her uncle shook his head. "Now who's upset?"

Rose returned with the kettle and filled their mugs. Minty steam billowed out of the cups. Resting the kettle on a trivet, she sat beside John, who handed her his hankie.

"What a fine bunch we are," he said. "Rosie's trying to do what's right for you, and you're trying to please your mom and Rosie, but what has that accomplished? Everyone's frustrated and no one's happy. Maybe it's time to stop worrying about everyone else and start doing the right thing, even if that means someone else doesn't like it."

With a whack of his cane, he stood. "Enough of this for now. It's going to be a beautiful day. Why don't we drive down to Venice and have dinner at that restaurant you girls like? We'll be there early enough to look around the shops and still be back before dark."

Her aunt sniffed but nodded. "I need to shower and change first."

"Then get moving. We've got to beat the crowd."

She patted Ashley's shoulder as she walked around the table, then disappeared into the bedroom.

"She'll be okay eventually," he said. "Give her time."

"I'm doing the right thing, Uncle John."

"I figured so."

"I feel peaceful when I think about marrying Russ."

"That may be, but you certainly don't look peaceful right now."

She didn't feel it either. "Telling you didn't go quite the way I'd expected. It was completely different when Russ told his family."

"How so?"

"He told them. They argued. He won."

"It's not about winning," he said. "Marrying Tom was what you wanted, but now you want to marry Russ for practical reasons, whatever that means. And a minute ago you said you wouldn't marry him for your aunt, but you think this would make your mom happy.

"I love Rosie, and your mother was one of my favorite people, but this is your life, no one else's. You've got to figure this out." He carried his tea to the couch. "I've never understood the female brain, but you're in a league of your own. The only other person I've ever met like you was your mom. You're more alike than that journal will ever show you."

"Really?" Ashley ignored her tea and joined him on the couch, always eager to hear stories about her parents. She settled beside him on the beige-and-gray tweed upholstery. Rose had tried to soften the look of the living room by crocheting pastel arm covers and afghans. The contrast reflected her and John's personalities, which comforted Ashley as she gave her uncle her attention.

"When your mom was in college, she had all kinds of ideas about what she wanted to do with her life. She changed her mind every few months, deciding to go here and do that. It made Rosie crazy, all of the uncertainty and change."

"But I've never been like that. I lived in the same house my entire life. I've had the same boring job for years."

"Until you found your mother's journal."

Three years ago, somehow hidden in a box Ashley had never fully emptied. She smiled. "Mom dreamed about all kinds of things. We never had a chance to talk about most of them, so reading about them was like meeting her for the first time."

"Ever since you found that thing, you've reminded me more of your mom, which is how I remember you as a child."

"What do you mean?"

"As a kid you were always trying new things, looking for something fun to do. You would play a different board game every day for a week, but when you found the game you liked, we couldn't pull you away from it. That's how your mom was. She took five and a half years to graduate from college because she kept switching majors until she found a subject she liked.

"You were like that before your parents died. I suppose it makes sense that you picked up some of Rosie's traits when we started seeing you more often, but you weren't always so practical."

"Did I really change that much?"

"Not all at once, but over the years. You've spent as much time being our girl as you were with your parents, so I can understand the change, but it's fun to see your spirit re-emerging."

John chuckled. "Your mom and Rosie used to get into awful fights. Your mom wanted to explore all of her options, and Rosie wanted her to settle down and figure her life out. The ten-year age difference didn't help either. You never met your mom's oldest sisters, but they grew up in a different era, much more traditional. Rosie was stuck between their influences and your mom's. She tried to accept their traditions and your mother's free spirit, but she usually came home all worked up."

"Do you think my mom would have married a man this fast? Is that why Aunt Rose is so upset?"

"I can't guess about what your mom would do, but these last three years have been wonderful watching you step back into yourself. It's more uncertainty than your aunt's had to deal with in years. Give her time. Your mother's starting to influence you again, so Rosie has to give up some of her influence. Not easy for a seventy-five-year-old beauty like her."

"Do you think I'm giving my mom's journal too much influence?

John shook his head, his face tense. "You're still too focused on what you think everyone else wants, honey. You did everything for your aunt, and then for your mom. *You* need to figure out what you need to do. This isn't about them. It's about you."

Ashley heard his words, but they rattled around in her heart. "I don't want to hurt either of them."

"You can't hurt your mother, and you can't keep trying to please everyone else. I promise you, though, if you're sure this is the right decision for you, Rosie will support it."

CHAPTER 29

Finally—silence. Russ peeked into the boys' rooms, confirming that all three were in their own beds before heading downstairs. His nephews had maneuvered their bedtime back by well over an hour, but *Monday Night Football* would still be on. Not how he'd imagined his evening, but better than a night alone. Or with Jess.

He flipped on the TV as his phone rang. Only Ashley called this late. Without taking his eyes off the game, he answered the phone. "I was hoping you'd call."

"I'm glad to hear that."

"Jess? Sorry, I thought you were Ashley."

"Are you sure? I heard she left town."

The referee blew his whistle. "Still engaged."

"We'll see."

"Did you need something?" The Cowboys lined up on the Eagles' twenty-five-yard line. Not his favorite teams, but a game was a game.

"Russ, did you hear me?"

"What? No, sorry. The game's on."

"I won't keep you long. I heard that Ashley skipped the wedding again, and I wanted to see if you're okay."

"Her uncle broke his foot, so she went to help out. Everything else is fine."

"Listen, I know the timing is weird, but I'm serious about the dinner invite, especially now that your fiancée's gone."

Whistles sounded, but they weren't coming from the television. "Jess—"

"It could be a good distraction."

"A distraction from what?"

"It's a big house, Russ. It can't be easy sitting there alone every night."

Which was one of the reasons he didn't mind babysitting. Of course, the other reason was on the other end of the phone.

"It's just dinner," she said. "We can catch up, talk about the farm. My parents heard you were working with Central Northern Michigan College on a new agribusiness program. I'd love to hear about it."

"Is there anything you haven't heard?"

"Small towns."

God bless Boyne Heights. "I don't actually know much about the program. I haven't looked through the paperwork yet."

"Bring it with you. We can figure out what they're proposing and see if it's anything you should consider."

That idea definitely had merit. While Jess might have made a mess of her social life, she had a great mind for economics, especially when it came to the farming industry. Even Tom had recognized it. Russ wouldn't mind hearing her opinion. "I could certainly use some advice on this one, but—"

"I know, I know. It's not a date. In fact, you can do it as a favor for me. I'm staying with my parents for the next few weeks, and they're already making me crazy. If you don't need the distraction, I do."

Russ kept his eyes on the game as he mulled his options. A quiet night at home with nothing to do except think about Ashley, or a couple of hours with an agribusiness expert and Wayne Dunville's information folder.

"Russ?"

"Honestly, I could use the help. As long we're clear—this is business only."

"Got it. And I really think I can help. Consider it an apology for the way I acted. Besides"—she chuckled—"we both know you'd rather move manure than papers."

He laughed. "The township supervisor tried to explain it, but I wasn't in the mood to talk. If you could give me your personal and professional opinion, I'd appreciate it."

"Done. I have a business meeting tomorrow night, but I'm free the night after. Why don't we go to that oyster bar in Charlevoix? I have to drive by your place on the way, so I can pick you up. I should be done around six."

"Sounds good. Meet me at the house and we'll carpool."

"I'll see you then."

Russ tossed his phone on the coffee table, never taking his eyes off the TV. Fumble, recovery, first down. Technically an exciting game, one of the best quarterbacks in the league versus a top-two defensive line, but he couldn't focus.

That didn't make sense. Good football. A stomach full of extra-pepperoni pizza. Free professional advice from one of the smartest business minds he knew. So why didn't it feel right?

PING.

Ashley! How could he have been so stupid? He'd just agreed to have dinner with a woman who wasn't his fiancée. The pizza punched him in the gut. Russ checked the message.

Rough day. Can we talk about it 2morrow?

His shoulders tensed. *R u ok?* The television crowd cheered, but Russ couldn't pull his eyes from the tiny screen in his hand.

I'm ok. U?

Babysitting for Rachel. What time 2morrow? Want 2 catch up. He glanced up long enough to see the right tackle sack the quarterback. Half of the stadium cheered.

Will text a time in the morning. Don't know 2morrow's plans yet. Shouldn't B 2 late.

Talk 2 u then. Russ was about to toss the phone back to the table when it pinged again.

Miss u.

His gut burned. How could two words stir so many emotions? He didn't want to push Ashley, but he couldn't help it. *Miss u 2.*

He set the phone on the couch beside him as he tried to refocus on the game, but those two words kept popping into his mind. And then he tried to imagine her rough day. How rough was rough? Could he help? He didn't like leaving the conversation like that. Even if they didn't talk about her problems, he wasn't going to ignore Ashley for the Cowboys. *Monday Night Football* wasn't that important.

PING.

☺ *How are the boys?*

His chest warmed. Not important at all.

CHAPTER 30

Ashley spread the brochures across the table. Greece. Hawaii. Alaska. Vietnam. Stark-white buildings surrounding crystal-blue bays. Pink leis on tanned skin. Brilliant, snow-covered mountains. Curved rooftops and straight-lined Asian buildings. The most beautiful places she'd ever seen, or dreamed of seeing.

John set a plate of cookies in front of her. She snatched up the cream-filled goodness. "Thank you. What's with the brochures?"

He picked up the Vietnam packet and flipped through the glossy pages. "This is a test."

"I'm pretty good at geography."

"But not decision-making. I've got some money saved up, and I'd like to send you and Russ on a honeymoon if you decide to marry him."

A chunk of cookie lodged in her throat before she choked it down. "You can't pay for my honeymoon."

"Of course I can. Your mom had a wedding account for you, and Rosie has been adding to it for years. If you're not going to use it all on this wedding, at least let me send you someplace nice."

"Uncle John, I can't—"

"You don't have a choice. You're taking a honeymoon, and I'm paying for it, but here's the catch. You have to pick the location. By. Your. Self."

Ashley looked at the booklets. Gratitude and love replaced the chunk of cookie in her throat. "I don't know what to say."

"You don't need to say anything right now. Read through the brochures and tell me where you want to go. I'll make all the arrangements for you. And when I say I'll do it, I mean Rosie will do it so it'll be done right."

A honeymoon. Ashley flipped through the Alaska book. Whales jumped out of midnight-blue seas. Moose grazed along winding rivers. Jagged mountaintops sliced into a cloudless sky. "My mom talked about going to Alaska."

He chuckled.

"What are these?" Rose appeared beside Ashley. "Hawaii! I've always wanted to visit the islands." She picked up the tropical catalog. "What an amazing place. Imagine, walking around on top of a live volcano. Is someone planning a trip?"

Ashley looked at her uncle, who shrugged. "I haven't planned anything yet, but I'm thinking about it."

"I vote for Hawaii. One of these days, I'll convince John to go with me." She tossed the book back on the table. "Of course, he'd go to Vietnam if he could. I'm not surprised he's holding onto that one."

The light bulb went on. Ashley's family's favorite places. "Uncle John—"

"Too many people think of the war when they think of Vietnam, but it's a beautiful place to see." He winked at Ashley. "Rosie, are we still going to the grocery store today? I have a few things I'd like to pick up."

"Let me get some paper so you can make a list."

As she walked away, Ashley smacked his knee. He winced, but she rolled her eyes. "Too late for the weak-and-feeble card. I'm on to you, and I see what you're doing. These are all your favorite places. And Greece, where my parents met during a semester abroad."

John's smile consumed his face, radiating equal parts mischief and delight. "You need to figure out what you want and why you want it. I'm done watching you settle because you think it's what someone else wants for you, and you'd better be able to convince me this is what you want, or I may not pay for your trip." He dropped a warm kiss on her cheek. "And don't tell your aunt, but I already bought our tickets to Hawaii."

Ashley wrapped her arms around his waist. "I've never met another man as wonderful as you."

He gave her hair a tug. "They're out there, but this kind of wisdom comes with lots of experience. I hope this young man of yours can live up to the standard."

"He's doing well so far."

"The two of you." Rose returned, shaking her head but smiling. "Hurry up and make your list. If we leave early enough, we can make it home before it heats up too much. Temperatures are supposed to be high this week. It might be a good time to work in the garden."

Ashley didn't need the unseasonable temperatures. The comfort and love of her family warmed her to her bones.

* * * * * * *

Russ peeked through the window as he tugged on the worn leather gloves. He would never complain about the heat again. Having to choose between frozen fingers or the bulky gloves while working on the truck was a nuisance. Either way, things took twice as long. Too bad his truck didn't care about the temperature. Oil needed changing.

He opened the front door and stepped into the biting wind. Exactly fifty-two steps and he'd be in the barn. Pressing his chin to his chest, he lengthened his stride. Halfway across the yard, his phone rang. Without pausing, he pulled it from his pocket.

Ashley.

Smiling, he swiped the screen. The phone kept ringing. Stupid smart screen. He yanked off his glove and answered the call. "Hey, stranger. I expected to hear from you yesterday. Is everything okay?"

"That's a matter of opinion." Ashley sighed. "I told my aunt and uncle about Tom ... and you."

"It doesn't sound like it went well. Is there anything I can do to help?"

"I don't think so, but thanks for offering. Do you have time to talk? Aunt Rose and Uncle John are playing cards, so I have some privacy."

"Sure. Let me head back to the house. It'll be warmer there than in the barn."

"Did I interrupt anything? I don't want to—"

"You're not." Russ spun around. "I'm just ... Jess."

"You're what?"

The familiar black Jetta rolled up the driveway, Jess behind the wheel. What was she—oh no. Dinner.

"Russ?"

"Jess is here."

Nothing.

"I'd forgotten all about it. She called the other night before we started texting."

"And you're ..."

"Having dinner tonight. It's a business meeting. She agreed to look at the farm proposal from the township and college."

"Farm proposal? What's that? You've never mentioned it."

"Honestly, I have no idea. It's an internship program with the college, but I haven't even opened the folder. Jess volunteered to look at it. It's only dinner. It's not as bad as it sounds."

"It sounds like you're having dinner with your ex-girlfriend so the two of you can discuss *our* farm without me."

"Okay, it's exactly like it sounds. I'll cancel."

"Why would you talk to her about it instead of me? I've been self-employed for almost two decades. I do have some business acumen."

"Jess works in the business development department of the MSU extension office. Her background is AgBioResearch, so—"

"Ag, what?"

The Jetta stopped in front of the house. Jess raised an eyebrow.

Russ pointed to his phone. "Basically, she's an expert at helping farmers get started and stay in business. She'll be able to tell me if the college's proposal is worth considering."

"And I don't know anything about farming, so you didn't think to include me."

"I didn't do it on purpose. This is all new to me. It's always been Tom and I making decisions about everything. I didn't mean to exclude you."

"Why are you considering this program? Is the farm in trouble?"

"No, but I'm going to need help eventually."

"From your stalker ex-girlfriend. Over dinner."

"I'll cancel."

Ashley let out a long, slow breath. "Don't do that, especially if she's already there. Get her expert advice, then tell me what you find out."

"I'll call you later tonight and tell you everything."

"Don't worry about it. We can talk tomorrow."

But he didn't want to wait that long, and he needed to show her he cared. "Jess can wait. What did you want to talk about?"

"Greece."

"What about it?"

"How do you feel about it?"

"I hear they've had some financial troubles recently. Why?"

"It's a project I'm working on. Would you ever want to visit Greece?"

"I've never thought about it."

"Gut reaction. Time and cost are not a problem, would you ever want to visit Greece?"

"Sure, why not?"

"Hmmm."

"Was that the wrong answer?"

"There's no wrong answer. What about Hawaii?"

"You're planning an escape, aren't you?"

"I told you, it's a project."

"I've heard good things about Hawaii."

"Would you ever want to go there?"

"If I didn't have to work, and money wasn't an option, sure. Why not?"

She sighed. "Is there anyplace you wouldn't go if you didn't have to work, and money wasn't an option?"

"Not really."

She groaned.

"Wrong answer?"

"Technically, there are no wrong answers."

It didn't sound that way. "Are you sure you're okay? I can cancel tonight so we can talk about this."

"I appreciate it, but this is my project, and you have yours. I should get back to it." Though the tightness in her voice didn't sound like she was looking forward to it.

"Call me if you need anything. At any time."

"Have fun with Jess."

* * * * * * *

Russ opened the restaurant door so Jess wouldn't bump into it, her eyes buried in the yellow folder. He grabbed her arm an instant before she stepped in front of a bustling waitress. "Would you like to take a second to pick a table," he asked, "or do you trust me to find a good spot?"

"I'm almost done. Give me a minute."

He steered her around the tables to an empty booth near the back, then slid into the seat while she continued reading. When she finally looked up, he held out her car keys. "You'll probably want these later."

She snagged the keys as she took her seat. "Thanks again for driving. I'm glad I got to read this." Jess slid the folder across the table to him. "This could be a great opportunity."

"Really?"

She laughed. "Don't look so surprised. CNMC may be small, but it's a good school. They've obviously put a lot of thought into this. If you don't take advantage of it, I may recommend a few other farms to them."

"Now you've made me curious." Russ leaned forward. "What are the benefits?"

A waitress stepped up to the table and smiled. Russ sat back and listened to her spiel, but Jess had piqued his interest. If she recommended this program, then it had to be good. If it was good, it wasn't something Wayne threw together a week ago to help after Tom's death. And if it wasn't the township's awkward attempt to support Russell Farms through a family tragedy, it might be worth considering.

The waitress finally walked away. This time Jess leaned forward. "You should talk with the college to nail down the details, but this looks good, Russ."

"A bunch of eighteen-year-olds running around the farm for the summer doesn't sound good."

"How old were you when you started working with your dad?"

"That's irrelevant."

She crossed her arms.

He scowled. "Five."

"Exactly. And don't Carrie's and Rachel's boys work with you during the summer? Age isn't an issue. Besides, this isn't an introductory-level course. It's a program the students will commit to for at least twelve months, and they'd consider making it a two-year program if things go well. It starts mid–school year in January and runs through December. It won't only be extra help. You'll get to teach."

"I'm not a teacher."

"You don't have to be. You'll have one or two students working with you all season. You'll get to teach them the way your dad taught you."

A chance to share his passion, to inspire someone. Anticipation coursed through him but, "What about the office? I can handle the trees, but I need someone inside."

"You need someone to do that anyway. You can't rely on the college to run your business."

Russ slouched in his seat. "I figured that was too much to hope for. What do you suggest?"

The waitress returned to take their orders, delivered their food, and topped off their coffees twice as Jess walked him through the internship program, referring often to the folder. When the waitress finally cleared their plates, Jess glanced at her watch. Her eyes widened. "It's nine-thirty."

"A night well spent. Anything that takes away the headache of office work is a good thing." As he reached for the check, she pulled out her wallet, but he waved her off. "Let me. It would have taken me two weeks to make sense of what you explained in two hours. Thank you."

Jess unleashed her traffic-stopping smile and tucked her hair behind one ear. "It was my pleasure."

A few minutes later, they braced themselves against the wind as they walked down the sidewalk. Russ stepped around Jess, putting himself between her and the wind as they headed toward her car. She slipped her arm through his.

"Do you think Ashley would mind if we did this again sometime?" she asked.

"As long as we keep this professional, I'm sure she'll be okay. And I wouldn't mind getting some more information from CNMC if you're still willing to help."

She leaned into him. "Of course. Are you busy Friday night?"

"I doubt it, but I'll check."

"Do that."

When they reached Jess' car, Russ opened the driver's door for her. "I'll try to get more information before then," he said.

She covered his hand with hers. "Bring it with you if you have it. If not, we can still eat. Either way, it's a date."

CHAPTER 31

"Rosie, stop fussing with me. I don't need you getting my coffee." Thump, thump, thump.

"It wouldn't hurt you to rest a little more. Give your foot time to heal properly."

The muted conversation drifted into Ashley's bedroom as she nestled deeper into her pillow. It wasn't yet nine, and they were already nagging each other, but Ashley could listen to her aunt and uncle's loving banter for hours. Of course, she had two weeks left in Florida, so it might not seem loving by the time she flew home. Then she and Russ could start their own banter.

Something clanked in the kitchen. The rich aroma of coffee slid beneath the door. Might as well get up. Ashley stayed in her pajama pants but pulled a sweatshirt over her head. Out in the kitchen, John and Rose stood next to each other in front of the stove. Rose tapped his cast with her toe. He pinched her side.

Ashley laughed. "I'm glad to see things are getting back to normal." She took her laptop off the table and made her way to the couch. "Did you want to go anywhere today, or can I plan on hanging out here?"

"It's supposed to rain today." Her aunt pointed a spatula at the darker-than-normal sky outside the window. "I can find plenty to do in the house, and I'm sure you've got work to do."

Ashley looked at the headphones and CDs at the far end of the dining-room table. She'd spent the last two days either shuttling her aunt and uncle or transcribing medical records. With her final assignments on their way back to her clients, she could finally give her photos some much-needed attention.

"I think I'll email Mr. Miller, the photographer in Michigan, to see if he needs anything else from me before I start. I don't want to overlook something." She flipped open her laptop and set it on the coffee table, then poured herself a cup of coffee. By the time she returned to her computer, wintery wallpaper greeted her. She checked her email first. Newsletters, two pieces of spam, an online order confirmation, russellfarms@mail.com. Fear and excitement crashed into her chest. Ashley clicked the last email.

Hi. This won't be long. I hate typing. I hope your uncle is okay. Are they doing better with everything? Can I do anything to help? I hope we can talk soon. Russ

Ashley read it again. Then again. Nothing romantic or revelatory. No confessions of love. Then why did her heart flutter, spurring her to memorize those simple words?

BLIP. A blue instant-message icon flashed on the bottom of her screen. She clicked it. *Contact request from Rachel Billings.* Ashley didn't recognize the last name, but she knew the adorable little boys in the profile photo—Russ' nephews. She accepted, then went back to her email.

How should she respond? If only someone would dictate a response for her to transcribe to Russ.

A ringtone blared from the laptop as the video-chat app popped up. Rachel's profile picture filled the screen.

"What in the world is that?" John walked out of the kitchen.

"A video call. I'll use my headphones so it doesn't bother you."

"Don't worry about me. I'm going out to clean the garage."

"You most certainly are not!" Rose followed him through the back door.

Ashley plugged in her headphones and answered the call.

Rachel's face filled the screen. "How are you? I would have called earlier, but these boys keep me running." She smiled, her hair piled up on her head and a large red sweatshirt hanging on her shoulders. "We've got fifteen minutes before their show ends. Do you have a second?"

Ashley adjusted her own sweatshirt and ponytail. "Sure. What's up?"

"We're putting together a wedding reception for you, and I have a few questions."

"Russ mentioned it. That's so generous. Thank you." Ashley looked at the garage door, where Rose stood, one hand on her hip as she waved the spatula, undoubtedly lecturing John about walking too much. Should Ashley plan a reception after promising not to commit to the wedding?

"Russ said you want to keep things small, so we're only inviting our family and Rob Kraft's."

"The lawyer?"

"He's a family friend, and he already knows about the wedding, so why not have another few guests, right?" Rachel produced a legal pad and pen. "We rented a private room at the resort. They'll let us order off a limited menu—beef, chicken, and veggie options, plus something for the kids. Will that work?"

"Yeah, if you think that's good."

"It'll be fabulous. Chad and I had a similar menu when we had our reception there. The food was fantastic, and there's a great view of the ski slopes."

A shiver ran over Ashley's skin. "Is there that much snow?"

"Not yet, but they'll start making it soon. Let's see." She scanned the page. "Flowers. What would you like?"

After flowers came colors, decorations, cake flavor. The list went on. Ashley answered what she could. She wasn't sure how she'd feel about her decisions in a week but wanted to give Rachel something to work with. They squeezed out twenty minutes of planning before Aiden ran into the frame.

"Leo's eating candy and he won't share. Can I have eggs?"

"Give me one minute. Why don't you get everything out for me, and I'll make breakfast when I'm done." The curly-haired mini-Chad ran away. Rachel's gaze followed, adoration written all over her face.

Longing pressed against Ashley. "He's adorable."

"I love him to pieces, but it won't take him long to get the food out, so I need to go." Rachel looked over the list one more time, then set it down, flashing the same smile as Russ. "Is there anything else you want? We could see about music for dancing. That's more for the kids, really. It's good for burning off as much energy as possible before going home."

"Anything you want will be great. It all sounds amazing."

"Are you getting excited?"

Rachel's energy practically pulsed through the monitor, but Rose's and John's voices carried in from the garage. They wouldn't be happy about this call, but Ashley didn't want to disappoint Rachel either. She forced her cheeks to cooperate and put on a smile. "I think so."

Rachel's face blanked, but she didn't look away from the camera. "Aiden, will you take your brothers upstairs and get everyone dressed?"

"I'm hungry."

"Grab a box of cereal and pour a bowl to share. I'll have breakfast ready when you come down." Shuffling and banging ensued, then a few loud yells and pounding before silence. "I bought us ten more minutes. What's going on?" Rachel sucked in a breath. "Are you having second thoughts?"

"Not really—"

"Russ's having second thoughts?"

"I don't think so. I haven't talked with him a lot since I've been gone."

"I told Russ this was too quick. Mom and Carrie have always supported him no matter how crazy the idea. He could decide to set up a chop shop, and they'd be there for him. I love my brother and everything, but you don't know him like I do. Why don't you wait? Everyone would understand."

"Jess would love that."

"What about Jess?"

"She and Russ have had dinner a couple of times."

Rachel's face blanked again. "What?"

"To talk about the farm and the college. I shouldn't be upset— he says she's the smartest about these things—but she's also beautiful, and she knows all about agri-business, and she may have been crazy once, but she seems pretty stable now, so why wouldn't they want to spend time together while I'm away? Maybe it's better that—"

"No."

"No, what?"

"No, it's not better for Russ and Jess to get together."

"But they already know each other."

"Yeah, and Russ knows it would never work. Obviously I'm in favor of you two taking your time, but that doesn't mean I want you to give up on my brother and leave."

Confusion and hope whirled through Ashley's heart. "You don't? I'm confused."

Rachel sighed as her neck and ears turned red. "I want you to slow down so *I* can get to know you too. That's selfish, I get it, but you're clearly good for Russ. He's more relaxed and smiley since you showed up. Whatever's going on between you two works. I just wanted some time to experience it myself."

Her confession could have knocked Ashley over. Rachel *liked* her? It shouldn't have mattered that much, but Ashley couldn't deny her growing sense of peace. "I'd like that too."

"Good, then don't worry about Jess. I'll take care of that. What else is bothering you?"

Ashley tried to smile, but her blossoming peace wilted. "With the reception planning, this whole thing became more real, and my uncle—"

"How is he? Russ said he'd talk to you about booking their flights. Is that set yet?"

"I haven't asked them to come."

"Why not? They're family."

She didn't call them Ashley's family. Rachel lumped them in with *her* family. Everything about Russ' sister—her friendly face, the warmth in her voice, her kind patience—confirmed Ashley's desire to go back to Michigan, but Rose. "My aunt's not happy about the engagement."

"Add her to the list."

"I guess, but she took it hard. She and my uncle started fighting about it, and ..."

"What happened?"

She slumped against the couch, the webcam showing every unflattering wrinkle and bulge, but she didn't care. Ashley finally had someone other than Russ and Rose to talk to. "I promised Russ I'd come back, get married, and start a life together, but then my aunt freaked out because she thinks I'm only doing this for my mom, so she and my uncle started arguing about it. I hate when they fight, so I promised her I wouldn't make a final decision until it was time to go back to Michigan. I promised Russ, and I promised her, and now I'm planning a reception with you, but what if my aunt doesn't come around? What if I have to call off the wedding?"

Ashley waited for the usual crush of a contrary opinion, but it never came. Instead, Rachel watched her, a sympathetic look on her face. "I'm sorry you're in this position. I can't imagine how hard this must be." With every word Rachel spoke, the peace returned, washing away bits of Ashley's worry.

"Thank you."

"Have you told Russ any of this yet?"

Ashley shook her head. "I don't know how to explain it to him."

"Have you changed your mind?"

"No, but I can't hurt my aunt. She's seventy-five years old. She's basically been my mother for the past seventeen years." How could Ashley repay that love and devotion with unnecessary worry? "But then there's Russ, and I don't want to hurt him either, but I can't stop wondering if maybe someone like Jess wouldn't be a better option for him."

"You need to tell him this."

"I suppose." But her heart didn't quite agree with her words.

Something crashed and the boys yelled. Rachel looked over the top of the webcam, then rolled her eyes. "I need to go. Will you please talk with Russ about this?"

"I will. I promise." As soon as she figured out what to say. Now Ashley understood why Tom had never mentioned her to his family. It wasn't an easy conversation to have.

Rachel smiled. "Call me if you need to."

Her picture disappeared, but Ashley didn't move from the couch. Muted chatter flowed from the garage. Why had she spilled everything to Russ' sister? Ashley couldn't explain her motivation, but her unplanned confession filled a void in her heart she hadn't realized was there. She'd had a few friends who listened and encouraged well, but she'd never had that familial bond she had with Rachel, even after only a few days. What else could she expect from a sister-in-law?

* * * * * * *

Chad stood in the driveway, shovel in hand. The boys ran around the yard making trails in the accumulating snow as Russ parked his truck behind his brother-in-law's. He couldn't remember the last time he'd visited his sister so many times in such a short period.

"What brings you back to the funny farm?" Chad asked. "I'm going to start charging you for food."

Russ shut his door, narrowly missing the top of Phin's head. "I was actually invited this time. Rachel called me."

"She told you, eh? I didn't realize she wanted to start telling people."

"Told me what?"

Chad swung the shovel over his shoulder. "Come on, kids. We need to clear off the deck." The boys screamed their way around the side of the house, their dad riding drag.

Subtle. Russ let himself into the house. Leaving his coat and boots by the front door, he followed his nose into the kitchen. Garlic bread and lasagna. His favorite. Rachel must be desperate if she cooked his favorite Italian food. He found her at the kitchen table with a notepad and a glass of milk.

"Chad took the boys out back to shovel off the deck. What's going on?"

She looked at him and smiled. "It's nice having you visit so often. Dinner will be ready in about fifteen minutes."

"Perfect." He pulled out a chair across from her. "What's up? Chad said he didn't realize you were telling people. Are you pregnant again?"

Her smile disappeared, eyes wide. "He told you?"

"He thought you told me. Am I right? Aren't you happy about this?"

"Yes, of course, but I wasn't expecting you to know." The corners of her mouth slowly crept back up. "It was such a surprise, but I can't wait."

"How's Chad handling it?"

Rachel rolled her eyes. "He's hoping for twins."

"That much closer to his baseball team."

"I'm willing to give him a basketball team, but five might be my limit."

"When are you due?" With so many nephews, Russ knew all of the questions his sisters expected from him.

"April first." She pointed her pen at his nose. "No stupid comments."

"I wouldn't think of it." Except he had, and he couldn't keep the smile off his face. "Congratulations. You didn't have to make me lasagna for this, though. I'd be happy for you anyway."

"That's not why I made lasagna."

Uncertainty pricked at the back of his neck. "What is it?"

"Are you dating Jess?"

"What?" The idea curdled in his stomach. "Of course not. Why would you think that?"

"Because Ashley told me you've been having dinner with her. Like people do when they're dating."

"They're business dinners." But if Rachel and Ashley weren't convinced of that, what were the chances Jess was? Oh no. "I swear, I'm not interested in her. I never should have agreed to any of this. What do I do now?"

"Talk to Ashley."

"I've tried. We keep missing each other."

"Then try harder. She's not doing well with all of this. She needs you."

"I can't make her answer the phone. What am I supposed to do?"

"Get creative. Think of another way to reach her."

"How do you know all of this?"

Rachel waved her notepad. "I talked with her today to get more details for the reception."

"What'd she say?"

"It's not my place to tell."

"Then why bring it up?"

"Because she *needs* you." Instead of giving an explanation, Rachel drank her milk.

A hundred different scenarios raced through Russ' head, none of them encouraging. "Is she at least safe?"

"Yes. I promise I'd tell you if she wasn't."

He believed his sister, but her reassurance didn't help. He needed to hear it from Ashley, but what else could he do? Whenever he didn't answer the phone, his sisters hunted him down, like the day they found out about the wedding. Maybe it was time to let them teach him something.

Russ pulled the wallet out of his back pocket. "I need to borrow your computer."

CHAPTER 32

"Where do you want these?" Ashley pulled another pair of beige pumps out of a cardboard box. She held up the shoes from where she sat on the cool garage floor surrounded by boxes, bags, and piles of her aunt and uncle's belongings. Meanwhile, the car sat outside so they could sort items for the church's rummage sale.

Rose wrinkled her nose. "Donate."

"How many pairs of shoes do you own, Rosie?" John motioned around the garage from his spot on a folding chair. The bright Florida sun shone through the open windows, spotlighting the boxes that still needed to be searched. "Didn't you already throw out a pair like that?"

"Don't you worry about my shoes. These are the old ones. The church can have them. Why don't you sort through your tools and see what you can donate?"

"I shouldn't be on my feet. Doctor's orders."

She rolled her eyes. "Convenient."

Ashley chuckled as she dug into the box again. When her phone rang, she picked it up off the shelf beside her. Her throat constricted. Russ. She hadn't figured out what to say yet, so she silenced the ringer and set the phone back down. She had no desire to discuss the wedding or his dinners with Jess, especially in front of her aunt and uncle.

"John"—Rose shifted boxes on a shelf—"where did you put that box of old golf stuff? We could donate that."

"I forget."

She punched her little fists on her narrow hips. "I didn't realize your ankle was connected to your memory."

"I'm an old man. What do I know about these things?"

Ashley chuckled, but she knew enough to stay out of it.

The house phone rang, interrupting the mock argument. When Rose walked inside, Ashley tossed a pair of wood-soled flip-flops into the donate box. Her aunt would never miss them.

"Get rid of those rain boots too." John pointed at the pair by the garage door.

"She still wears those."

"Yeah, but they squeak when she walks."

"Aren't you both supposed to be donating things?"

"Sweetheart?" Rose stepped into the doorway, the cordless phone in hand. "It's for you."

"Me?" Her curiosity piqued, Ashley brushed off her pants and stood. No one called her on the house phone. "Who is it?"

"Edgar Russell."

Her steps faltered. What could be so urgent that he would call her on the house phone? As images of the boys flashed through Ashley's mind, she rushed to the door, tripping over boxes and shoes. Steadying herself, she avoided her aunt's gaze as she tore the receiver from her grasp. "I'll take this inside, thanks." Once she cleared the garage, Ashley ran to her bedroom and shut the door. "Russ? Are you okay? What's wrong? How did you get this number?"

"I'm fine. Nothing. It's in the phone book."

Thank heavens. She sank onto the bed, relieving her weak knees. "I'm sorry I didn't answer your call earlier. We've been working in the garage this morning, and—"

"I'm on the front porch."

The phone slipped through her fingers and thudded against the thick carpet. This wasn't happening. Her worlds weren't really colliding in Lakeland, Florida.

Someone knocked on the front door.

Ashley ended the call, then raced through the living room, tossing the phone on the couch as she passed. When she opened the front door, her heart stopped. "Russ."

He smiled. "Hi." The warm breeze stirred his curling hair, picking up his woodsy scent. How had he gotten more handsome in two weeks?

She leaned against the door frame, trying to look casual but desperately needing the support. "What are you doing here?"

"We keep missing each other's phone calls, so I came to see you."

"You flew all the way down here to talk to me?" Warmth flooded her veins. "How long are you staying?"

"A few days. I booked a room in town. I thought maybe I could help chauffeur your uncle around and get to know your family."

Her family. The warmth and strength drained from her.

"You're white as a ghost." He took her arm, pulling her onto the porch and closing the door behind them. "Should I not be here?" he asked as he led her to the rocking chairs at the end of the porch.

Should he? How would Rose react when she saw him? Probably not with the tingles and excitement that raced through Ashley's body.

They sat beside each other on the smooth, wooden seats. "They still don't like the situation, do they?" he asked.

"We haven't talked about it since I told them." Ashley slid all the way back on the chair, pulling her knees up and tucking her feet under her legs.

Russ, on the other hand, sat on the edge of his seat, elbows on his knees and fingers entwined. He blew out a slow breath. "I didn't think about how your aunt and uncle would react to seeing me. All I could think about was getting here to see you."

"Really?" She held her breath.

Russ grinned. "Really."

A thousand miles to see her? So much for practicality. No matter how much she denied it, she cared. She cared deeply for Russ. How could she walk away from that? "I want you to meet my aunt and uncle. I'll tell them you're here."

As she hopped out of the chair, one foot caught in the arm rail, tossing her forward. Russ caught her shoulders, then stood in front of her, holding her as she adjusted her feet. Her chair rocked, pitching her forward again, and she crashed into his chest as she struggled to balance herself.

Russ laughed. "Stop moving before you hurt yourself."

Warmth flooded her cheeks. "This is embarrassing."

"Hold still."

She clung to his shoulders, bracing herself. A tangled mess of extremities and wood slats, she tried not to move herself or the chair. Russ wrapped an arm around her waist, then secured her ankle. He shifted. The chair moved. Her foot popped free. Russ held her against his chest, anchoring her to his strength and stability.

"Sorry about that," she said, unable to look away from his too-close face.

"I don't mind." Instead of releasing her, he settled her against him. "I missed you."

Every insecurity melted away. How could she have doubted this? "I'm glad you came. I'm sorry I've been avoiding you."

His eyebrows shot up. "I didn't realize it was deliberate."

"I wasn't sure what to say."

"I honestly don't know what's going on, but Rachel said you needed to talk to me, so here I am."

Ashley's body tensed. "What did she say?"

"That it's not her story to tell. I hoped we could talk about it. I also wanted to meet your aunt and uncle, help them see that I'm not a bad guy. Give your aunt some peace of mind."

If only he knew how badly Ashley needed that peace of mind too. Everything might work out if she didn't mention her promise to get married, coupled with her promise to not get married. She hadn't meant to lie, but how could contradicting promises not be lies? She played with the hair on the back of his neck, loving the thick, silky texture. When had he slipped so completely into her life? She hadn't realized how much she'd missed him until she opened the front door. Smelled him. Touched him. Ashley needed him. She wanted him with her. Refocusing on his mesmerizing eyes, she smiled. "I'd like to introduce you."

His face brightened. "I'd like that too."

"You should probably let me go, though."

"Probably."

His arms tightened, closing what little space remained between them. Her pulse quickened. He lowered his head toward hers, his breath brushing across her face.

The front door opened. "Ashley?"

Rose.

Russ turned to face the door, keeping an arm around Ashley's waist. "You must be Rose Dodge. I'm Edgar Russell, but everyone calls me Russ."

"Ashley's mentioned you." She stepped outside, flashing Russ a genuine smile. "She didn't tell me you were coming."

"Actually, I didn't tell her. I hope you don't mind the interruption."

"Of course not. We could use the distraction. Please, come in."

They entered the house, Russ' hand resting on Ashley's waist. In Rose's presence, Ashley couldn't decide whether she wanted to shrug away or lean into him. Her aunt motioned to the table before heading to the kitchen. Ashley touched Russ' shoulder. "I'll be right back. I'm going to get my uncle."

"Should I worry about your aunt?"

"She's barely five feet tall, and I doubt she weighs a hundred pounds. You should be able to handle yourself." Ashley rushed away before she could overanalyze the feelings rising in her chest. She raced past the kitchen, where her aunt was arranging glasses on a tray.

When she stepped into the garage, John held up a pink plastic umbrella. "You remember this? Rosie's oldest sister bought it a million years ago. They kept passing it through the family, hoping someone would use it. I wonder how it made it back to our house?"

"We've got company."

"Company?" He tossed the umbrella on a pile, hopefully the donate pile, and practically jumped to his feet. "Who's here?"

"Russ."

"Ah, your young man."

"Uncle John." She smacked his arm.

He chuckled. "Let's get inside before Rosie talks his ear off."

CHAPTER 33

Russ opened the car door and offered Ashley his hand. "We have two hours until we pick up your aunt and uncle. What do you want to do?"

Ashley took his hand, her fingers cool but soft, and climbed out of the rental car, shivering against the breeze. She pulled him up the front steps and across the porch. "Whatever we do, let's go inside. You didn't need to bring the Michigan weather with you."

Russ moved ahead of her and unlocked the front door. "This is barely coat weather."

She stepped on his heels as she pushed past him and into the house. "How long before there's snow in Boyne Heights?"

"Five days ago."

She spun around, her face shriveled like she'd eaten a rotten pickle.

He chuckled. "You realize we get a lot of snow up north, right?"

"Sure, but it's hard to imagine snow on the ground while I'm here."

He kicked the door closed while helping Ashley slip out of her jacket. When his hand brushed her shoulder, she shivered again. He stifled a smile. "It won't stick. We usually have a few weeks of snow and warm-ups before it gets cold enough to pile up."

"Snow in November? That's a long winter."

"They don't all start this early."

"Really? How lo—" Ashley turned, nearly bumping into him. Pink brightened her cheeks. "Do you want a drink or snack?"

She stepped back, but Russ took her hand. "I fly out first thing in the morning, and we still haven't talked."

"I know."

"We need to have this conversation."

"I know." Ashley sighed and straightened her shoulders.

For two days the sparks had continued between them when they were alone, but with her aunt and uncle, Ashley sat back, put on a smile, and treated him like an old friend. Russ didn't want to admit what he saw in her eyes and posture, but he needed confirmation. "You aren't coming back to Michigan, are you?"

She pursed her lips.

Silence punched him in the gut. He inhaled deeply, battling an onslaught of emotions as he pulled Ashley to the couch. "What's going on?"

She sat on the cushion beside him but far enough away that they didn't touch. She rubbed the tops of her thighs, her gaze intent on her hands. "I'm not sure what to do."

"About what?"

"About everyone."

"What does this have to do with everyone? This is between you and me. Do you want to get married?"

"Yes?"

"That's not an answer. What's confusing you?"

She shrugged.

Frustration built in his chest. "Is it me?"

"No."

"Is it because of Jess?"

Her gaze slammed into his. "What about Jess?"

"I messed up. I get that now. I should have talked with you about the farm, about everything, first. I won't make that mistake again."

"She's a better match for you."

"In what universe?"

"She understands farm life and finances, and she seems to have gotten the stalking out of her system."

"Yeah, sure. What does any of that have to do with us?"

"When you had a problem, your knee-jerk reaction was to call her. That should tell me something."

"It tells me she's good at her job. Give it a few years, and you'll understand it too."

"I can't learn a lifetime's worth of experience in a few years, but Jess—"

"Is gone! I told her I wouldn't be able to meet with her again until you could meet with us. Last I heard, she's working on the other side of the state. Why are you trying so hard to match us up?" His heart skipped. "Did you change your mind?"

Ashley sagged back against the couch, arms crossed over her chest. "I have no idea what to do. I made such a big deal of making sure you wanted to get married, but when my aunt freaked out, I promised her I wouldn't commit to anything right now. Then Rachel called to plan the reception, so I did commit, but I didn't tell Aunt Rose." Ashley glanced up at him, her face deflated. "I don't want to let you down, but I don't want to make my aunt worry. My mom would like you, so I know this would make her happy, but maybe Jess is better suited for you."

"Would you forget Jess? And what does your mom have to do with this?"

"I know it sounds silly, but I want her to be proud of me, even if she's not here to see me. Sometimes I do things because I think she would have wanted me to."

"Like get married?"

"Yes."

The immediacy of her response caught him off guard. Would she really marry him for her dead mother? "Ashley, what do *you* want to do?"

She folded into herself against the tan, tweed couch.

The uncertainty of the situation pressed against Russ. He'd never considered himself a talker, but somehow Ashley inspired him, probably because he'd never cared so much what someone else had to say, even if it broke his heart. "Ashley, I need to know. Why do you really want to marry me?"

"It makes sense, doesn't it? We co-own the house and possibly the farm. We're both alone. My mom was—"

"This doesn't have anything to do with your mom."

She looked at him like he'd sprouted horns. "Yes, it does."

"No, it doesn't. You're a grown woman. You can make your own decisions. You either want to marry me or you don't, but you can't blame this on your dead mother." She flinched. Maybe he'd crossed a line, but it needed saying. So did his own frustrations. "I don't want someone to marry me because she thinks her mother would like me. *You* have to like me."

"This isn't about emotions."

"It wasn't at first, but you can't deny that something is happening between us. Something beyond our agreement."

Ashley sucked in a sharp breath but didn't respond.

Reality slapped Russ. "This really is all about everyone else, isn't it? Does it have *anything* to do with us?"

"Of course it's about us. How could it be about anyone else?"

How indeed, yet everyone else had a say in this relationship. Russ scrubbed a hand over his face, trying to rub some understanding into his head. "I don't understand what you're doing, and I don't think you do either. I don't care that our arrangement is unconventional, but I thought it was what we both wanted. I don't want to spend the rest of my life with someone who's looking to please her mother."

"That's not the only reason I want to marry you."

"Then give me another."

"Well, I ..." Her gaze shifted as she twisted a piece of hair around her finger. "I told you that I would."

He waited for more, but she kept twisting her hair. His gut clenched. "That's it? You're going to marry me because you told me you would?"

"Of course. We're committed, remember? I mean, I thought you wanted it too. Don't you?"

"That's not good enough for me."

She popped upright, finally focusing on him. "What? Why not?"

"I'm honored that you think your mom would like me, but I want more. This is supposed to be about companionship and a future. I didn't realize it was a mission to appease the memory of your mom." Anger pooled in his heart. "Did Tom know?"

Ashley's mouth opened and closed, her face a shade of red Russ couldn't identify. "He didn't, did he? And this is what you couldn't tell me. That you want to marry me for your mom, and you don't want to marry me for your aunt."

"That's not true."

"Isn't it?"

"I just ... I don't know."

Russ shoved himself off the couch, trying to reconcile the information with his emotions, which surprised him more than anything. It shouldn't bother him that a woman he met a month ago didn't want to marry him. This should be his way out of an unusual marriage, but he didn't want out. Despite their agreement, his heart was involved. He wanted her living at the house, sitting beside him at church, exploring the farm together, but he didn't simply want her presence. He wanted Ashley. Their conversations. Fixing meals together. The softness of her hair between his fingers.

Now what? Russ paced the room. He cared for her more than he'd realized, but what was the point in telling her now? If he told her, she might marry him to make him feel better, but that wasn't good enough for him. Not anymore. He turned back toward her. Ashley had curled up on the couch, arms wrapped around her legs and eyes closed. He understood how she felt. He'd consider clamming up too, but all of his pent-up anger and frustration would probably launch him off the couch like a rocket. Part of him wanted to comfort her. The other part wanted to walk out the door.

A tear rolled down her face, crushing the remains of his heart.

Fool. He never should have agreed to this arrangement. He'd already lost too many people he cared about. Then he invited Ashley in and gave her his heart without realizing it, and she was leaving him too. He couldn't stop the ache, but for once he had some control. "It's time for me to go home."

Ashley's eyes popped open. "Now?"

"I need to think. So do you."

She slid to the edge of her seat, hands clenched and eyes wide. Sympathy overwhelmed him. She must have noticed, because her mouth tightened and eyes narrowed. "Don't pity me, Edgar Russell. I'll survive."

"Probably, but you're *only* surviving. You're trying to fulfill everyone else's dream for you, but what about your dream? What about the people you're pulling in with you? Have you considered them?" Or their hearts? He shook his head as he walked to the door.

"What do you want me to do?" Desperation dripped from her voice.

"Figure out what you want." He looked over his shoulder. "I care about you, Ashley. I still want to marry you, but I won't do it for your mother or your sense of duty. This is between you and me, no one else."

Before he could change his mind, Russ walked out the door.

* * * * * * *

The door closed, and he was gone. All of the air rushed out after him, sucking the breath from Ashley's lungs.

He was gone.

Her chest burned. "Russ?" An engine revved. Tires squealed. Ashley ran to the window in time to see the rental car drive around the corner.

Now what? She needed to talk to someone, needed to get some advice, but who was she supposed to call? She craved her mother's journal, but it wouldn't reveal anything. Besides, wasn't it the reason Russ left?

No, she couldn't blame the journal. Russ was right. She had no idea what she wanted, and the thought of figuring it out alone caused her insides to quiver.

What had she done? Ashley dropped onto the cushion Russ had vacated, desperate for any remaining essence of him. He knew exactly what he wanted. Maybe some of his confidence would rub off.

Did she want to move to Michigan? Her mom had wanted to.

Did she want to marry a farmer? Tom had wanted her to, and Russ liked the idea.

Should she stay in Florida? Aunt Rose would stop worrying.

She couldn't please all of them.

Ashley looked around her aunt and uncle's home. Black-and-white photos of relatives she'd never met hung on every wall. Photos covered the walls of Russ' house too—her house—but she'd met Kathleen, her girls, and their kids. Florida offered a life of familiarity surrounded by memories of a life Ashley could never live. In Michigan, she had the chance to add her picture to the wall. Maybe add a new branch to the family tree. She'd still have Rose and John, but she'd also have Russ.

Overwhelming peace surrounded Ashley, calming her to the core of her being. Every thought of him brought peace, but was it enough?

CHAPTER 34

Alarm bells clanged. Silence. Bells. Silence. Was it an emergency or wasn't it? Ashley rolled over, and something slick stuck to her face. No, not alarm bells. The phone.

John and Rose!

She jumped up, slipped on a brochure, and landed back on the floor, burning her palms as they slid across the carpet. Ignoring the sting, she shuffled over to the phone. "Hello?"

"Sweetheart, are you okay? Why are you still at the house?" Rose's voice trembled.

"I fell asleep. I'm leaving right now."

"Don't speed. We'll be fine until you get here."

Despite her aunt's wishes, Ashley struggled to keep the accelerator off the floor. It wasn't even dinnertime yet, and she'd already pushed Russ away and forgotten to pick up her family. How selfish could she be, mistreating the three people closest to her? On the plus side, she'd run out of loved ones to hurt, but there were plenty of strangers in Lakeland who didn't deserve her carelessness. She tapped the brakes as she took a deep breath.

Approaching the movie theater, she spotted her aunt and pulled up to the curb, rolling down the passenger window. "How was the movie?"

"It was delightful." Rose beamed as she slid into the back seat.

John sat beside Ashley and huffed. "I'd like my ten dollars back."

"It wasn't that bad." They bickered all the way home, correcting each other's summaries of the plot. When they walked through the front door, vacation brochures covered the floor.

"What's this?" Rose walked to the nearest pamphlet and picked it up. "Are you still trying to plan your vacation?"

"Sort of." Ashley sank to the floor in the midst of the mess.

Her aunt handed her the booklet and looked around the room. "Where's Russ? Did he go back to his hotel?"

"Not really." Might as well get it over with. "He went back to Michigan."

John hobbled his way toward Ashley. "What happened?"

"He asked me why I want to get married, and he didn't like my answer."

Rose sat beside her. "What did you tell him?"

"I don't know."

"You don't know what you told him?"

"No, I told him I don't know why I want to get married."

"Oh, sweetheart. Maybe it's a good thing you're not rushing into this. If you can't answer that question, you need time."

Her uncle snorted. "Hogwash."

"John!"

"This is nonsense, Rosie. She knows exactly why she wants to marry him, but she won't admit it to you."

"What's that supposed to mean?"

"It means she's so busy trying to make you and her mother happy that she's not thinking about herself or that young man who flew down here to meet you."

"That's ridiculous. Ashley would never—"

"I would." A familiar weight settled on Ashley's shoulders. "I didn't want to disappoint anyone, but I ended up disappointing everyone."

Rose rested a hand on Ashley's knee. "This isn't about anyone other than you and Russ. You can't decide whether to get married based on someone else's feelings."

"That's what he said, but you were so upset. I couldn't let you worry about me."

"Ashley." She chuckled. "I'd worry about you even if I handpicked a husband for you. That's my job."

"But you and Uncle John were fighting about it."

He pulled a chair toward them and sat down. "And tomorrow we'll fight about how much salt to put in the eggs."

"Sweetheart, I could never live with myself if you made life-changing decisions for me and not yourself. I appreciate that you're willing to consider a longer engagement, but you can't change your mind for me. We're different people. That's what makes us special. I love everything about you, not just the things I understand and agree with."

The pressure eased, but Ashley's need to please nipped at her like an anxious chihuahua. "I want to live a life my mom would be proud of."

"She would be proud of *you*, no matter what you do."

Hope simmered. "Do you think? I mean, she wanted me to have a career and a family and—"

"And you're getting all of your information from a journal she wrote when you were fifteen years old, and she thought she'd be around to talk with you about all of these things." Rose smiled. "She never saw your face light up when you went to your first Tim McGraw concert, and she didn't know you'd fall in love with military biographies. Your mom was talking to the child Ashley, but you need to live as the adult you are. Now, what do you want to do?"

"I want to be happy."

"Everyone wants that, sweetheart. Your uncle's right. You need to figure out what *you* want. If I don't agree, I'll get over it, but you can't live my life. It's your turn."

A door opened, and possibilities rushed in. Ashley picked up a brochure. She didn't want to go to Vietnam or Hawaii. She wanted to see the Italian countryside, take a cruise, or spend a week in Boston. Honestly, she didn't care. Russ said he'd go anywhere.

Her heart raced. None of those trips mattered without Russ. She didn't want to plan her honeymoon alone. She wanted to plan *their* honeymoon with him. A week on a tropical beach with Russ? Ashley fanned her face.

Rose giggled. "That's quite the blush."

"What's wrong?" John pressed the back of his hand to Ashley's forehead. "Are you running a fever?"

"Hush, John. She's considering her options." She patted Ashley's knee. "Take all the time you need, but this decision has to be yours."

* * * * * *

The extra helpings of mashed potatoes, stuffing, and gravy filled Ashley's stomach like a sandbag. She stared at the ceiling above her bed. Her bedroom door muted all signs of life. Rose would probably enjoy some company in the living room, but it would take a few more minutes for the Thanksgiving feast to settle before Ashley could move. Comfort food should come with a warning.

She checked her watch. Five minutes later than the last time. Would Russ be available to talk? She should have called him the day he left, but she didn't want to lead him on if she was wrong. After two days of pros and cons, however, the pros were winning. The doubts had faded. She wanted to tell him everything but didn't want to hurt him again. Maybe one more day, just to be sure.

PING.

Without looking, she pulled the phone off her nightstand. Russ and Kristy, asleep on the couch, filled the screen. *Post-Thanksgiving nap* ☺ *Rachel.*

Karin Beery

Tears flooded Ashley's eyes. She recognized that living room.
Had stroked Kristy's soft cheeks, snuggled into the scratchy blue
pillow on that couch, and awakened in the warmth of Russ' arms.
Every cell in her body ached to return. John and Rose wouldn't
need her soon, and Ashley needed Russ.

Her heart fluttered. She'd tell him she was coming back, but
not the whole truth. Ashley wanted to see Russ' face when she told
him she was falling in love with him. Thinking about it warmed
her cheeks, then flooded her body. This time she didn't need Rose
to point out her blush.

One week. The doctor said her uncle could drive again in seven
days. Then she'd be on a plane to Michigan. She could make it that
long. It had already been—she checked her watch—two minutes.
She'd never make it.

Rolling off the bed, she headed toward the kitchen. Maybe
mint tea would help her stomach while killing a few more minutes.
Snores rattled through the other bedroom door as Rose sat on the
couch crocheting, the original *Miracle on 34th Street* playing on the
TV.

She spotted Ashley and smiled. "The only time that man snores
is after a holiday meal. I should be happy we don't celebrate more
of them. Are you going back for more?"

"No way. Do we have any mint tea? I need something to settle
my stomach."

"I'm not sure, but there are peppermints in the cupboard."

Ashley found the bag and popped one in her mouth, then
another. A little extra comfort couldn't hurt before she shared the
news. With a deep breath, she headed into the living room and
dropped onto her uncle's overstuffed recliner. "I'm going back to
Michigan to marry Russ."

Rose's fingers paused for a moment, then continued. "You're
sure about this?"

"Yes."

"Do you love him?"

"I think so. Every day I miss him more, and I can't wait to see him again."

"You may look like your mom, but this situation reminds me of Harriett."

"Your oldest sister?" Ashley grabbed the remote and muted the TV. "Why?"

Rose's fingers moved steadily as she watched the silent screen. "When your mother was in elementary school, Harriett was nearly thirty and had just gotten engaged to Lewis."

"I thought her husband was Stanley."

"He was, but she didn't meet him until after she broke off her engagement to Lewis."

"What happened?"

Rose shrugged. "Harriet could never explain what it was, but she said she knew in the pit of her stomach that she wasn't supposed to marry him. She prayed and prayed and prayed about it, but that feeling never went away. He was a good man, a kind person, but something wasn't right. It broke her heart, but she called off the wedding. She cried for six months."

"Did she ever say why?"

"Only that she wasn't supposed to marry him. I can't say that I understood it. I was in high school and thought Lewis was amazing. I was still trying to figure out what happened when she met Stanley. One day she announced that she'd grieved long enough, so she went to a dance with her girlfriends and met him. They got married four weeks later."

"What?" Ashley nearly jumped off the chair. How did she not know that about her aunt? Maybe Ashley wasn't crazy—it was genetic. "What happened?"

"That first night, Stanley asked if he could court her, and she said yes. One week later, she told me she was going to marry him, and she did."

"Did she love him?"

"Absolutely, but it was different than with Lewis. With Lewis, she giggled all the time and burned dinner while she daydreamed about him, but with Stanley, she said it was comfortable. She said he felt like home, and she wanted that more than butterflies."

"Were they happy?"

Her fingers finally stopped, and she looked at Ashley. "I've never seen a happier couple. They were married for fifty-six years when Stanley died."

There was hope! Ashley wasn't losing her mind. She was following in Aunt Harriett's footsteps. Excitement swirled through the air but crashed into a wall of confusion. "If it worked for them, why were you trying to stop me from doing the same thing?"

"Harriett was older than me, and I looked up to her. I look *out* for you. You're a braver woman than I am, but I'm not sure that's the best way to start a marriage. If you want to marry this man, though—if you've considered everything and are certain this is the right decision—then I can't argue with you. Harriett made it work, and you're so much like her."

That was the closest thing to a blessing Ashley could hope for, and she let it wrap around her like a warm hug as a hopeful smile spread across her face. In one week she would be with Russ, and she could go with John and Rose's support. "I want this, and I'm committed to Russ. I care about him … a lot."

Rose resumed crocheting as Ashley imagined her homecoming. Russ' deep laugh. His calloused hands. His strong arms around her. The pain in his eyes when he walked away from her. What if he changed his mind? What if he had decided he was better off alone? Or with Jess?

"Sweetheart?"

"What if it's too late? Russ was so angry, and he was right to be, but what if he can't forgive me? What if he changed his mind?"

"Ashley, calm down. You—"

"I played with his heart, and he caught me. He was right to leave."

"Sweetheart."

"I hurt him, and—"

"You're overreacting."

"What do I do?"

"Why don't you fly back tomorrow?"

"I need to apologize, to tell him how I feel. I should … wait, what? I can't leave tomorrow. Uncle John's still in his cast. Someone has to drive you around."

Rose dropped her hand onto her lap. "Nonsense. We can survive for a few days. Besides, next week we'll be on a plane to Michigan for your wedding."

An extra week with Russ? Ashley's heart skipped. "Do you think I can change my flight?"

"If not, we can buy you another ticket. After all, we have that wedding money saved for you, and it certainly doesn't sound like you'll be using it all."

Anticipation trickled through Ashley's veins. "Will you be—"

"Ashley Elaine Johnson, John and I have survived for decades without your assistance. We will make it through the next week. Now do you want that ticket or don't you?"

Ashley dove at her aunt and wrapped her arms around her. "Thank you, thank you, thank you! I love you."

"I know. Now—"

"I'm on it." Ashley planted a kiss on her cheek before racing back to her bedroom. Grabbing her phone, she punched in Rachel's name.

Flying back 2morrow! Don't tell Russ—want 2 surprise him!

CHAPTER 35

Snow covered the front steps, erasing any evidence that Russ had shoveled. Typical Michigan weather. Next week's storm would blanket the state, but last night's lake-effect snow took everyone by surprise, including him. Any sane person would stay inside today, but he had a stomach full of holiday leftovers to burn off and frustration to release. Clearing his own porch wasn't going to cut it.

He pushed the snow off the steps again before propping the shovel against the house. He opened the front door far enough to grab his truck keys off their hook on the wall, locked the house, then cut a path through the yard toward his truck. Time to swing by Mom's house and shovel her out. That should provide at least another hour of manual labor and distraction, not counting the drive over. If he was lucky, he'd get to engage the four-wheel drive and take his frustration out on some snowdrifts along the way.

Without any other cars on the road, Russ let the silence of the drive seep into his bones. Normally he needed a few hours of quiet after the chaos of a family holiday, but today the emptiness taunted him. It reminded him that Ashley was in Florida. They hadn't talked since before Thanksgiving, and the uncertainty of their relationship gnawed at him. How had he let himself get into such an insane situation?

That stupid will. All of this because of the family house. No, he couldn't blame the will or the house. Russ couldn't care less where he lived. His heart had never hurt like this because of his living arrangements.

It might be time to consider his alternatives. Lifting his foot off the accelerator, Russ coasted to a crawl, cranked the wheel to the left, and headed to town. He passed a handful of cars, most of them inching their way through the blizzard. As he rolled down the street, blowing snow obscured the buildings and people, but he recognized Rob's Jeep parked in front of his office. Parking behind it, Russ hopped out of the truck and leaned into the wind, hiding his face from the pelting snow. He fought his way over the drifted sidewalk and into the warm law office.

An unoccupied receptionist desk greeted him in the well-lit, yet seemingly empty, office. "Hello?"

"I'll be right there!"

Russ plopped himself on the pleather couch. He stomped the snow off his boots and was brushing flakes off his coat when Rob walked out front.

"Did we have an appointment today?"

"No, I was driving out to my mom's and decided to swing by. Do you always work the day after Thanksgiving?"

"Kelly and her mom go shopping every year, so I try to put in a few hours in the morning."

"They're out in this weather?"

"It would take more than a blizzard to cancel Black Friday. Something about a new bedspread." Rob sat in an armchair across from the couch. "My office isn't exactly on the way to your mom's. What's up?"

"I'm not sure. I think it's time to seriously look at the will and consider my options. Have you had any luck with your research?"

"I, uh …" Rob scratched his neck, suddenly very interested in the carpet.

"You have been looking into it, haven't you?"

"It hasn't really been a priority."

"Where exactly does it rank on your list of priorities?"

"It wasn't my idea."

"What wasn't your idea?" Russ crossed his arms, trapping the growing frustration in his chest. "I'm not going to be happy about this, am I?"

"Your mom asked me to do it."

"Do what? What are you talking about?"

"Your mom called after Tom's memorial. She told me the family would figure the house situation out and asked if I could sort of … ignore it for a while."

"What the …? Are you working for me or my mom?"

Rob held up his hands in surrender. "I didn't actually agree to it," he said. "I was looking into things and had it on my calendar to call you and schedule a meeting. Then I heard about your engagement. Congratulations, by the way. At that point, I figured it wasn't urgent, so I sort of let it slide down the list."

Unbelievable. Mom had been plotting against him from the beginning. The wind howled outside, whistling past the door as the office groaned against the pressure. He could relate. Clenching his fists, he jumped off the couch, looking for an outlet before he showed his frustration all over Rob's face.

"You're looking a little purple there. You okay?"

"No! You and my mom lied to me. You're messing with my life, and you're messing with Ashley's. She deserves better than that!"

Rob laughed. He actually laughed! Every muscle in Russ' back stiffened.

"Calm down, man. Are you even listening to yourself? You're engaged to Ashley. You should be focusing on her right now, not worrying about whether or not the house is technically yours or hers."

"Don't try to reason your way out of this. It still doesn't excuse what you did."

"Maybe not, but I think you'll forgive me after the honeymoon."

A honeymoon. With Ashley. A completely different rush of emotions slammed into Russ. She may not know what she wanted, but he did, and he was tired of waiting. "You're right. I'll worry about you and my mom later. Right now, I need to talk to Ashley." No more waiting for her to decide. If she wasn't sure that she wanted to marry him, then he'd go convince her.

Rob's phone rang.

"Kraft Law Offices, this is Rob." His eyebrows pinched together. "Yeah, he's right here. It's Rachel."

"What?" Russ grabbed the receiver, pulling the entire phone off the desk. "What's going on? Why are you calling me here?"

"You're not answering your phone. I've been calling for over an hour."

"I must have left it at home. How did you know I'd be here?"

"I didn't. I called everyone I could think of. Don't tell Robbie, but he was number twelve on the list."

Russ smiled. "What's so important that you're tracking me across the county?"

"Ashley's on her way here."

His legs wobbled. "When?"

"Now."

"In this storm?" Outside, snow piled up on the sidewalk, covering his footprints. All the warmth evaporated from the room. "How do you know?"

"I just talked with her. She's in Detroit. They delayed her flight, but apparently there's a break in the weather, so they're taking off now. She wanted to surprise you, but Chad said the roads are bad, and she's planning to rent a car and drive to your house. You saw what she rented last time. I asked her to wait in Traverse City, but she insisted."

"I'll pick her up."

Rachel sighed. "Thank you. I didn't want to ruin her surprise, but—"

"Chad's right about the roads. I wouldn't go out without my truck. I'll head to the airport now. Thanks for calling."

"Tell her I'm sorry I ruined the surprise."

"I will." Russ hung up and smiled. "Ashley's flying into Traverse City."

"In this storm?"

"I'm going to get her."

Rob snagged a business card from the desk and pointed at the bottom line. "See that? Estate planning." He gave the card to Russ. "I suggest you and Ashley put everything in writing. And file it properly this time. Call me if you need help."

Russ shoved the card in his back pocket. "If you're nice, we'll give you all the paperwork and let you figure it out." Without waiting for a reply, he ran outside, disregarding the wind and snow. If he drove straight to the airport, he should arrive at the same time as Ashley's plane. Maybe he'd be on that honeymoon sooner than he'd expected.

The truck fired right up and slipped into gear. He loved that truck, and today he loved it more than ever. Nothing would stop him from being the first person to welcome Ashley home.

****

Ashley finally understood Russ' winter warnings. A gust of wind pushed the compact car to the right, to what she assumed was the side of the road. The car rumbled on the way over and again when she drove back into her lane. The blowing snow and solid-white ground hid everything. She flipped on the high beams, throwing herself into simulated warp speed, then switched back to low.

How did anyone get to work in this weather?

The wipers swung about uselessly but somehow calmed her nerves. The car rumbled again, the hard, rubber steering wheel vibrating in her grasp. Ashley strangled the wheel as her pulse picked up. She should have called Russ. His ridiculous truck made so much sense now.

She lifted her foot off the gas as the road took a familiar turn. Squinting, she tried to find the road sign. Between blasts of white, she spotted it, but the front half of the car had passed the intersection, so she hit the brakes. The car swerved. She tapped the brakes again. Skidded. Slowed. Stopped.

Her heart raced. It couldn't be more than a mile to the house. She could do it. Sliding the car into reverse, she maneuvered back onto the road.

She turned into what she hoped was her lane, clipping a mailbox with the passenger-side mirror. Ashley pulled on the wheel, her heart pounding as she swerved left. Every nerve wanted to stop, but she couldn't see a thing, and no one would see her blocking the road. She had to find the driveway.

Tapping the accelerator, she inched the car forward. She steered toward where she thought the driveway should be, keeping her eyes on the side of the road. The car crept along as the wind whistled around it. Another mailbox crawled past.

By the time Ashley turned onto the driveway, her fingers ached, but her insides warmed. She only had to make it to the end of the drive. One more mile to Russ.

She had imagined watching the house grow larger as she drove nearer, with Russ standing on the porch waiting, but a wall of white blocked her view. The longer she drove, the slower she went.

She hoped Russ would be happy to see her, but that wouldn't happen if she accidentally drove into the front porch. Finally, a shadow broke through the storm. The snow whirling around her had nothing on her crazy pulse.

She pulled up to the steps but could barely see the house. Why were all the lights off? Odd. She left the car running, headlights on, as she zipped her coat. She'd be inside and warm in no time.

Ashley forced the car door open and leaned into the powerful wind. As she stepped into a snow bank, snow spilled into her shoes. Four giant steps later, she climbed onto the porch and grasped the door handle.

Locked. She pressed the doorbell twice. Nothing. The skin on her ankles burned. In July, she might run around the house and try the back door, but the stiffness in her fingers begged for warmth. Abandoning her surprise, she struggled back to the car. Ashley pressed her hands to the vents, the hot air creeping into her skin. Where was Russ?

As soon as she could bend her knuckles, she dialed his number. *You've reached Russ of Russell Farms. Please leave a message, and I'll call you as soon as I can.* She hung up and called Rachel.

"Ashley, did you make it to Traverse City, or did they cancel your flight?"

"I'm here, but the door's locked. Do you know where Russ is?"

"Here where? Aren't you at the airport?"

"No, I'm at the farmhouse, but it's locked, and Russ isn't answering his phone. Is there a hide-a-key somewhere?"

"What? Where's Russ?"

"I don't know. That's why I called. I don't trust myself or this tiny car to get me into town to find him. I thought I'd let myself in and wait for him to come home."

"He was supposed to meet you at the airport. I didn't want you driving in the storm, so I asked him to pick you up. He should have been there hours ago."

The panic in Rachel's voice echoed Ashley's. "He wasn't there. I haven't seen him."

"Chad!"

The wind continued to scream, but something in it changed. Ashley pulled the phone away from her ear and listened to the low howls, the shrill whistle, the—honking. In her rearview mirror, two dull orbs bobbed up the driveway.

Russ! "Someone's here." Ashley turned around, wedging herself between the seat and steering wheel. "Someone's coming up the driveway. I can't tell if it's him, though."

"Ashley?" Chad's voice cut through the noise. "Is Russ there yet?"

The lights came closer—much faster than she dared drive—but the beams were too low to the ground to be Russ' truck. "I don't recognize the vehicle." A black Jeep slid to a stop beside her. The overhead light popped on, and someone ran in front of the headlights, straight to her door. "It's Rob Kraft."

He yanked her door open, then ducked his head inside. "Good, you're here. We have to go. Russ was in an accident."

CHAPTER 36

Two nurses walked past Ashley, their clogs squeaking against the linoleum floor. Closed captions scrolled across the bottom of a muted television screen as a monotone voice paged another doctor to the emergency department. A dozen scattered people chatted among themselves as they sat on short, firm couches waiting for their names to be called. Unable to sit any longer, Ashley paced the length of the waiting room. Thirty minutes at the hospital, and she still hadn't seen Russ.

Rob sat on a brick-red, vinyl couch, talking on his phone. As he slipped it into his coat pocket, he caught her gaze and smiled. "I talked to Kathleen again. She promised not to drive in the storm, but she'll be at your house tomorrow morning to check on Russ."

"You're sure he's okay?"

"He was awake and responding at the scene, but he cut his head, so they needed to bring him in to run a few tests."

"And Rachel?"

"I talked with Chad. He's calling the girls. We can call him with news, and he'll take care of the grapevine." Rob grabbed Ashley's arm as she walked by. "I'll stay with you until you find out what's going on."

"Thank you, but I'll be okay."

"Maybe, but Kathleen and my wife would never forgive me if I left you here. Besides, I'm your ride home."

"Your wife! I didn't mean to pull you away from your family." Then it hit her. "Why are you here, anyway?"

"Russ had my card on him, and he didn't want to worry his mother, so he asked the responding officer to call me instead."

His thoughtfulness wrapped around her. "Thank you for being here."

"Miss Johnson?"

Ashley turned toward the sound of her name. "I'm Ashley Johnson." An EMT approached and offered his hand.

"Matt Pillsbury. I'm one of the EMTs who arrived at the scene. Mr. Russell asked me to find you."

Sweet relief. "Is he okay?"

"He'll be fine. He has some cuts from the broken windows, and he'll be sore for a few days, but there are no major injuries. He can go home as soon as they discharge him."

The news practically knocked her off her feet. Rob caught her arm, letting her lean into him. "Can I see him?" she asked.

"I don't see why not. One of the nurses should be able to take you to him."

"How did the accident happen?"

"He was driving through an intersection when a truck missed the stop sign and hit him. Luckily, they were on a main road, so they were spotted pretty quickly. They were both wearing their seatbelts, and their airbags deployed, which saved them from major injuries. It could have been a lot worse."

Rob and the EMT continued talking, but Ashley couldn't pay attention. Russ was okay. He was talking. He was thinking about her. Tears clouded her eyes. She needed to touch him and see for herself that he was okay.

A tall, brown-haired man in scrubs stopped beside Rob. "Are you Ashley Johnson?"

"Yes, sir. How's Russ? Can I see him?"

"He's banged up but alive. The cut on his head is from broken glass, so there's no need for a CAT scan. We're busy right now, so it could take a while before he's discharged, but you should be able to take him home tonight. I can take you back to see him now."

Ashley rushed ahead of the nurse, then paused at the emergency entrance. Instead of walking through the doors, however, he pointed down the hall. She followed him through the labyrinth, practically stepping on his heels as they walked around a corner and to a room. He pushed open the door, then stepped aside for Ashley to enter.

Her throat constricted. Russ reclined on the bed, a tube and wires attached to his arm and a bandage on his temple. He opened his eyes and turned his head toward the door. A smile spread across his face. "You're safe."

Her chest tightened. "You're in a hospital."

"Only until they let me out." Even in the hospital bed with his face bruised, his eyes twinkled at her. "I'm glad you're here."

She stood there, memorizing the sight of his overgrown beard, broad shoulders, and long legs. His face blurred. God had spared him. She'd never know why, but she wouldn't waste time questioning it.

"Hey, don't cry." Russ reached toward her, but she couldn't move. Relief. Love. Thankfulness. A torrent of emotions raced through her. Tears ran down her cheeks as a sob escaped her lips. Russ sat up and winced. "Give me a hand here."

Rob appeared beside Ashley, wrapped an arm around her shoulders, and escorted her to the bed. Russ took her hand and wove his fingers between hers. With a gentle tug from Russ, she collapsed onto the bed, falling against his warm chest. She trembled as his strong arms wrapped around her. Rob retreated, and the door swished shut behind her, but the only sound that mattered was the rhythmic beating beneath her ear. Russ was alive.

"Shhh." He nestled her against him, and she rested her head on his shoulder. A warm kiss brushed her forehead. "It's okay. I'm all right."

"I thought you died." Ashley wrapped her arms around him and sobbed into his shirt. "The police ... my parents ..."

"It's okay. I'm okay." He rubbed slow circles on her back, holding her close and whispering assurances in her ear.

The tension eased from her shoulders as she listened to the strong, steady beat of his heart. "You're alive."

"And if I hadn't cut my head, they would have sent me right home." One arm anchored her close to him while his other hand trailed over her hair, smoothing away the rest of her fears. "I was more worried about you than myself."

She leaned back, savoring the gentle gaze from his fathomless eyes. "I couldn't believe it when Rob told me you'd been in an accident. I don't know what I would have done if you'd ..." He cupped her damp cheek. Ashley closed her eyes, relishing every contour of his strong, calloused hand. Another kiss feathered across her forehead, then her temple. Her insides quivered.

She took in a calming breath. "There are so many things I wish I could have told my parents, and I was afraid I wouldn't get to talk to you again either." She opened her eyes, needing to see his face. "I love you." His hand froze, his gaze locked on hers. "I wanted to surprise you, but I should have told you as soon as I realized it. This isn't about anyone or anything but me and you. I love you, and I want to be with you. Please tell me I'm not too late."

Russ' chest rose and fell beneath her hand. Maybe she'd said too much, but she didn't care. At least she'd said it. A broken heart would heal, but she couldn't live with any more missed opportunities. Of course, that didn't mean she had to sit there awkwardly while Russ tried to figure out what had just happened.

"I should let you rest." Ashley leaned away, wiping the wetness from her cheeks. "You must be tired, and you'll probably be sore tomorrow."

Russ slid a hand behind Ashley's neck and pulled her close. He pressed his forehead against hers, his warm breath tickling her lips. "I love you too."

"You d—"

His mouth covered hers, answering her question as he threaded his fingers through her hair. She snuggled against him, tilting her head to deepen the kiss. Russ' lips nipped at hers. His beard tickled her cheek as he trailed kisses along her jaw. Tingles followed his lips.

"I'm so glad you're here." He kissed the skin below her earlobe. "I never thought I'd be so happy to wind up in the hospital."

"Shouldn't I be the one comforting you?"

Wincing, he shifted her in his arms but didn't relent.

"I'm hurting you," she said. "Let go, and I'll pull the chair over."

"No," Russ said, his jaw tight but his arms tighter. "Nothing could hurt as bad as walking away from you in Florida. I'll live." With one quick motion, he moved her to his lap. "I kind of like this situation. Since I'm the one with the head injury, I should get to call the shots."

She snuggled against him again. "So far I like your thinking." His throaty chuckle rumbled beneath her ear. "I'm so glad you're okay. I just can't imagine …" But it was too late. She'd already imagined life without Russ, and she hadn't liked it. In a few days, she wouldn't have to worry about it anymore. "I can't wait to marry you."

"I can't believe this is actually happening."

"Can't believe *good* or can't believe *bad*?"

"Good." He pressed his lips to the top of her head, then yawned. "Very, very good."

"You should rest." She sat up, but Russ held on. "You have to let me go eventually."

"No I don't. I have friends here." His hand slid up her arm, gently pulling her back into his embrace. "Now that I have you, I'm not letting you go. Can't believe I said that. I sound like one of those pop songs Liz listens to. You have a strange effect on me."

Ashley's skin tingled where he touched her, but her bones melted in the warmth of his arms. This was what she wanted, even if it took an unconventional agreement to figure it out. "You do strange things to me too."

The whoosh of the door startled Ashley. She sat up, careful to give Russ room as he turned toward the door.

"Oh, I'm sorry." Pastor Stanford raised his hand. "Your mother called. I was already in town, so I told her I'd check in on you. I see you're feeling well."

Ashley scrambled off the bed, but Russ grabbed her hand and tugged her back toward him. He turned her to face him and wrapped his hands around hers. "Everyone planned a wedding, but I don't want to walk away from you ever again. We can celebrate with family next week, but right now I only want you." Her chest tightened as Russ kissed her fingers. "Ashley, will you marry me? Right here, right now?"

"All by ourselves?"

"It's your decision."

She threw her arms around his neck, leaning into the life and love he offered, but she pulled back and pressed her lips to his. The kiss didn't last long because she couldn't stop the smile that consumed her lips. "I just want you." Clasping his hand in hers, she faced their visitor. "Pastor Stanford, could you get a nurse? We're going to need a witness."

CPSIA information can be obtained
at www.ICGtesting.com
Printed in the USA
LVHW091202131019
634055LV00002B/398/P